P9-DNZ-970

STARRY MESSENGER:

The Best of Galileo

STARRY MESSENGER:

The Best of Galileo

Edited by Charles C. Ryan

St. Martin's Press/New York

C.2

Copyright © 1979 by Charles C. Ryan for *Galileo: Magazine of Science & Fiction.*
All rights reserved. For information, write:
St. Martin's Press, Inc., 175 Fifth Ave., New York, N.Y. 10010.
Manufactured in the United States of America
Library of Congress Catalog Card Number: 79-16604

Library of Congress Cataloging in Publication Data

Main entry under title:

Starry messenger.

Twelve stories from the magazine Galileo.
1. Science fiction, American. I. Ryan, Charles C.
II. Galileo.
PZ1.S798 [PS648.S3] 813'.0876 79-16604
ISBN 0-312-75599-6

Apr. 80 B+T. 6.42

Contents

Acknowledgments

"Django" by Harlan Ellison, Copyright © 1978 by Harlan Ellison. Reprinted from *Galileo Magazine* by permission of the author.

"Where the Lines Converge" by Brian Aldiss. Copyright © 1978 by Brian Aldiss. Reprinted from *Galileo Magazine* by permission of the author.

"Samaritan" by Connie Willis. Copyright © 1978 by *Galileo Magazine*. Reprinted by permission of the author.

"Ye Who Would Sing" by Alan Dean Foster. Copyright © 1976 by Avenue Victor Hugo. Reprinted by permission of the author and the author's agent, Virginia Kidd.

"Do Not Go Gentle" by Kevin O'Donnell, Jr. Copyright © 1978 by Kevin O'Donnell, Jr. Reprinted from *Galileo Magazine* by permission of the author and Kathryne Walters Literary Agents.

"The Midnight Bicyclist" by Gene DeWeese and Joe L. Hensley. Copyright © 1978 by *Galileo Magazine*. Reprinted by permission of the author.

"The Best is Yet to Be" by M. Lucie Chin. Copyright © 1978 by *Galileo Magazine*. Reprinted by permission of the author.

"On the Road" by Gregor Hartmann. Copyright © 1978 by *Galileo Magazine*. Reprinted by permission of the author.

"Three Soldiers" by D.C. Poyer. Copyright © 1978 by D. C. Poyer. Reprinted from *Galileo Magazine* by permission of the author.

"The Silver Man" by John Kessel. Copyright © 1978 by *Galileo Magazine*. Reprinted by permission of the author.

"The Children of Cain" by Eugene Potter. Copyright © 1978 by *Galileo Magazine*. Reprinted by permission of the author.

"The Oak and the Ash" by John Alfred Taylor. Copyright © 1977 by *Galileo Magazine*. Reprinted by permission of the author.

Introduction

"Some have believed that this structure of the universe should be rejected as impossible."

—GALILEO GALILEI, *The Starry Messenger*, 1610

I'm a journalist, a newspaper reporter by profession, which is why stories fascinate me. They always have. And this book has a history behind it which is probably more curious than most. Because of my involvement, it has been a story I've been unable to relate—until now....

In the spring of 1975, the future of Avenue Victor Hugo Publishers (AVH) was still trapped in the bleakness of winter. The eighth issue of *Fiction* magazine had prompted a disastrous financial setback when commitments to distribute it fell through. Bill collectors were waving their scalpels over the magazine's barely breathing body like so many morticians waiting for the death certificate.

Begun in 1971 as Publisher Vincent McCaffrey's ill-fated attempt to create a national magazine dedicated to "the art of storytelling," *Fiction* was grossly undercapitalized, published irregularly, and never drew more than 2,500 subscribers. Even though it had been launched with enormous hopes and dreams and staffed with inexhaustible volunteers, the ideal never came to be.

When the weather improved that spring, McCaffrey took to pushing a book cart along the historic streets of Boston in an attempt to raise enough money to get things rolling again.

It was an unacceptable situation. If *Fiction* had succeeded—and the stubborn publisher refused to consider failure—he had optimistic plans to unleash a series of sister publications: *Now Voyager*, a children's storybook; *Baker Street*, a mystery periodical; *Sundown*, a Western publication; and *Galileo*, a magazine of science and fiction—all focused on the craft of entertaining through storytelling.

While hawking books to passersby at the corner of Boylston and Exeter streets, the thought occurred to him that it might be easier to obtain financial backing for special issues of *Fiction* than it was for the magazine in general. He was partly right. The special Western issue ended up being the death knell for *Fiction*. The science-fiction issue metamorphosed into an entirely new publishing venture.

Four volunteers survived the transition: the publisher; Thais Coburn, the assistant publisher; and assistant editors Thomas L. Owen and Charles C. Ryan. McCaffrey was the glue that held everything together. A 1969 graduate of Mark Hopkins College with a degree in creative writing, he never seemed to sleep. The feisty publisher kept scheming to convert the total lack of assets into an asset in and of itself. Thais Coburn put her B.A. degree in International Affairs from George Washington University to good use acting as the sounding board for some of the more exotic ideas the magazine's founder continually generated, and kept a close eye on production schedules. Tom Owen, an Alaskan and a graduate of Reed College in Oregon, flourished in the Boston climate and used his talents as a general coordinator. Later, his knowledge of the science fiction fan scene became a valuable resource. Charles Ryan, a former Peace Corps volunteer, was experienced in dealing with impoverished conditions. A professional journalist and a Boston College graduate, he had been a science fiction buff since the age of five.

Ryan and Owen were assigned the task of collecting material for *Fiction*'s science-fiction issue. Offering a whopping 1¢ per word, they began writing letters to authors and fan publications. The response was unexpectedly positive. There was clearly a lively, interested readership out there. Several skull sessions were held and plans for *Galileo* were formalized.

Ray Bradbury, Arthur C. Clarke, Hal Clement and Carl Sagan were among those who responded to the plea for material. Through contacts he had made as a journalist, Ryan began discussions with Fred and Carmen F. Zollo about financing *Galileo* as an independent company. Carmen Zollo, the proprietor of a leather import-export firm, had brought Ingmar Bergman's film *The Magic Flute* to this country for a highly successful run, and in recent years, had become deeply involved in several award-winning Broadway productions.

Plans coalesced, schedules tightened, and by the spring of 1976 letters were sent out announcing *Galileo's* debut as a quarterly magazine of science and fiction at the 34th World Science Fiction Convention (dubbed the MidAmericon) in Kansas City, Missouri, on the coming Labor Day weekend. The announcement initiated a trickle of subscriptions and advance orders from specialty bookstores.

The staff of AVH was excited. Even before the first issue was published, *Galileo* had generated almost as much interest as *Fiction* had in its entire existence. *Galileo*'s welcome at the convention was cordial and even enthusiastic. More experienced professionals and fans, however, were skeptical. The stated goal of Publisher McCaffrey and Editor Ryan to make *Galileo* into the "biggest and best" magazine of its kind drew many knowing glances and amused shakes of the head. On the face of it, the goal was impossible. The magazine had only modest financial backing, it was not produced by a major publisher and—what seemed the most quixotic of all—it would not be distributed on the newstands. They proposed to sell it by subscription only. In truth, it was the only way AVH could go. Newsstand distribution would have required a minimum press run of 100,000 copies, and the budget was barely adequate for the 8,000 copies which had been printed. Because of limited distribution and the fact that the first issue was produced on newsprint stock, certain fans referred to *Galileo* as a semiprozine—not quite professional. A bit more than 800 copies were sold at the convention.

The absence of an advertising budget necessitated the negotiation of trade ads with existing SF publications, pro and fan alike. Subscriptions continued to seep in, and by its third issue, the magazine had accumulated two thousand subscribers and *Galileo*'s first issue was practically sold out. At that point, what had been an agonizing decision the year before became *Galileo*'s greatest legacy. Budgetwise, it had been hard for the magazine's staff to justify a four-color, wrap-around cover. It pushed a skimpy $3,000 budget well beyond $4,000. But every other SF magazine had color covers, and the staff agreed it would be impossible to compete without it. In the spring of 1977, eight thousand extra covers were printed and mailed as the magazine's first direct-mail solicitation. It was moderately successful, encouraging additional mailings with even larger responses.

Around the same time, several computer firms were approached to handle subscription fulfillment. It was becoming increasingly difficult for *Galileo*'s small staff to process each new subscriber and type individual labels to mail each issue. Over the next two years subscription fulfillment became a very costly problem.

The magazine continued to grow. By the time the 35th World Science Fiction Convention came along, the staff was optimistically talking about reaching 20,000 readers with the fifth issue. It turned out to be 29,000. The original computer firm had become unreliable and a second was contacted, lasting four issues before it, too, began to cause more problems than it solved.

By the spring of 1978, *Galileo* had over 40,000 subscribers, and continued success with direct-mail campaigns goaded the publisher into a nearly fatal mistake. Test mailings amounting to nearly a million pieces were scheduled over the next six months. They did poorly, losing money the magazine could not afford. At practically the same time, the third computer firm went bankrupt, tying up the list of subscribers. It was impossible to mail the next issue and equally impossible to send out renewal notices due at that time, which were needed to compensate for the floundering of the direct-mail effort. The loss of money on the mailing and the computer foul-up handcuffed the entire operation. Cash flow dropped depressingly low and little could be done to correct the situation. Gradually, enough money was scraped together to print the next issue, but it took nearly three months before the fourth computer firm was able to reprogram the subscription list. And when the issue was mailed in early October of 1978, thousands of returns swamped the office because of improper labeling. Incredibly, the new computer firm was even worse than its predecessors, and the list had to be entirely redone for the fifth time. Cash flow became even worse than before. Renewal notices could not be mailed, and it was difficult to add new subscribers to the list. The eleventh issue was held back from the printer. Even if it had been printed, it couldn't be mailed.

Ironically, the magazine should have been at its healthiest. It had 57,000 subscribers and was selling 3,000 copies through bookstores. A few months before, at the 36th World Science Fiction Convention, *Galileo* was deluged with congratulatory comments. It had become the third largest magazine in the field.

In the fall of 1978, it became painfully obvious that the magazine could no longer rely solely on computer firms to decide its fate. The decision was made to put *Galileo* on the newsstands, and negotiations were initiated with several major distributors. Dell provided the best offer, and arrangements were finalized to release the first newsstand issue in May of 1979. With 110,000 copies being put out for sale and a press run of close to 200,000, by the time these words appear in print, *Galileo* will have finally attained the threshold of its seemingly impossible goal—it will have become one of the largest magazines in the field.

Through it all—the minor successes, the delays, the costly computer problems—McCaffrey and company kept plugging away. Working for little or no pay, they continually upgraded the magazine. Originally an eighty-page publication, it grew to ninety-six pages or more. What started as the lowest rate of payment for stories and articles became one of the highest. The quality and variety of editorial material improved from issue to issue, and the magazine's reputation blossomed.

The Galileans are stoic about the future. Prepared to cope with success *or* failure on the newsstands, they aren't about to relax. They long ago learned to ignore the odds against them. If they have anything to say about it, *Galileo* will, tenaciously, inevitably, become "the biggest and best." They won't settle for anything less.

The appearance of a *Galileo* anthology—this anthology—is only one of several projects primed for the launching pad, and in the science-fiction field, it is not such a long step from concept to reality.

That's the story—a bit biased, perhaps, but the basic facts. Which brings me to the stories which follow. They *are Galileo.* In the magazine's first year, a reviewer in *Library Journal* said *Galileo* was, "one of the best among SF mags." *We* feel each story in the magazine *is* well done. The ones which follow are prime examples. But I do not intend to comment on them. They speak well enough for themselves. These, and the other authors we have published, helped us become what we are. If you like this collection, tell them about it. They deserve the kudos. If you don't, blame me.

—Charles C. Ryan, Editor
March 1979

STARRY MESSENGER:

The Best of Galileo

Django

Harlan Ellison

Copyright © 1979 Harlan Ellison

He stood in the Portobello Road and screamed up at the closed windows. "Anatole! Anatole, hey! Come to the window! Open up, hey, Anatole! The war's started!"

London, on that Sunday morning, was filled with the sound of air-raid sirens. Unearthly wailing. Foreshadowed sounds. He stood there and screamed louder. Finally, a window on the third floor squeaked up in its tracks and Anatole's white hair and white face were thrust out into the morning chill.

He stared down at Michel, trying to focus him with sleep-bleary eyes. He worked his mouth to get the mugginess thinned. "Are you insane? It's very early! Everyone is asleep!"

Then he actually heard the sirens. He had *been* hearing them for some time, but had not codified the cacophony. Now he *heard* it. "What is that?"

Michel shouted. "War. It's the war; come down; I'm leaving!"

"Leaving? Leaving where, you fool?"

"I'm going. Back to France. The war!"

"Don't be a fool, Michel. We have a concert tonight."

"Piss on the concert. I'm leaving! Come down now. I didn't know war had been declared, but I'm off now!"

"What do you expect *me* to do about it? Do you think I can go off and stop it like Chamberlain? I'm a violinist, not a political person!"

"If you don't come down straightaway, I'm off without you!"

"We have contracts! The tour! We will be sued, you fool! Stay in England, play your guitar! You're no young boy, you're no soldier ...they have enough young boys to play soldier...you're a musician...come back...Michel! *Michel!* Come back, you idiot!"

But he ran down the road and fought in the underground with the *maquis*, and he lost the ring finger and the little finger on his fretting hand, his left hand, and he never saw Anatole, the combo's violinist, ever again. He became a jazz legend.

His name was Michel Hervé and he died honorably.

Silver droplets fell on the black river. Spattering and then shattering as moonlight carried the molten silver downstream. He sat by the edge of the river, contemplating onyx. He held his guitar tightly, as he had held the manila rappelling sling during that last suspension traversal before the others fell to their death. He thought about them, Bernot and Claudeville and little Gaston, lying dead at the bottom of the crevasse, and he clutched the guitar more tightly. He wanted to play something for them, but he had lost his sentimentality at least a year before, in the face of withering fire from a water-cooled machine gun; and playing a new composition for broken corpses was beyond him now.

He sensed movement at the edge of the river, almost directly across from him where silt had built up the shore and a crossing was possible. He sat very still, hoping the shadows cast by the trees still cloaked him from the eye of the moon. It was an animal. Something sleek and quick. It dipped its head and thrust its muzzle into the black water. And drank.

Something oily and thick extruded itself from the water and wrapped itself around the animal's neck. There was a moment of slithering, tightening; then the cracking of a twig. The tentacle withdrew below the onyx surface of unrippled water, dragging the dead animal by its neck. A courteous plash of water, and the bank of the river was silent again.

He edged back.

Now he was afraid to play in the darkness. Calling up that killer from the river was a terrifying possibility. And so he sat quietly, holding the guitar tightly; and finally, he slept.

Beside him, the canister of radioactive isotopes cooked, holding death, promising nirvana.

There were wolves in the hollow, and they were eating. Whatever was being eaten was screaming, still alive and very much in pain. He detoured around the rim of the bowl, dragging the canister behind him through the golden sand at the end of a twenty-five foot length of climbing rope. He had been travelling exclusively by night, burrowing into the sand during the day, hiding from the roaming skirmisher packs of Nazi *stürmerkommandos*, the canister leaking its death in a pit fifty yards away.

On the rim, someone had erected a cairn of stones, pried out of the desert from God only knew where. He had not seen a rock or stone for days. The cairn seemed to be an altar of some sort. He decided to pause there, and have something to eat. He fancied strawberries, but all he had left was the heel of the rye bread and some carrots. He settled slowly to the ground, leaned back against the cairn of dark stones, and took the bread from his jacket pocket.

He ate with his eyes closed, pretending to rest. Perhaps there would be a sun tomorrow. For many days now he had been hoping for a sun, any kind of sun. It might tell him where he was. He had the carrots lined up like pens in his inside jacket pocket, with the bushy leaves bunched against his armpit. He withdrew one and took a bite. If there was a sun tomorrow, he would see what color it was, and that might at least tell him if he was still in the world. But what if the sun came up green or blue?

He lay back against the altar with eyes closed and thought about little Gaston. His smile, the dimple that appeared in his chin when he smiled. Lying dead at the bottom of the crevasse now, unsmiling. They shouldn't have used manila. Would hemp have been any better? Probably not. But climbing had been the only way to escape.

He had trouble putting it all in sequence. Every time he tried, the music would run through his head and he would make up a new tune. He wanted to play a few of them, but there was always the chance that the Nazis were on his trail, following the sound of the music in his head.

It was still bothersome to him that *they* had managed to pull themselves through when Claudeville and Bernot and little Gaston had fallen and died. It wasn't right, it wasn't fair. He wanted desperately to play them a going-away song.

He shifted around and unslung the guitar. He laid it on his lap and touched the strings. He wasn't sure he could even play with two fingers missing, but the healing had somehow been speeded up by the passage through to this place, and he had been thinking for many days about how he could lay his hand on the neck to do what he wanted to do. It would be a different sound, but it might be a fine sound. He wanted to try, and to try this first time as a going-away song for them.

Knowing he was taking a terrible chance, he raised the guitar and fitted himself to it. Then he began to play, very softly. It wasn't one of the new tunes from his head, it was one little Gaston had enjoyed. "Rosetta."

It worked. The fingers that were left accommodated themselves and the song jumped up and out.

He sat there on the golden sand, a carpet of black beneath him, without moon, and the bright snowfall of too many stars above, with his back to the dark altar, and he played. And the shapes that had waited in the darkness came to listen.

One was a creature without eyes that sank its filaments into the sand and absorbed the sound by vibration. Another rolled into a ball and pulsed with soft pastel colors through its scales. Another looked like a flower but had feet and pods where hands should have been. There was a tall, thin one that hummed softly; and a snakelike creature with a woman's face; and a paper-thin flying wing that swooped in to pick up the sound of *Rosetta* and then sailed away into darkness, only to return again and again as though refilling itself.

After a long while, Michel Hervé realized he was not alone. Because his eyes had been closed, and because he had been living with the music, he had been in their company and had not known. He stopped playing.

The flower began to wilt, the ball of pastel scales went gray, the flying wing sailed away and did not return, the creatures grew silent and hummed no more. He understood, and began strumming softly. They perked up. He smiled.

"Do any of you speak?" he asked.

There was no answer, but they listened.

"We had to climb to escape the *Boche*," he said, talking to them, not to himself, and letting the music of one of the new tunes flow along as background. "I'll have to tell Bernot's daughter how he died if I ever get back. I could hear him asking for absolution as he fell. He was much older than Gaston, and I didn't know him as much, but I think that long after I've forgotten certain things about Gaston, I'll be able to smell Bernot's pipe tobacco."

The flying wing sailed back overhead, dipped, caught a downdraft, swooped and filled itself with sound, and rose on its forked tail. It went straight up and was lost among the spilled milk of the stars.

"The rope was frayed. I think it must have rubbed against some rocks. We didn't see. We could have gotten away, I'm sure of that. Hemp. Perhaps we would have done better had we used hemp instead of manila. Some day they'll make better ropes."

A gentle purple light began to seep out of the dark stones of the altar. Michel felt warmth at his back. He looked over his shoulder and the glow was growing, enveloping him. It was like a tepid bath. It cut off the chill of the night, but not the darkness. The darkness remained and the silent creatures remained, but the *maquis* were dead and could not return.

"They fell. And I fell with them. But something very peculiar happened. There was a place in the air, and I fell through it, and the others went down, but I didn't. You may think it odd that I don't question what happened. My mother was a Gypsy. I don't question such things. Or the music. Magic shouldn't be questioned. If this is magic. I don't know. But, listen, all of you, listen for a moment longer, then I'll play you many songs, *Avalon* and *Nuages* and even a lovely song I know, *Star Dust*, that you will enjoy. What I need to know is the way back. I don't question, you understand, but I want to get back, to tell some people what happened to little Gaston and Claudeville; and I really must tell Bernot's daughter that he died for her and for France. Can you understand what I'm asking? Do any of you speak?"

But there was only silence.

So he played the songs for them, because they would have spoken if they could. He knew that. And they enjoyed the music. He was a wonderful musician.

And the *stürmerkommandos* did not come.

The purple glow settled around Michel Hervé and the silent creatures watched him, and suddenly he stopped playing. They watched him for a time, but he did not seem inclined to play more, and they went away silently, one by one.

He dragged the canister wearily. If he had known why he was

compelled to burden himself so, it might have been easier. But he had no idea. The canister had been there in the golden sand when he had drifted down through the air from the space where the peculiar passage had occurred. He had understood, without questioning, that this was a thing he had to keep with him. He even knew it was leaking death, but he had attached the rope and had assumed the burden.

And when he came to the second altar, a much larger but exactly identical altar to the tiny one of dark stones where he had rested, he knew he should bury the canister there.

So he did, and he lay down a good distance from the leaking metal container, and he waited for someone to come and tell him what he should do. He perceived that he had no control over what was happening to him, that where he was and what it meant would probably never be revealed to him, but that he must be patient.

All through the night that stretched on without end, he waited; sometimes sleeping, sometimes letting the music have its life. And in the night the dark stones of the great altar let loose the purple glow, and he was bathed in the radiance. When he awoke, there was day all around him, and the purple glow was faintly discernible, but there was still no sun, not of any color.

But Claudeville and Bernot and little Gaston were there. They sat around him, cross-legged on the golden sand, and they waited for him to awaken. For just an instant he was happy to see them, but then he understood that they were dead, and he sat up with pain in his face.

"Now I must make the choice, is that it?" he said.

They watched him. They did not plead nor did they try by their deaths to shame him. They merely sat quietly, as the animals had sat. They presented him with the other side of the question by their presence.

"If the music, then you cannot go home, eh, Gaston, little friend? Claudeville? Bernot, I'll never smell your pipe tobacco again? Is that it? If I want to make the music?"

The glow from the altar surrounded them, because the time for making the decision was at hand.

"And what of this metal thing with the death in it? Does that come with me and my music, or does it stay here where no one will ever suffer from it?"

Spectacular runs of notes cascaded through his mind.

He began to breathe very heavily. He felt himself about to cry.

He didn't want to cry; he knew what that would make him decide.

"I *have no* choice," he said. "It is the music. It was always the music. Forgive me. You understand, perhaps you won't understand, but you died for something you loved, and I would do the same. But to live for it is even better."

And he made the choice, and was returned, and the dead remained dead, and the canister came soon after, but not soon enough for the *stürmerkommandos* to use it.

And he made great music for a while, for just the little while that he bought in that peculiar place of silent animals and dark stone altars. And it was *great* music, because he became a jazz legend, even with two dead fingers, and buying those few years was the only brave thing he could do.

His name was Michel Hervé and when he died, he died honorably.

This story is dedicated to the memory of Django Reinhardt, the greatest jazz guitarist who ever lived; and to the music that he left us.

—Harlan Ellison

Where the Lines Converge

Brian W. Aldiss

Anna Macguire drove to see her father whenever she could. The opportunities grew fewer and fewer, although she knew he needed help. She said to herself, "I go as often as I can because I love him as much as I am capable of doing, given the limitations of my nature. Since those limitations were to large extent fixed by the dreadful way he and my mother brought me up, then he has only himself to blame if I do not turn up as often as he would like."

She had another excuse ready to explain why she went to Crackmore less often than formerly. Since the new airport had been built, Crackmore had become extremely difficult to reach. The old main road, the A394, had been severed. It ended at Ashmansford now, and a lengthy detour was needed, meandering through all the lesser roads skirting the west side of the airport. True, a new spur had been added between Packton and Bucklers Wick, but that was only useful for traffic approaching from the west. Then again, the fast new airport road ran really in the wrong direction. Anna had used it once, driving right into the airport and out again at the north side; but she had lost her direction and was forced to make a detour through Plough and North Baldick.

She had said to her boyfriend, as she called him, in one of her small flat jokes, "It's all sort of symbolic of the way old people are cut off. Every time you improve a means of transport—i.e., build a new airport—you lose a generation. I'm sure Pop sees it that way."

She actually said "i.e.," as Trevor reported to his buddies in the office the next day. That was a Friday. By then, Anna, having scrounged a day off from the lab, was turning off just north of Ashmansworth, watching anxiously for the sign to Watermere.

Felix Macguire was due to retire from King Aviation Systems when the plan for the new airport was passed officially. Judy had been alive then.

"We'll be able to flog this property for twice what it's worth," he said. "How'd you like to go and live in the Algarve, my love?"

"I'm getting too old for change," she said.

"We could swim nine months of the year."

"I'm too old to get into a swimsuit," she said.

He smiled at her then, as part of the plan he had carried out tenaciously for over thirty years to keep her as happy as possible, for his own sake, and said gallantly, "I'd rather see you swimming in the nude."

Eventually, the representative of a firm of land developers came and made an offer for Macguire's house and gardens. The offer was disappointingly small.

Felix and Judy hung on for a bigger offer. "We'll force them to improve their bid," he said. "We can wait as well as they can."

They waited. They were only on the margins of the new development. A new offer never came. Felix wrote and accepted the old offer. The firm wrote back five weeks later (addressing the letter to P. McGuine) to say there was no longer any necessity to purchase the property referred to. Judy died before the first runway was completed.

The barriers of the airport came swinging along, mile after mile of green-plastic-clad chain link unrolling, munched off the road that passed Macguire's drive, and strode over the ditch that drained his pathetic little piece of orchard. There was one house still occupied next to Macguire's, owned by a pleasant, retired art auctioneer called Standish who kept three Airedales. He had misplayed his hand much as Felix had, and was stuck with deteriorating property. On the evening of the day that the fence went by his land, secured by an enormous roaring machine that spat ten-foot concrete fence posts into the ground at five-metre intervals, Standish shot his dogs, poured petrol all over the ground floor of his house, lit it, ran upstairs to his bedroom, sat himself down at a desk before a faded portrait of himself as a little boy, and blew his brains out. Felix heard the shots, even above the roar of a SST coming in.

From then on, he let weeds grow in his garden and the beeches become shaggier in the drive. He stayed indoors, concentrating on developing an advanced system of vision screens he called the Omniviewer, and thinking about the growing inhumanity of man.

"Oh, piss!" said Anna. She steered the Triumph into the side of the road and pulled the map over to her. She had gone wrong somewhere. She didn't recognize this stretch of road at all. She should have been through Wainsley by now. The map remained inscrutable.

She climbed out and stood in the road. There was no traffic. Anonymous countryside all round. Being a townswoman, she could not tell whether or not the fields were properly tended. The only landmark was an old railway station down a lane, its ruined roof showing across the nearest field. No rails served this monument to an obsolete transport system. Huge elms choked by ivy stood everywhere; she watched a transport plane appear to blunder between them like a huge moth.

A man stood in front of her. He might have materialized out of the ground. She thought immediately, "It's true, I wouldn't mind being raped, if we could go somewhere comfortable, but he might have all sorts of horrible diseases. And he might strangle me when he'd finished."

But the man simply said, "You aren't going to Casterham, are you?"

"No, I don't think so. I want to get to Crackmore. Do you know if I'm going the right way?"

He'd never heard of Crackmore. But he set her right for Wainsley, and she drove on again. At the last moment, she offered him a lift, but he refused; he wasn't going to be led on.

"I'm so isolated," she said aloud, "so isolated," as she drove.

But she had to admit to herself that it was a half-hearted protest; after all, she could always have *asked* the man if she wanted it that badly. People did, these days.

The self-focusing cameras were his especial contribution. Light-and-motion-sensitive cells ensured that lenses focussed on him whenever he entered a room. Working slowly, spending a generous part of every day out in the workshop-laboratory next to the disused garage, Felix built himself a spy system which would record any movements within the house.

When he had a few thoughts to express, Felix uttered them aloud and the house swallowed them as a whale swallows plankton—and would regurgitate them later on request.

"The Omniviewer is designed purely for self-observation: it is introspective. All other spy systems have been extrovert, designed to watch other people. Their purposes have generally been malign. The parallel with the human senses is striking. Human beings are generally motivated throughout life to watch others and not themselves, right from the early days in which they begin to learn by imitation and example...I must remind the grocer when he calls that that last lot of tinned meat gave me diarrhea."

Leaving the workshop, he went through the garage into the hall, which he crossed, and entered the living room. This he had bisected with partitioning some while ago, when he had been feeling his way towards a correct method of procedure for his experiments. It was in the far corner of the living room, the south-pointing corner of the house, that he had built his main control console. The workshop contained an auxiliary console.

From the main console, he could direct the movements of the nine cameras situated about the house, mainly on the ground floor. On monitor screens before him, he could keep zealous eye on most corners of the house—and above all on himself. Several times, he had detected movements that roused—indeed, confirmed—his suspicions, and of these he kept careful note, recording place, time, and appearance and gesture of the alien pseudo-appearance. "Alien pseudo-appearance" was his first, half-joking, label for his early discoveries.

As usual, when he began work in the morning, he ran through a thorough check of all electronic equipment and sightings. That took him till noon. It was more than a check. It was a metaphysical exploration. It was a confirmation both of the existence of his world and of its threatened disintegration.

He switched the cameras on in turn, according to the numbered sequence he had given them, beginning with Number One. In this way, organisation was held at maximum. Not until much later in the morning would he get round to testing Camera Nine, perched outside on the chimney stack of the house—none of the other cameras, except Five and Three, were situated for looking beyond the confining walls; that was not their province.

As Camera One briefly warmed, a scatter of geometrical patterns flashed like blueprints across the small monitor, grew, grew, burst, and were instantly gone. An unwavering picture snapped into being on the tiny screen.

This camera was located on its pivot in the wall behind Felix and some two feet above his head. As it was at present directed, beamed downwards and ahead (he carefully read off its three-dimensional positioning on a calibrated control globe), it showed the control console itself, with its switches and monitors, and Felix's right hand resting on the desk; the back of Felix's head was visible in one corner; so was the lower half of the partition, on which a giant viewing screen had been erected. Also visible were the edge of the carpet, part of the wall, and a section of the window sill. The pattern on the monitor was a restful one of converging angles, relieved by the greater complexity covering about a third of the screen of the console.

Felix scrutinized the view in a leisurely and expert manner. In many ways, One always provided the most absorbing view, if not the most interesting perspectives.

After a thorough scrutiny, he switched on the large viewing screen. Before viewing it direct, he watched it light in the monitor screen, via One.

The scatter of particles cleared and the tiny screen showed him the lower strip of the large screen, on which part of the console with the monitors was visible. On Number One of these tiny monitors, he could see the image of the lower strip of the large screen, with its lineup of monitors on the console. On the first of those monitors was a blur of light which the definition, however good, would not resolve into a clear image. Better lenses were probably the answer there, and he was working on that.

Satisfied at last with optical details, he set the camera controls to Slow Scan.

Camera One had a scan of two hundred and ten degrees laterally and little less in the vertical axis. Among the many pleasures of its field of vision—to be taken in due turn—was the view at 101.40N, 72.50W, which gave the corner of the room, where the southeast and southwest walls of the house met at the ceiling, as well as an oblique glimpse of the right-hand of the two windows in the front (southeast) wall. The merging and diverging lines were particularly significant, and there was the added pleasure of the paradox that although almost all the window could be seen, the view was so oblique that little could be observed beyond the window, except an insignificant stretch of weedy gravel; this seemed to reduce the window to a properly insignificant stature.

Also desirable, and considerably more complex, was the view at 10.00N, 47.56E. It gave one insignificant corner of the console, looking over it toward one of the two doors in the L-shaped room which led into the hall passage. Through this door, the camera took in a dark section of the passage, the doorway of the dining room beyond, and a segment of the dining room including a bit of the table with a chair pushed in to it (the dining room was never used), the carpet, a shadowy piece of ceiling, something of one of the two windows, and Camera Six, which stood on a bracket set in the wall at a height slightly less than that of One. 10.00N, 47.50E became even more engrossing when Six was functioning, since it then showed One in action; and, when One was in motion, its slight and delicate action was the only observable movement.

There was automatic as well as manual controls for each camera, so that "favourite" or "dangerous" or "tranquil" views could be flicked over to at a moment's notice. There were also programmed automatics, by means of which the eight indoor cameras ran through a whole interrelated series of sightings of high complexity and enfiladed the entire volume of the house—for Felix had his moments of panic, when the idea that he had caught an unsuspecting movement, a figure all too like his own, would send his adrenaline count rocketing and his heart pounding, and he would snap into a survey of the whole territory. His recording system allowed him to play back and study any particular view at leisure.

Frequently, he saw shots which filled him with grave doubt, as he played them back and allowed his heart rate to ease. Although no figures were revealed—his opponents were very clever—their presence was often implied by shadows, dark smudges, mingled fans of light and shade on carpet. They were there, right enough, meddling deliberately; and although no doubt some of the discrepancies in the visual record could be ascribed to aircraft passing low overhead, they were unwise to think he would always use that excuse as a pretext for believing in their non-existence.

When he had thoroughly tested out Camera One through its entire sphere of scan, Felix left it running—and it would run now until he closed down after midnight—and switched on Camera Two.

Camera Number Two was on the far wall of the workshop. It had been the first of the series of cameras to be installed. It overlooked the length of the narrow workshop, including the screens of the auxiliary console, and the door at the far end, which always stood open (not only for security reasons but because the coaxial cable running to the rest of the house prevented its closure) to give a view into the garage, piled high with its old grocer's cartons and crates of tapex.

Although none of the cameras offered a very colourful scene, Two gave the grayest one. As, under Felix's control, it commenced its slow scan, it had nothing bright to show, although rolling towards the roof like an upturning eye, it picked up a patch of blue sky through the reinforced glass skylight.

When it lit obliquely on the three blown-up photographs on the inner wall, Felix slowed the motor until the view was almost steady and stared with satisfaction at the images of the photographs thrown on the big screen before him. There he saw three gigantic sea-going creatures, each remarkably similar to the next in its functional streamlined form. Something of his original thrill of horror and discovery came back to him as he looked.

He said aloud: "My evolutionary discovery is greater than Charles Darwin's, or his grandfather's... greater and far more world-shaking. Darwin revealed only part of the truth, and that revelation has ever since concealed a far greater and more awesome truth. Do you hear me out there? I have the patience and courage of Charles Darwin... I too will wait for years if necessary, until I have incontrovertible proof of my theories."

Still staring at the images of the photographs, he switched to playback. He sat listening to his own voice, filtering softly through the house.

"—man beings are generally motivated throughout life to watch others and not themselves, right from the early days in which they begin to learn by imitation and example... I must remind the grocer when he calls that that last lot of tinned meat gave me diarrhea... My evolutionary discovery is greater than Charles Darwin's..."

He heard himself out and then added, "The proof is mounting slowly."

He smiled at the pictures. They were more than a statement of faith; they were a defiance of the enemy. In truth, he inwardly cared little for his own bombast broadcast through the silent and possibly unoccupied rooms; yet it gave him a certain courage—

and courage was needed at all times by all who moved towards the unknown—and of course it had a propaganda value. So he sat quietly, breathing regularly under his tattered sweater, as he watched the viewpoint of Two crawl lethargically past the marine shapes and up the formless areas of wall.

When Anna reached what was left of Crackmore, the morning was well advanced. She stopped the car at the filling station and got petrol. She had a headache and a sniffy nose. The pollen count was high, the midsummer heat closed about her temples.

"Oh God, don't say I'm going to get one of my streaming colds! What a bore!"

With a feeling of oppression, she saw as she left the untidy station that the village had entered a phase of new and ugly growth. A big filling station was under construction not a hundred metres away from the one at which she had stopped. Next to it, a pokey estate of semi-detacheds was going up. A new road to the connecting road to the airport was being built, cutting through what was left of the old village. Although, admittedly, the old village was nothing to get excited about, at least it had preserved a sense of proportion, had been agreeably humble in scale. Now a gaunt supermarket was rising behind the old square, dwarfing the church. Everywhere was cluttered and uncomfortable. She was amazed—as so often before—at how many people showed a preference for an inhuman environment. As she drove by the road-making machines, a jet roared overhead, reminding her of her headache.

"Piss off!" she told it.

It was so senseless. There could now be nobody remaining in Crackmore who desired to live there. Most of them would be attached to the ground staff of the airport or something similar, and lived where they did purely for financial interest. Anyone with any spark of humanity in them had fled from the area long ago.

She turned off by the old war memorial ("Faithful Unto Death" 1914-1918, 1939-1945) and headed towards her father's house. The road shimmered in its own heat, creating imaginary pools and quagmires into which she drove.

Round the last corner, she passed the burnt-out shell of the Standish mansion. Burdock grew along its drive, rusty with July, and eager green things had sprung up round what was left of the structure. Sweet rocket flowered haphazardly. The shade under the high beeches behind was as dark as night. Ahead, lopping off the road, the airport fence. The fence put a terminator on everything—beyond was only the anticyclonic weather, breaking into slatey cumulus, which began to pile up the sky like out-of-hand elms, growing above low cloud and threatening a chance of thunder before the afternoon died.

The drive gates stood open. As the Triumph turned in, Anna saw that the drab green fence was closer to her father's house than she recalled. It was too long since she last visited Felix; her neglect of him was part of a greater neglect, of the wastage of everything.

On the other side of the fence, the road had been eradicated; machines had wiped it out of existence; on this side of the fence, nature was at work doing the same thing, throwing out an advance guard of wild grasses and buttercup, following up with nettles, dock, thistles, and brambles. Soon they would come sprawling their way along the road. It only needed a year or two, and they would be at the house.

Anna drew up before the front door, noting how the trees about the drive, beech and copper beech, had grown more ragged and encroached more since she was last here. She blew her nose before climbing out, not wishing her father to suspect she might have a cold developing.

The house had been solidly built just after the turn of the century, with gray slate roof and red brick, and a curious predilection for stone round the windows. It had never been fashionable or imposing, though perhaps aiming at both; nevertheless, even in its old neglected age, it manifested something of the rather flashy solidity of the epoch in which it had been designed and constructed.

Before entering, Anna let a certain dread provoke her into stepping across the weedy gravel to peer through the living room windows. Through the second window, she saw her father crouched in his swivel chair, looking fixedly at something beyond the range of her vision. She stared at him as at a stranger. Felix Macquire was still a powerful man, the lines of his face were still commanding, while the recessing of his gums lent more emphasis than at any other stage in his life to a determined line of chin and jaw. His white hair, hanging forward over his brow, still contained something of the boisterousness she recalled in her childhood. All in all, he, like the house, had weathered well, retaining the same flashy solidity of the Edwardian Age.

Feeling guilty for spying on him she turned away, thinking in a depressed way that her father seemed scarcely changed in appearance from when she could first remember him in childhood; yet she herself no longer had youthful expectations of life, and was moving towards middle age. With her habitual quick shift of thought, she ironically pronounced herself resigned to her own listless company.

She tried the handle of the front door. It opened. Hinges squeaked as she entered the hall.

Despite the heat outside, the feeling in the house was one of cold and damp; a comfortlessness less physical than an attribute of the phantoms haunting it. But the lengths of coaxial cable running boldly over the carpet or snaking up the stairs, the doors—to the garage, lavatory, coat cupboard, and living room—wedged open, all contributed to the discomfort—not to mention the slow stare of Camera Four, situated knee-high on its bracket on the corner of the coat cupboard, where it could survey front door, hall, passage, and stairs.

"Are you there, father? It's me, Anna."

She went down the passage and through the second door of the living room. He had risen from the console and stood awaiting her. She went over to him and kissed him.

"How are you? You're looking well! Why didn't you write or send me a few words on a tape? I've been worried. I'm sorry it's been so long since my last visit, but we've been terribly busy at the labs—trade's bad, and that always seems to mean more work, for me at least. I had to go up to Newcastle with one of the partners last weekend or I would have come over then. Did you get my card, by the way? I'm sure I've sent you that view of the Civic Hall before, but it seems to be the only view they had at the tobacconists..."

She paused and her father said, "It's good of you to bother to come at all, Anna. I'll get you a cup of coffee, or something, shall I?"

"No, no, I'll get it. That's what I'm here for, isn't it? And may I open a window or two? It's terribly stuffy in here—it is July, you know, and you need some warm air circulating. And why don't you keep the front door locked when you are alone in the house? Suppose someone broke in?"

"If the front door is unlocked, I can get out quicker if I need to, can't I?"

They stared at each other. Anna dropped her gaze first.

"You aren't exactly welcoming, are you, father?"

"I said it was good of you to come. I'm pleased to see you. But it's no good complaining about the way I live directly you get in the house."

"I'm sorry, father, really. I didn't mean to nag, of course. Just a motherly instinct—you know what women are!" She put on a smile and moved to embrace him, then clumsily cut off the gesture. "Father, you're alone far too much. I know what you think about me, but you don't make it easy—you've never made it easy. Even when I was a little girl and I used to run to you—"

"You are grown up now, Anna!"

"Oh God, don't rub it in! You took care of that! What does being grown up mean but being even more isolated than as a child? What made you so inhuman, father? You never really loved me, did you? Why do you still expect me to come all this way up here to visit you, and it's terribly difficult to get here, just to make fun of me?"

"I don't expect you to visit me, Anna. You have to come now and then just to reproach me. You know very well that what you say hurts. You have in some way failed to achieve a mature personality and so you blame me for that. Perhaps I am to blame. But what use is blame? Was it worth coming this far just to deliver it?"

"Nothing's of any use to you, is it?" she said sulkily. "I'll go and make coffee, if there's any in the house."

Her father went back to sit down before his monitor screens. He switched Camera Eight on to the big screen and sat looking at an image of the inner wall of the second bedroom which included part of a wardrobe and, hanging from the picture rail, an engraving of Sir Edward Poynter's "Faithful Unto Death", which had belonged to his mother.

In a minute, Anna poked her head round the door.

"Coffee's ready! Come and have it in the kitchen—it's a bit fresher in here."

He went through and took the cup she offered him. Anna had opened the door to the side drive. Sunlight lay there in patches between trees.

"I'm pleased to see you have plenty of provisions in the house. At least you keep yourself fed properly. Prices of everything keep going up and up. I don't know where it will all end."

"I live very comfortably, Anna. I nourish myself, I exercise myself. I am entirely dedicated to my research and mean to keep myself as healthy as possible in order to pursue it. Did you manage to get that volume on convergence by Krost?"

"No, not yet. Foyle's had to order specially, and still it hasn't come through. Sorry. Everything takes so long. How's the research going?"

"Steadily."

"I know you aren't very keen to tell me about it, but you know I'm interested. Perhaps I could be of more help to you if you would tell me a bit more."

"My dear, I appreciate your interest, but I've told you before—the work has to be secret. I don't want it blabbed about and, in the sphere in which I'm working, you could not possibly be of any help."

"Ignoring the insulting suggestion that I should blab your secrets everywhere, couldn't I approach someone—"

"You know what I mean, you might tell one of your boyfriends casually—" He paused, knowing he had said the wrong thing, blinked, and said hastily, "You shall have, perhaps, a small demonstration of what I'm doing. But I must keep it all secret. I'm on the brink of something extraordinary, that I know...one of those discoveries—revelations—that can completely overturn the thinking of all men, as Galileo did when he turned his telescope to the sky. There were telescopes, there was sky. But *he* was the man who had the original thought, *he* was the man who looked in a new direction. I am doing that. To you—though you may be my daughter—I'm just an old eccentric, spending his days staring at television screens. Aren't I, admit it? Well, that's much what they thought of Galileo...The name of Felix Macguire, my child...a few more years...I can't tell you..."

"Don't let your coffee get cold, father."

He turned his back to her and stared out of the door at the unkempt bushes.

"I understand, father. I mean, I understand your aspirations. Everyone has them. I know I have."

Her pathetic words, intended to contain a charge of reassurance through shared experience, died on her lips. In a more practical voice, she said, "All the same, it's not good for you to live here alone like this. I don't like it. It's a responsibility for me. I want you to come and live near me in Highgate where I can keep an eye on you...Or, if you won't do that, then I want a medical friend of mine to be allowed up here to see you. Robert Stokes-Wallis. He's a follower of Laing's. Perhaps you know his name."

She sniffed and blew her nose. Felix turned and watched her performance.

"I warn you, Anna, I want no interference with my routine. Tell your man to stay away. You think I'm cranky. Maybe I am. It's a cranky world. Whether I'm mad or not is really a question of no importance beside the magnitude of the questions I am confronting. Now, let's say no more on that subject."

"Drink your coffee," she said pettishly. "And what's this demonstration you want to give me?"

Felix picked up the mug and sipped. "Are you, in fact, particularly interested?"

Making an effort, she laid a hand on the arm of his sweater. "I'm sure that you understand that I really am interested, father, and always have been, when allowed to be. I am really quite an intelligent and loving creature to my friends. So of course, I am keen to see your demonstration."

"Good, good. You need only say yes—speeches aren't necessary. Now, I don't want you to be disappointed by the demonstration, because there is a danger it may seem very flat to you, you understand? Let me explain something about it first."

He pulled a book off the top of the refrigerator.

"Milton's poems. *Paradise Lost*. I read it sometimes when I'm not working. A marvellous poem, although it contains a view of reality as a theological drama to which we no longer subscribe. When Milton was in Italy, he visited Galileo Galilei, and something of the astronomer's involvement with the heavens has got into the poem. Galileo is the greater man, because the scientist must take precedent over the poet; but either must have a measure of the other for real greatness."

"Father, you forget that you read me most of Book IV of *Paradise Lost* last time I came up here. It is not my favourite poem."

"'What seest thou else in the dark backward and abysm of time?' Let me come to the point, which is not exactly Milton. We are talking about views of reality to which we no longer subscribe. The geocentric view of the universe prevailed for over a thousand years—needlessly, since a heliocentric view had been advanced before that. How can anything be correctly understood when such a great thing is misunderstood? It was not just a minor astronomical error—it was grounded in Man's erroneous view of his own importance in the universe.

"Nobody believes in the Ptolemaic geocentric view nowadays, and yet nevertheless thousands—millions of people have found a way of clinging to that ancient error by maintaining a belief in astrology: that the movements of remote suns can control a human destiny, or that, vice versa, human behaviour can provoke eclipses or similar signs of heavenly displeasure. Clear views of reality are at a premium. Indeed, I've come to believe something always distorts our vision. Bacon comes very close to the same conclusions in his 'Novum Organum'.

"Take mankind's idea of its own nature. In the west, the view prevailed until the nineteenth century that we were God's creatures, especially made to act in some obscure drama of His making. Your grandmother believed in the tale of Adam and Eve, and in every word of Genesis. She preferred that version of reality to Darwin's. Darwin showed that we were different from the animals only in degree and not in kind. But the opposite view had prevailed practically unchallenged for centuries, and men still prefer to behave as if they were apart from Nature. Not only is the truth hard to come by—it's often refused when available."

"I see that but, surely, in this century we have had our noses rubbed in reality uncomfortably enough."

"I don't think so, Anna. I believe we have escaped again. Look at the way in which the so-called side effects of technology are universally deplored. Everyone who pretends to any degree of civilization agrees to condemn nuclear warfare, the pollution of air, sea, and land, the sort of dreadful fate that has overtaken Crackmore, the hideous tide of automobiles which chokes our cities. Yet all these things are brought about by us. We have the power over technological and legislative processes to end all such abuses tomorrow if we wished. Instead, we continue to stockpile nuclear weapons, we go on making thousands of automobiles per day, we continue to destroy every accessible environment. Why? Why? Because we wish it. Because we *like* it that way, because we crave disaster. That is the truth—that we think we feel otherwise is yet another proof of how incapable mankind is of coping with reality."

"Oh, but to argue like that—that's silly, father! After all, growing numbers of people—"

"I know what you are going to say—"

"Oh, no, you don't—"

"I know what you are going to say. You are going to say that there are increasing numbers of people who are showing by action that they hate what technology is doing to us. Perhaps. I do not suggest all men feel the same. Indeed, part of my thesis is that man is divided. But by and large there is a mass wish for catastrophe, hidden under mass delusion. So a considerable amount of my time here is devoted to bringing reality under better control."

She shook her head. "Father, honestly, you just can't—"

He shut the door to the drive. "We must bring reality under control. The technology we turn against ourselves can be turned to fortify that weak link in our brains which always seeks to deceive us about our own natures! I'll show you how. You've had the lecture—now the demonstration. Go and sit in the other room at my chair and watch Number Five monitor screen."

Putting his hands on her shoulders, he guided her from the kitchen. He noticed how stiff and lifeless her body felt, and hurriedly removed his hands. In time to catch the expression on his face, Anna turned and said, "Father, I do want to be of help to you—desperately! It's awful how people in families get all tangled up with their relationships, but I do want to be more of a dau—"

"Demonstration first!" he said briskly, pushing her forward. "Get in there and sit patiently watching Monitor Five. That's all you have to do."

Sighing, she went through into the living room. Most of its original furniture had been pushed back into one corner. An old sofa covered the unused fireplace. There were cushions, occasional tables, a magazine rack, and an old box piled on top of the sofa. The room had been further reduced in meaning by the partition across it, with the television screen burning on it. Past the side of the partition, she could see through the other door of the room and out through the discomfort of the hall, the eye perforce following the intertwined snakes of black cable, into the garage, with its empty crates and wall of breeze blocks.

She sat at the console, took a tissue out of her handbag, and blew her nose. The headache was there in full force, despite two aspirins she had swallowed with her coffee. The atmosphere was leaden.

On the large screen burned an image which she recognised as one of the bedrooms, although it was years since she had been upstairs. Despite herself, she was interested and, as she scrutinized the picture, tried to reason why she should be. She could see through an open door to a landing across which light and ill-defined shadows of banisters lay, to a corner of wall; the continuation of landing had to be deduced from the chiaroscuro eclipsed by the bedroom doorpost. From this glimpse, Anna deduced she was seeing a view from the spare bedroom at the top of the stairs.

Inside the room, she could see the foot of a bed, part of a wardrobe, and a picture hanging against a patterned wallpaper. She leaned forward instinctively, interested to see if the bed were made up. It appeared not to be. She also stared at the picture on the wall. A man, perhaps a soldier, was holding a pike or a spear and gazing fearfully upwards at the entrance to a forbidding alley; behind him, something awful was going on; but she could make little of it.

All, on the surface, was dull and without any power to enchant; yet she felt herself enchanted.

The colours were of high quality, conveying an impression that they were true to reality but perhaps enhanced it slightly. For instance, the landing carpet: mauve: but did it actually present those tender lavender contrasts between shadowed and unshadowed strips? Or was it that the colours on the screen were true and one merely paid them a more attentive respect because they were images of the real thing? Was there an art about the reproduction that the reality lacked?

She noted belatedly that the sound was on, so that she was actually listening to this silent vista as well as watching it. And she noted something else: that the viewpoint was low, as if the camera was fixed just above the skirting. So one was forced into the viewpoint more of a child than an adult. That might explain why the shadows radiating from the wardrobe seemed both somewhat emphatic and somewhat menacing, as well as accounting for some of the fascination of the picture as a whole.

But was it a live picture or a still? Anna was convinced it was no still. Some quality about it suggested a second-by-second congruence with her own life. Yet how to be sure? Of course, a long-enough vigil would reveal movement in the shadows, or a diminution in light towards evenings; but she found herself looking for a spider crossing her field of vision, perhaps a fly trapped in the room, circling vaguely under an overhead lampshade. Nothing moved.

With an involuntary shiver, she thought, "That room's as lifeless as the top of Everest! It's not a real room anymore—it's just a fossil!" Her attraction changed to revulsion and she looked down at the row of monitor screens to obey her father's directions.

Eight of the nine small screens were lit. All showed static views of rooms and, in the eighth, she saw duplicated—in miniature and in black and white—the view projected on the big screen. Its smallness gave it an even more hypnotic quality. It frightened her. As she averted her eyes, she caught sight of her father in the fifth screen, moving purposefully across it. Almost as soon as he was lost to sight on that screen, he was caught advancing in Number One screen, coming from a shadowy passage, and then he materialised in the room in person.

"Did you watch closely? What did you make of the demonstration?" he asked.

She stook up, vexed with herself.

"I was so fascinated with the view on the big screen... I was only just about to watch Number Five monitor."

Felix frowned and shook his head. "Such a simple thing I asked you to do—"

"Do the demonstration again, father. I will watch this time, honestly! I'm sorry!"

"No, no, it was just a small thing, as I warned you. To do it after this fuss would make it meaningless."

"Oh, no, that can't be so, surely. I wasn't making a fuss. I won't find it meaningless. You didn't give me enough time. You didn't give me a proper chance—" To her own dismay she began to cry. Angrily she turned her back on him, fumbling in her bag for a tissue.

"Always these overheated personal nonsenses!" Felix shouted. "Isn't it enough that you should have been stupid without compounding it by bursting into tears? Dry your eyes, woman! —You're as bad as your mother!"

At that, she cried the louder.

When she turned round at length, he had left the room.

She stood there in a melancholy containment, with the unwinking monitors by her right hand. Should she leave, despite her headache, so much worse after the fit of weeping? Did he expect her to leave? And how much did his expectations influence whether she would actually leave or not?

In any case, it was past lunchtime. She could either rustle up something from the kitchen, where she had found a surprisingly well-maintained range of food, or she could go down to the pub in Crackmore. She had meant to take him along to the pub, but his insufferable behaviour put a different aspect on things.

She glanced at the screens to see if she could catch sight of him. The view on Number Seven monitor was moving slowly; she looked and realised that the movement of the camera was automatic. The screen showed another bedroom, evidently her father's from its state of occupation. There was a cupboard, one door half-open to reveal suits within, and an untidy pile of clothes on a chair. She supposed the laundry man still called every week. The bed was unmade. The viewpoint was moving beyond it in a slow arc, taking in blank wall, an angle between walls complex with diffused shadow, then a window—seen obliquely, but revealing the tops of unkempt trees in the drive by the front gate—then the wall between windows, then the next window, rolling gently into view...No father there.

He had built neat switchboards; she realised that everything could be controlled from here. If she could set all the cameras tracking, then presumably she would detect him in one of the rooms. Tentatively, she pressed one of the piano keys nearest to her.

His voice came out at her. "—st lot of tinned meat gave me diarrhea...My evolutionary discovery is greater than Charles Darwin's or his grandfather's...greater and far more world-shaking. Darwin revealed only part of the truth—"

She switched him off.

He was mad. No doubt of it. Madness suited him—there had always been a madness in the distance he had kept between himself and everyone else.

He was probably dangerous too. Men with monomania were generally violent when opposed. She'd better be careful. But she'd always been careful. And really—she told herself in the thick ticking room—she had hated him since childhood.

She saw him On Number Four screen. He must have rushed outside to avoid her crying; now he was entering the house, turning to close the door—my God, was locking it! Locking it! What did he mean to do?

Anna ran out of the nearer living-room door and into the kitchen. Panic momentarily overcame her. She ran across the kitchen and pulled open the door. Surely he was intending to trap her, or else why lock the front door? He had said he never locked it—What was that ghastly phrase? — "If I don't lock up, I can escape faster"? Nutty as a fruitcake!

She ran from the kitchen. The gravel outside had sprouted so many weeds, so much grass, that it hardly showed anymore. She hurried through them, thinking she had better get to her car and clear off, or at least go and get a drink and then return, cautiously, and plead with him to let Stokes-Wallis examine him...As she turned the corner and came to the front of the house, her father emerged from the front door and—no, it was not a run—*hastened* to her car.

Anna stopped a few yards away.

"What are you playing at, father?"

"Are you going already, Anna?"

She went a little nearer.

"You aren't trying to stop me leaving, are you?"

"You are leaving, then, are you?" His hair almost concealed his eyes.

She paused.

"It's best if I leave, father. I don't understand your work, you refuse to explain it to me, and I interrupt it in any case. It's not just a question of that, either, is it? I mean, there's the question of temperament, too, isn't there? We've never got on. It was your business—the way I look at it—to get on with me if you could, since I was your daughter, your only child, but, no, you never fucking well cared, did you? I was just an intrusion between you and mother. Okay, then I'll get out, and as far as I'm concerned you can sit and goggle at your empty screens till you fall dead. Now get out of my way!"

As she came forward, Felix stepped back from the car. He let his gaze drop so that his eyes were completely hidden by the overhanging lock of his hair. His arms hung by his side. In his stained grey trousers and his torn sweater, he looked helpless and negative.

Proud of her victory, Anna marched forward and grasped the door handle of the Triumph. As she pulled it open, he seized her fiercely from behind, locking his arms round her so that her elbows were pinned against her sides.

She yelled in fright. A passenger jet roared overhead, taking up and drowning the note of her cry while he spun her round and dragged her into the house.

Even in her fury and fear, she found time to curse herself for forgetting that mannerism of her father. How often as a child had she seen him doing as he did then, suddenly turning deceptively limp and passive before springing on her like an enemy! She should not have been deceived!—But of course memory so often worked to obliterate the miseries of reality!

Once he had got her into the hall, he pulled her toward the side door into the garage. Anna recovered her wits and kicked backwards at his legs. He was immensely strong! Together, they tripped over the cables in the entrance and half-fell down the concrete step into the garage. As she broke from his grip, he caught her again and momentarily they were face to face.

"You're the enemy!" he said. "You're one of the non-humans!"

Above their heads were unpainted wood shelves, crudely fixed to the wall with brackets and loaded with boxes and spools of plastic covered wire. Pinning his daughter to the wall, Felix reached up and dragged down one of the spools. The action tumbled a couple of boxes, and nails cascaded over their heads. Tugging savagely at her, Felix commenced to bind her round and round with wire, securing her ankles as well as her wrists.

He was just finishing when they heard a distant knocking.

Felix straightened. He pushed his hair from his eyes.

"That'll be the grocer. Don't make a sound, Anna, or I'll be forced—well, you know what I'll be forced to do!" He gave her a hard straight look which included no recognition of her as a human being.

As soon as he had got into the hall and was making for the kitchen, from which the knocking came, Anna struggled upright and hobbled towards the door. It was impossible to climb up the step into the hall with her ankles bound; she fell up it. Before she was on her feet again, her father was coming back. He had a letter in his hand, and was smiling.

"A Glasgow postmark—this will be from Professor Nicholson! The grocer kindly brings my mail along from the post office. He's a good fellow. He recognised your car; I told him I was having the pleasure of a visit from you. Now, my dear, we are going to get you upstairs. If you help yourself a bit, it won't be so painful."

"Father, what are you going to do with me? *Please* let me go! I'm not a little girl anymore, to be punished when I disobey your orders."

He laughed. "No, you are far from being a little girl, Anna. Just how far, I intend to discover for myself."

She stared at him in shock, as if for the first time the helplessness of her position was made real to her. He read her expression and laughed again, a lot less pleasantly.

"Oh, no, my dear, I didn't mean what you think—whatever fantasies you entertain in the depths of your mind!"

"You don't know what I'm thinking!"

"I don't want to know what you're thinking! What a miserable generation yours was, obsessed by sex, yet totally unable to come to terms with your own sexuality. Your mother and I had a far better time than you or any of your friends will ever have!"

By dint of pushing and lifting, he got her upstairs and trundled her past the bathroom into the bedroom whose door stood open opposite the head of the stairs. She found herself in a bedroom at the back of the house, recognising it indifferently as the room she had seen on the viewing screen.

"Now!" he said, looking round, frowning.

He loosed some of the wire from her ankles, led her over to the bed, and tied her legs to the bedpost, so that she was forced to sit there. Then he disappeared. She heard him going downstairs. A minute later, he was back, a tenon saw in one hand. He knelt by the door and started to saw low down on the leading edge. When he had got six inches in, he stood and kicked vigorously at the bottom of the door. The wood splintered and a piece sagged outward. He kicked at it until it was loose.

The door would now shut, despite the cables trailing over the floor. Looking meaningfully at her once, he went out, and she heard him turning the key in the lock. She was properly imprisoned.

Impotently listening, she heard him march downstairs. Silence, then the sound of the Triumph engine starting up. What a fool she was to have left the key in the ignition—by no means for the first time! But he could always have taken the key from her bag; she had left it in the kitchen.

She heard the car engine fade almost immediately; so he had driven it round the side of the house, parking it beyond the kitchen door, where it would not be noticed from the road.

The grocer might see it when he called again—but how long ahead would that be? Evidently no postman called—the grocer had agreed to deliver her father's post. Perhaps no other tradesman came up this cul-de-sac; her father might well rely on the friendly grocer for all supplies. Of course, she had told Trevor and some of the fellows in the labs where she was going, but Trevor was not to be relied on, while the rest of them would not give her another thought until Monday, when she did not show up for work. She was on her own.

Well, that was nothing new. It was just that the situation was more extreme than usual.

Anna was already working to free her hands. It should be possible. She had already noticed that her father had left—carelessly or by design?—the saw on the floor by the door. It might come in useful.

The front door slammed.

Of course, he could watch her over the Omniviewer. She glared across the room at the dull lens of the camera, bracketed in the wall against the disused grate, a foot above floor level. She would just have to hope that he was unable to watch all the time.

Her feet were less tightly tied than her wrists and arms. After working away carefully, she managed to slip one of her brogues off, and then to wriggle her stockinged foot from the coils. The other one came out easily, and she could walk round the room.

Still pulling at her wrists, she ran over to the window and looked out.

Clouds had piled up in the sky. The afternoon was torpid. She was looking over what had once been a vegetable garden. Impenetrable weeds grew there. They stopped at the high wire fence, drab green and stretching away into the distance. Beyond the fence lay the airport, flat and featureless. She could see no building from this window, only a distant plane, deserted on a runway.

The view was blank and alien. It offered her no courage.

Hooking her wrists over the catch of the window, she pulled and wriggled to such effect that in a minute her hands were free. As she rubbed her hands together, she listened for his footstep on the stair.

Just how dangerous was he? She could not estimate. That he was her father made it all more difficult to calculate, more bizarre. If he came up, would he not, this time—at last—put his arms round her and love and forgive her for all her shortcomings?

No, he bloody well wouldn't!

The door was locked, as expected.

Anna crossed to the single picture on the wall above the bed, a sepia reproduction mounted and set in a solid oak frame. As she pulled it down, she saw that it represented a Roman sentry in armour standing guard before a gateway leading into a luridly lit court in which people were dying and dead—flares of some kind were falling from the skies onto them. The picture was called "Faithful Unto Death." She swung it in front of the camera, propping it against a chair so that the view was obstructed. Then she opened the window and looked out.

Felix Macguire was standing among the weeds aiming a gun of some kind at her. A rifle, possibly. Aimed at her. Half-fainting, she sank back inside the room.

Leaning against the wall, she heard him shouting. She began listening to his words.

"I'd have fired if you'd tried to jump. I warn you, Anna! You may not fully understand the situation, but I do. The fact that you are my daughter makes no difference. You are not going to leave here, or not until I say you can. Professor Basil Nicholson is coming tomorrow, and I want him to look at you. Behave yourself and you'll come to no harm. If you don't behave yourself, I'll lock you in the landing cupboard without food. Forget you're my daughter—remember you're my captive. Now then—shut that window. Do you hear, shut the window!"

She summoned enough presence of mind to look out and say, though without all the spirit she hoped for, "Try and realise what you are saying and doing, father! You are now formally renouncing me as your daughter, which is what you have wished to do all your life. You are also threatening to shoot me!"

He said angrily, "This is a French carbine, used against rioters. I'll fire if you don't get back. I mean every word." A few drops of rain began to fall.

"I'm sure you do! I don't doubt that. I'm sure you do! I'm sure you'd love to fire. But you should recognise what it means. You have now crossed the dividing line between sanity and madness. You are also committing a criminal act!"

"Get your head inside and close—" His words were drowned by the roar of an airliner coming in to land, but his threatening gestures were enough for her. Anna pulled her head back and wearily shut the window. She laid down on the bed and tried to think what she should do. Her stomach rumbled like thunder.

It was a problem to understand how matters between them had deteriorated so rapidly. Was it just because she had forgotten to watch his demonstration on the monitor, or because of some other fault of which she was unaware? And what had the demonstration been? Something minor, despite its buildup, that was clear: perhaps merely watching her father in the kitchen over the closed-circuit. Instead, she had been hooked into watching an empty room—this room. "Getting control of reality": that had been his phrase. Had he, her all-powerful and untouchable father, been rewarded for his years of isolation—whether unwished for or self-imposed—by some amazing insight into the physical conditions governing man? Had he really stumbled on an equivalent to Galileo's proof of the heliocentric system? It was not past the bounds of credibility—but nothing was past the bounds of credibility these days. And if he had so done, he would naturally be impatient (though *impatient* was scarcely the word) with any silly girl who failed to follow him closely when he attempted to explain.

She lay looking up at the ceiling. She could hear rain outside, and another slight sound. The camera was still working.

Warmth and comfort overcame her. Perhaps the aspirins were taking effect; her headache had gone. She began to recall summer days in their old house, before she had grown up, when her mother was alive, and she had lain as she was now lying on her bed, idly reading a book; the window was open to the summer breezes, and she could hear her parents down in the garden, exchanging an odd sentence now and again. Her mother was gardening, her father working on a monograph on lacunae in the theory of evolution which never got published. Evolutionary theory was always his hobby—a complete contrast from the pushing world of electronics into which his job took him. She had put her book down and gone over—yes, she had been barefoot—gone over to the window and looked out. He had waved to her and called something...

"Can you hear me, father? I didn't mean to miss your demonstration, whatever it was, if that is why you're punishing me. If possible, I'd like to understand and help. It could be that when watching the big screen I had a useful insight into what you meant about reality. A view over the screen is different in some undefined way to a view direct, isn't it?"

No answer. She lay looking up at the ceiling, listening. She had often listened like this before going to sleep as a child, wondering if someone would come up and visit her. The ceiling blurred; suggestions of warmth and other modes of being moved in; she slept.

Felix MacGuire sat at the console, resting his elbow on the desk and rubbing his chin, as he peered at the big screen. It showed part of a scene at the Herculanean Gate of Pompeii in A.D. 79, with the inhabitants about to be destroyed; a soldier in close-up stood at his post, eyes raised fearfully towards the unknown.

The light values on the soldier's face changed almost unnoticeably as Felix ran back the tape and played over again the words his daughter had spoken.

"...had a useful insight into what you meant by reality. A view over the screen is different in some undefined way to a view direct, isn't it?"

He ran it back again, listening mainly to the tone of her voice.

"I didn't mean to miss your demonstration, whatever it was, if that is why you are punishing me. If possible I'd like to understand and help. It could be that when watching the big screen I had a useful insight into—"

He clicked her off. Always that pleading and cajoling note in her voice which he recalled from her childhood. A jarring note. No wonder no man had ever married her.

Silence in her room. But it was not the usual silence he received from Number Two bedroom. The usual silence had a sort of thin and rather angular dazed quality unique to itself, resembling the surface of a Vermeer canvas, and with a similar sense almost of *planning* behind it; he thought of it as an intellectual silence and, of course, it differed from the silences in the other rooms. With Anna's occupancy, the silence took on an entirely different weight, a bunched and heavy mottled feeling which he disliked.

The sound levels were so good that he could detect when she was drifting towards sleep. It was her way of eluding reality; a little editing of tape would soon bring her back to her uncomfortable senses.

She roused, sat up suddenly, aware that her mouth had fallen open. Someone was whispering in the room. She had caught the sound of her own voice.

"...a useful insight..."

Then her father's voice, indistinct, and then her own, perfectly clear:

"Can you hear me, father?" And his reply:

"Why didn't you watch what your mother and I were doing? You're old enough to learn the facts of life."

"I didn't mean to miss your demonstration, whatever it was, if that is why you're punishing me."

"What do you mean, 'whatever it was,' Anna? Come back into the bedroom and watch—we're just going to start again."

"If possible, I'd like to understand and help."

"That's better. Jump in with your mother. You'll soon learn."

She sat on the edge of the bed, flushing with shame.

"You're right round the bloody twist, father!" she said aloud. "For Christ's sake let me out of here and let me go home. I'll never bother you again—you can be sure of that!"

He came in the bedroom door, grinning in an uneasy way.

"Forget all that—just a bit of innocent fun! You see what can be done with reality! Now look, Anna, you present me with a bit of a problem. I'll have to keep you here overnight, so you'd better resign yourself to the fact. Basil Nicholson is coming tomorrow—his visit is very important to me, because for the first time I'm going to present my findings to an impartial outside observer. Nicholson and I have been in communication for months, and he's sufficiently impressed by what I've told him to come and look for himself. You could be useful in more than one way. So you'll have to stay here and behave. If all goes well, you can go home tomorrow afternoon. Okay?"

She just sat and stared at him. The whole business was too horrifying to be believed.

Felix picked up the framed engraving and hung it back on the wall. As he went towards the door, he picked up the saw. He smiled and waved it at her, a gesture part friendly, part menacing.

"Why don't you kill me, father? You know I can never forgive you—pointing a gun at your own daughter. I saw murder in your eyes, I did."

He paused with a hand on the door. "Never forgive? You can't say that. Never Forgive? Never? Think what a long journey it is between birth and death. Anything is possible on the way."

"Go to hell!"

"Think what a long journey you and I have come, Anna! Here we are together in this house; perhaps in one sense we have always been here. Perhaps it doesn't matter that we don't understand each other. Perhaps we hate each other, who knows? We make the journey together. It's like crossing a glacier—in moments of danger, all the various differences between us become unimportant and we are forced to help each other to survive.

There's no way of making sense out of such testing journeys until we have the tools to understand what human life is about."

Anna fumbled in her pocket for a tissue. One nostril was blocked with incipient cold. "I don't want your philosophising."

"But you must understand what I'm saying. Nobody lives out their life without being brought up against a sudden moment when they see themselves as in a screen or mirror and ask themselves, 'What am I doing here? Once, it used to be a religious question. Then people started to interpret it more in socio-economic terms. Your generation tried to answer it in terms of individual escape, and a poor job they made of it. I'm trying to provide an evolutionary solution which will take care of all the other aspects."

He sounded so reasonable. She was baffled by his changes of mood, always had been.

"If you didn't want to have me here, you should have phoned and told me so. How can you ill-treat me so? I've never harmed you. Pointing that gun at me! I just want to go away— I don't know whether I can recover from what you've done to me."

"You keep saying that. Try and pull yourself together, Anna. We're father and daughter—nothing can ever come between us, not even if I had to kill you."

He had put his arm round her, but now she drew away, looking at him with a face of dread seeing only a blackness in his eyes and a cruel estrangement round his mouth.

"I want to go now, father, if you don't mind. Back home. Please let me go. I've never done you any harm. Let me go and I'll never bother you again!"

He was unmoving as stone.

"Never done me any harm? What child has not harmed its parents? Didn't you, every day of your life, come between your mother and me with your insatiable craving for attention? Didn't you drive her into an early grave with your perpetual demands? But for you, wouldn't she be here, on this very bed, with us now?"

"Your evolutionary theory, father—are you sure you ought to talk about it with Nicholson? Shouldn't you publish a paper on the idea first? Or write to *Nature*, or something?"

He was standing now and looking down on her. She had hunched herself up on the bed with her legs tucked under her.

"You're frightened, aren't you? Why should you be interested in my theories? As—"

The roar of a plane swamped his sentence. For a moment, the room was darkened as the machine passed low overhead. It seemed to distract Macguire's attention. He wandered over to the window.

"The sooner we get control of reality, the better. One of these days, they're not just going to fly over—they'll drop an H-bomb on me, right smack down the chimney, since they can see their warnings don't scare me off." He turned back to her. "I must prepare my notes for Nicholson's arrival tomorrow. You'd better come down and clear the place up. If there's time, I'll give you the demonstration I plan to give him and see how you like it. This time, you'd better attend."

"Oh, I will, I will, father."

He walked out of the room, still clutching the saw in his hand. She hesitated, then climbed off the bed and followed him downstairs.

"The front door's locked, by the way, Anna, and I have the key in my pocket."

"I wasn't thinking of going out."

"No? Well, its raining, but just in case you were."

He went into the living room, pushed past the partition, and sat down at his console as if nothing had happened. She went into the kitchen, leaned her elbows on the window sill and buried her face in her hands.

After a while, the involuntary shaking in her limbs died away and she looked up. The house was absolutely silent. No, not absolutely. The camera made a faint registration of its presence. With very intent listening, she could hear slight movements from her father in the next room. She looked at her watch, decided to make a cup of tea, and started the soothingly traditional preliminaries of filling the kettle, switching it on, and getting down teapot and tea caddy from the shelf.

"Like a dutiful daughter, you are making me a cup too." A loudspeaker.

"Of course, father."

How could she persuade him that she loved him? It was impossible, because she did not love him. She had failed to love him. Shouldn't love have sprung up in her spontaneously, however he behaved, the way spring flowers—the modest and incorrigible snowdrops—bud and blossom even in the teeth of chilly winds? The truth was that she understood so little about herself; perhaps she even hoped that he would carry out his direct threats.

When the tea was made, she put everything on a tray and carried it through to him. Felix smiled and motioned her to put it on a side table.

As she did as he indicated, she saw the carbine. Her father had stood it in the corner behind him. It was ready for action, she thought—was he secretly planning to grab it up and shoot her?

"There are some chocolate biscuits in the cupboard over the sink, if you'd like to get them. You always enjoyed chocolate biscuits, Anna."

"I still do, as it happens." She fetched the biscuits.

He drank his tea absently, staring into the miniature screens, switching the view from one or another onto the larger screen scrutinising his static universe. Finally he settled on a panorama of the dining room through Camera Six, with the table, loaded with electronic gear, to one side of the screen and most of it filled by wall and desolate fireplace. This cheerless scene held his attention for so long that his tea grew cold by his elbow.

Anna sat staring towards the carbine.

At last, he sighed and looked up at her.

"Beautiful, isn't it? Human environment with humans abstracted. Almost a new art form—and utterly neglected. But that's neither here nor there."

Silence.

"Father, would it annoy you to explain to me what you see in the screen?"

"I see everything. The history of the world in that one shot. The grate, designed to burn fossil trees trapped in the earth since they grew in the jungles of the Carboniferous Age. Look at its Art Nouveau motif on the black lead canopy. All obsolete. A great age of mankind gone forever. Fires will never burn there again, prehistoric energy never be released there. Now the only function of that fireplace is to form part of this picture. The function of the picture is to activate part of my brain. My brain has been activated by retinal designs, formed in this house, never viewed before. I view them every day. They have made me conscious of my own brain structure, which in turn has modified that structure, so that I have been able to fit together facts—facts available to anyone through evolutionary study—and make them into a new whole. A new whole, Anna. You'd never understand."

He paused and drank down his cold tea.

Keeping herself under control, Anna reflected on the virtue of sanity; it was not half as boring as madness. With sudden impatience, she said, "Spare me the reasoning, please. Give me the facts. What exactly *is* this theory you keep bragging about?"

He looked rather guiltily up at her. "You must let it all soak in gradually. It needs practice to understand."

"I'm sorry, father, I have a job to go back to. You may not think it important but it is important to me. If you will not show me straightforwardly, then I shall have to leave before it gets dark."

He digested that. "I hoped you'd stay and have a bite of supper with me." His mild manner suggested he had forgotten his earlier threats.

"Why should I, after the way you have treated me? Explain at once or I shall go."

He shrugged. "As you will. If you feel up to it."

Pushing his teacup out of the way, he fiddled with various switches, rose, and messed about behind the partition, before saying, "Right, then, watch this carefully."

She dragged her eyes from the weapon in the corner.

The big screen lit. Anna looked with interest, but there was nothing except yet another view of the interior of the house. This was Camera Three working, moving slowly, so that the viewpoint descended from the upper landing to the hall, to a slow-moving shot of the hall cupboard and the ever-open door through to the garage. In the small section of the garage revealed, the door into the workshop could be seen. Only the eternal gleaming black cables, running across the floor, gave any sense of life. Then she saw a shadow move in the workshop. A man came through into the garage. She gasped.

"It's all right. This is tapex you're watching."

The man emerged into the hall. It was Felix, rather blank-faced, hair slanting across forehead. Without pausing, he moved forward and along the corridor towards the kitchen.

Now the scene was a blank again, unpopulated. The camera eye travelled over it in a leisurely and dispirited fashion. A shadow moved in the depths of the picture and a man passed from workshop to garage. Anna instinctively leaned forward, expecting something—she did not know what: something to frighten her. The man came out of the garage into the hall. It was her father, somewhat blank-faced. Without pausing, he moved out of camera range in the direction of the kitchen.

"Keep watching," Felix ordered.

The screen still showed only the view of the hall, its shadows, and the angles and perspectives created by the doorways beyond—a pattern that, by constant wearying repetition, seemed at once to annihilate sense and to acquire an ominous significance of its own; just as the single note of a dripping tap, listened to long enough, becomes an elusive tune. When something stirred in the shadows beyond the furthest doorway, she was prepared for it, prepared for the man who stepped from the workshop to garage and then, after a pause, from garage to hall. It was her father, wearing his old sweater. Without pausing, blank faced, he walked towards the kitchen and was lost from view.

The hall was empty. In a brief while, the whole insignificant action was repeated as before. Then it was repeated again. And again. Each time, the same thing happened.

At last the screen went blank, just when Anna thought she would have to scream if it happened once more.

"What have you seen, Anna?"

"Oh—you know. You coming out of the garage a million times!"

"Live or on tape?"

"On tape, obviously. The first time round, I thought it was live—well, except that you were here beside me. What does all that prove?"

"If I'd been hidden in the kitchen, you couldn't have told what you saw from live. Or any of the re-runs, if they had been shown first."

"I suppose not."

"How many times did you see me come into the hall?"

"I've lost count. Twelve? Eighteen?"

"Nine times. Do you imagine they were all re-runs of one occasion on which I came into the hall?"

"Obviously."

"It's not obvious. You're wrong. What you witnessed was me coming into the hall on three different occasions—three different days, in fact. Each was re-run three times. And you didn't spot the difference?"

"One time must have been very like another." She was weary of the nonsense of his solemnity. "You always looked just the same. The light always looked just the same. Obviously the house always looked just the same."

"Okay. You're talking about the scientific theory of convergence."

He pressed a key, ran the videotape until he was once more stepping from the garage to hall; then he froze the action. Staring out at his image, he said, "Obviously, ways of getting from one room to another are always closely alike. Right? So close you mistook them for identical. But they aren't identical. I've tried to remove the difference between one day and the next in this environment, as nearly as I can. Yet I—the living!—am aware of the change between one day and the next, as you were not when witnessing that change on the screen.

"Animals that adapt to similar environments and pursue the same inclination also tend to resemble each other. However alien the animals themselves may be from each other, there are only a limited number of ways of getting through a doorway or living in a desert or swimming in a sea. To fly, you have to have wings; there are animals which mimic birds in that respect, and they are examples of convergence."

He pressed a key in front of him, and a shot of the wall of the workshop came up, a grey view with nothing on which to fix attention except three blown-up photographs ranged one under the other on the wall. The photographs depicted three gigantic sea-going creatures, each remarkably similar to the next in its functional streamlined form. Felix left them in view for a while before speaking.

"This is part of the big game I have been hunting for forty years, you might say. You know what these creatures are?"

"Are they all sharks?" Anna asked.

A plane roared overhead. The house vibrated, the picture on the screen shimmered and split into a maze of lines and dots. When it reassembled and the noise died, Felix said, "The top one is a shark. The next one down is a porpoise. The bottom one is an ichthyosaur. They all look alike—prime examples of convergence; yet one is a cartilaginous fish, one a marine mammal, and the other an extinct marine reptile—inwardly, they are nothing alike."

She fidgeted a little. It was growing dark and she wanted to be away from the house and its insane pedant. The rain had ceased; all was still outside, with the stillness of dripping trees.

"That's hardly a discovery, father. It has been known for a long time."

His head drooped, his shoulders slumped. She feared that he was about to burst into one of his insane rages. When he looked up again, his face was distorted with anger, so that she hardly recognised him, as if he had undergone some uncharted Jekyll-Hyde transformation. Instintively, she took a step back. But he spoke with a measure of calm.

"You do not believe in me, you stupid vegetable... Have the wit at least to hear me out when I try to explain everything in layman's language and by analogy. My discovery is that there are creatures as strange as fish and extinct reptiles that go about the world under the same forms as man!"

Anna's first terrified thought was that he was living proof of his own hypothesis. Was there not, in that mottled jowl, that prognathous face, those blazing eyes, something that argued against idiothermous origin and whispered of a reptile brain lurking like an egg inside that bony nest of skull?

He stood up and stood glaring into her face, so that they confronted each other only a few inches apart.

"Reptiles structurally similar to man," he said. "Forms almost identical, intentions entirely different. Why is our world being destroyed? Why are the seas being polluted, why are nuclear weapons proliferating towards a holocaust, why do human beings feel increasingly powerless? Because there is an enemy in our midst as different from us as moon is from sun—an enemy intent on wiping out human civilization and reverting to a Jurassic world it still carries in its mind. These enemies are old, Anna, far older than mankind, still carrying a heritage from the Mesozoic in which they were formed, still hoping to bring the Mesozoic back down about our ears!"

With a mingling rush of light and dark in the room, another plane roared overhead, making everything in the room shake, Anna included.

Felix rolled his eyes up to the ceiling. "There they go! They are gradually assuming power, and power for destruction. Men develop the technology, reptile-men take over its results and use them for destructive ends!"

She clutched at her throat to help bring out her voice. "Father—it's a terrifying idea you have... but... but it's—isn't it just your fancy?"

The clouded swollen look was still on his face. "There is archaeological evidence. Nicholson knows. He has some of it. Evidence from the past is all too scarce. There's my quarrel with Darwinism— a fine picture of evolution has been built up on too little evidence. The layman believes that deceptively whole picture of dinosaurs dying out and mammals developing, and finally *Homo sapiens* rising out of several extinct man forms; but the layman fails to realise how the picture is in fact conjured up merely from a few shards of bone, a broken femur here, a scatter of yellowed teeth there... And the picture we now accept is wrong in several vital instances.

"You may know that there is no understanding of why all the species of the two dinosaur genera, the *saurischia* and the *ornithischia*, suddenly died out. Ha! The reason for that lack of understanding is that they did not die out. Both the saurischians and the ornithischians were capable of tremendous variety, adapting to all kinds of conditions, even achieving flight, covering the globe. Both produced creatures which walked on their hind legs like man. But the saurischians also produced a man-creature, evolving from the theropod line."

"Is there physical proof of the development of this creature?"

"There is no physical proof of the development of any dinosaur—for all we know to the contrary, the brontosaur and tyrannosaur may have popped *out* of existence overnight... But a few remains of a late development of reptile-man have been found. You have heard of Neanderthal Man, I presume?"

"Certainly. You aren't going to tell me that Neanderthal Man was a development from a dinosaur!"

"He evolved from the same original stock as the dinosaurs. He was probably always few in number, but he helped kill off the big dinosaurs. The popular folk idea that men were about when the dinosaurs lived is nothing less than the truth—perhaps it's a sort of folk memory."

"Can I put the light on? It's getting dark in here. But you say the line died out?"

"I didn't say that. The so-called Neanderthal is popularly said to have died out. There's no evidence, though. The Neanderthal reptile-men merged with humanity—mammal-humanity—and we have never been able to sort them out since."

She stood by the door, hand on the light switch, again thinking of flight. When the overhead light came on, it made the images of the three marine creatures on the screen appear faint and spectral, more suited to move through air than water.

"Father, my headache has come back. May I go upstairs and lie down in my room to think about what you have told me?"

He moved a little nearer to her.

"Do you believe what I have told you? Do you understand? Are you capable of understanding?"

"How is it that modern medicine has not tracked down these reptile-men if they still exist, by blood analysis or something?"

"It has. But it has misinterpreted the evidence. I won't go into the whole complex question of blood-grouping. Another problem is that reptile-men and human stock now interbreed. The lines are confused. There is reason to think that venereal disease is the product of interbreeding—another intravenous way in which the two species seek to destroy each other. Do you want some aspirins?"

"I have some eau-de-cologne in my case in the car. May I go and get it?"

"You go upstairs. I'll get your case for you."

Hesitating, she looked at him. Not liking what she saw, she moved reluctantly and walked along the hall corridor, turned right, and went up the stairs under the eye of Camera Three, holding to the banisters as she went. She paused again on the landing. Reptile-men! Then she went ahead into the bedroom, glanced hopelessly up at "Faithful Unto Death," sullen in the twilight, and lay down. She could have locked herself in but what was the point? In his madness, her father would break the door down whenever he felt like it. Perhaps he would come up and kill her; perhaps he imagined she was of reptilian stock.

She played with that idea, imagining the strange and aberrant allegiances it might give her with gloomy green unflowering plants, with damp stones, with immense shapes that moved only when prompted by the sun, and with languid spans of time which could find no true lodgement within the consciousness of man. The idea of being cold-blooded alone made her tremble where she lay, and clutch at the blankets for warmth.

There was a dull light in the room, gloomy, green, and unflowering. Another plane blundered over, shaking the house.

Downstairs, he heard and felt the plane go over. He raised his heavy eyes up towards its path, imagining it furry and coleopterous while the room vibrated, saying to it, "One day, you too will lie broken and stoney in a shattered layer of sandstone."

He stood before the big screen, Camera One trained on him, throwing his image over his body. Eyes, mouth, head, limbs, vibrated, became double and detached, then settled back as the noise died.

A memory came back to him from far away that he had said he would go and get Anna's case from her car.

Moving with lethargy, he crossed to the console and set Camera One moving until it was trained through the living room door to the dining room door. This was the nearest he could get to covering the back door; some day, he must install a tenth camera in the passage, so that the back door was surveyed. All he could see on the screen now was the ugly concatenation of angles formed by the two doors between them. He walked out into the passage and headed down it, to the door with two glass panels in its frame which he always kept locked. He unlocked it, opened it, went out.

To his right stretched the length of the back of the house. At right angles to it, another wall stood along the left, punctuated by scullery and pantry windows. An uneven path flanked this walk. He moved slowly along it. There had been flagstones of good York stone underfoot, but weeds and grass had covered them. Blank eyes of scullery and pantry surveyed him.

The light was leaden now. Time and twilight were congealed and fixed like a murdered eye. Like something viewed in a long mirror, he was embedded far in the past, together with gymnosperms, woodlice, the first ungainly amphibians and things still unidentified by the peeping gaze of man.

When he turned left round by the corner of the woodshed, Macguire was only a few feet away from the sterile green wire fence. He knew a lot of things about the colour green; it, more than any colour, was involved in the guilty story of downfall.

He turned left again, pushing aside overgrown branches of elder. They still flowered, individual florets looming up before his eyes like galaxies in some dim-lit and cluttered universe. Now he was stalking along the southwest side of the house. The weeds of high summer crushed and sprang under his footfall.

There was her car, low under the overhanging branches of trees. Every year, the beeches grew nearer and nearer to the house. Some of them already nuzzled their first tender branches against the brick.

He stood glaring through the windows at the seats within, awaiting people. It was shabby and vacant in there, another unwelcoming human environment, depopulated. On the backseat lay a small case Macguire pulled open the rear door, grasped the handle of the case, and dragged it out. He stood with it where he was, his other hand touching the car, staring at his daughter. Anna had come round the front of the house; she held his carbine in an efficient way, and was pointing it at his stomach. He looked at her face and saw it too belonged with the lost gymnosperms, woodlice, and amphibians hidden long ago behind the pantry, engendering only extinction.

"You can go if you don't shoot me, Anna. I'm the only one with the theory complete, although there are people everywhere piecing it together. It's a matter of time... It's not a race. I mean, there's no excitement—it's too late now for man to beat the reptile-men; they've had too long and they are virtually in control. Look at the light under these trees—if you understand such things, the light alone will tell you we're defeated. So there's no point in shooting."

"I'm going to shoot." The words came from her mouth. He watched the diagram of it, thinking how easy it was to understand human speech once you had the basic knowledge of the working anatomy of jaw and thorax and the formation of phonemes in the larynx by careful control of air, and how these sounds were carried into the listening labyrinths of those present. His daughter had the science of the whole thing off perfectly.

"I could show you yards of tapex—proof. Proof of all I say. I'm the only one who has studied a human being long enough. I've seen myself, caught myself off guard; I have to regard myself as heteromorphic. The reptile moves in my veins, too."

"Move away from the car."

He said, feeling the stiff discomfort of fear contort his lips and teeth and tongue, "Anna, this isn't the time of day... Just when I'm getting control of reality... Look, you're alien too. It's strong in you. Believe me. That's why you're so hostile. You're more lizard than I. Let me go! I won't hurt you! Let me show you!"

The gunpoint lowered slightly. A moth blundered through the space between their two ghastly faces and fell under the trees.

"What do you mean?"

"I got it on tapex. You can come in and see for yourself. Camera Number Eight. It's betrayed in certain movements. Unhuman movements. The gesture of the hand, the way a knee hinges, spinal tension, hip flexibility, a dozen details of facial expression. Oh, I've observed them all in myself. One hundred and thirty-one differences docketed. Throughout life, human beings are motivated to watch others and not themselves, right from early years when they begin to learn by imitation. I realised years ago I was not fully human. With age, you become less human, the antique lizard shows through more and more—after all, it's the basic stock. That's why old people turn against human pleasures. Now, in your case, you've never had much time for human pleasures—"

"Father—"

Afterwards, she wondered if he had begun to fall before she fired. The first shot curved the top half of his body forward. She fired again. This time he jerked backward, still standing, so that she saw how long and dark and lined his throat was. His mouth opened a little. She had a thought that he was looking down his nose and laughing at her, totally unharmed. She fired a third bullet, but was already trembling so violently that it missed.

An airbus came sizzling over the property so low that she fired again in sheer panic. The bullet whistled into the leaves of the trees, and still her father stood there, rocking a little, hands like claws digging into his belly. Then he fell over backwards, legs straight. When he hit the ground, the force of the fall caused his arms to spring out sideways. He lay there among the midsummer weeds in that attitude of unknowing, and never moved again. The beeches dripped on him, the erosions of his last July.

His hair was quite wet before Anna managed to move again.

She dropped the gun, then had the presence of mind to fumble it up again and toss it into the car. She picked up the little case and tossed that into the car. She stood over the body.

"Father?" she asked it.

It continued to make its gesture of unknowing.

Fighting her palsy, she climbed into the driving seat of the car. After several attempts, she got the motor going and managed to back away to the front of the house. She gave a last look into that deep grey-green past under the beeches where time had ceased, and drove towards the front gates.

As she passed through them, bumping on to the cul-de-sac road, she experienced a flash of memory. She thought of the electricity still burning, the camera still processing the spirit of the empty house, the big screen still registering daylight dying between an ugly angle of doors, the inhuman sequence of mounting time slithering into tapex.

But she did not pause, certainly did not turn back. Instead, she pressed her foot more firmly to the accelerator, flicked on the side lights, hunched herself over the wheel to control her shaking, forged ahead toward the tangle of tiny roads between her and Ashmansford.

She stared ahead. The shaggy elms outside the car, blue with advancing night, were reflected momentarily in her eyeballs. Overhead, another plane roared, its landing lights blazing, coming in to roost.

Samaritan

Connie Willis

The people of the Countrie, when they travaile in the Woods, make fires where they sleepe in the night; and in the morning, when they are gone, the Pongoes will come and sit about the fire, till it goeth out: for they have no understanding to lay the wood together.*

–Andrew Battell, 1625

Reverend Hoyt knew immediately what Natalie wanted. His assistant pastor knocked on the half-open door of his study and then sailed in, dragging Esau behind her by one hand. The triumphant smile on her face was proof enough of what she was going to say.

"Reverend Hoyt, Esau has something he wants to tell you." She turned to the Orangutan. He was standing up straight, something Reverend Hoyt knew was hard for him to do. He came almost to Natalie's shoulder. His thick, squat body was covered almost entirely with long, neatly brushed auburn hair. He had only a little hair on top of his head. He had slicked it down with water. His wide face, inset and shadowed by his cheek flaps, was as impassive as ever.

Natalie signed something to him. He stood silent, his long arms hanging limply at his sides. She turned back to Reverend Hoyt. "He wants to be baptized! Isn't that wonderful? Tell him, Esau."

*Orangutangs.

He had seen it coming. The Reverend Natalie Abreu, twenty-two and only one year out of Princeton, was one enthusiasm after another. She had revamped the Sunday school, taken over the grief-counselling department, and initiated a standard of priestly attire that outraged Reverend Hoyt's Presbyterian soul. Today she had on a trailing cassock with a red-and-gold embroidered stole edged with fringe. It must be Pentecost. She was short and had close-cropped brown hair. She flew about her official duties like a misplaced choirboy in her ridiculous robes and surplices and chasubles. She had taken over Esau, too.

She had not known how to use American Sign Language when she came. Reverend Hoyt knew only the bare minimum of signs himself, "yes" and "no" and "come here." The jobs he wanted Esau to do he had acted out mostly in pantomime. He had asked Natalie to learn a basic vocabulary so they could communicate better with the orang. She had memorized the entire Ameslan handbook. She rattled on to Esau for hours at a time, her fingers flying, telling him Bible stories and helping him with his reading.

"How do you know he wants to be baptized?"

"He told me. You know how we had the confirmation class last Sunday and he asked me all about confirmation and I said, "Now they are God's children, members of God's family.' And Esau said, 'I would like very much to be God's beloved child, too.'"

It was always disconcerting to hear Natalie translate what Esau said. She changed what was obviously labored and fragmented language into rhapsodies of adjectives, clauses, and modifiers. It was like watching one of those foreign films in which the actor rattled on for a paragraph and the subtitle only printed a cryptic, "That is so." This was reversed, of course. Esau had signed something like, "Me like be child God," if that, and Natalie had transformed it into something a seminary professor would say. It was impossible to have any real communication with Esau this way, but it was better than pantomime.

"Esau," he began resignedly, "do you love God?"

"Of course he loves God," Natalie said. "He'd hardly want to be baptized if he didn't, would he?"

"Natalie," he said patiently, "I need to talk to Esau. Please ask him, 'Do you love God?'"

She looked disgusted, but signed out the question. Reverend Hoyt winced. The sign for "God" was dreadful. It looked like a sideways salute. How could you ask someone if they loved a salute?

Esau nodded. He looked terribly uncomfortable, standing there. It infuriated Reverend Hoyt that Natalie insisted on his standing up. His backbone simply wasn't made for it. She had tried to get him to wear clothes, too. She had bought him a workman's uniform of coveralls and cap and shoes. Reverend Hoyt had not even been patient with her that time. "Why on earth would we put shoes on him?" he had said. "He was hired because he has feet he can use like hands. He needs them both if he's going to get up among the beams. Besides which he is already clothed. His hair covers him far more appropriately than those ridiculous robes you wear cover you!" After that Natalie had worn some dreadful Benedictine thing made of horsehair and rope until Reverend Hoyt apologized. He had not given in on the matter of clothes for Esau, however.

"Tell Esau to sit down in the chair," he said. He smiled at the orangutan as he said it. He sat down also. Natalie remained standing. The orangutan climbed into the chair frontwards, then turned around. His short legs stuck out straight in front of him. His body hunched forward. He wrapped his long arms around himself, then glanced up at Natalie, and hastily let them hang at his sides. Natalie looked profoundly embarrassed.

"Esau," he began again, motioning to Natalie to translate, "Baptism is a serious matter. It means that you love God and want to serve Him. Do you know what serve means?"

Esau nodded slowly, then made a peculiar sign, tapping the side of his head with the flat of his hand.

"What did he say, Natalie? And no embellishments, please. Just translate."

"It's a sign I taught him," she said stiffly. "In Sunday school. The word wasn't in the book. It means talents. He means..."

"Do you know the story of the ten talents, Esau?"

She translated. Again he nodded.

"And would you serve God with your talents?"

This whole conversation was insane. He could not discuss Christian service with an orangutan. It made no sense. They were not free agents. They belonged to the Cheyenne Mountain Primate Research facility at what had been the old zoo. It was there that the first orangs had signed to each other. A young one, raised until the age of three with humans, had lost both parents in an accident and had been returned to the center. He had a vocabulary of over twenty words in American Sign Language and could make simple commands. Before the end of the year, the entire colony of orangs had the same vocabulary and could form declarative sentences. Cheyenne Mountain did its best to educate their orangs and find them useful jobs out in society, but they still owned them. They came to get Esau once a month to breed him with females at the center. He didn't blame them. Orangs were now extinct in the wild. Cheyenne Mountain was doing the best they could to keep the species alive and they were not unkind to them, but he felt sorry for Esau, who would always serve.

He tried something else. "Do you love God, Esau?" he asked again. He made the sign for "love" himself.

Esau nodded. He made the sign for "love."

"And do you know that God loves you?"

He hesitated. He looked at Reverend Hoyt solemnly with his round brown eyes and blinked. His eyelids were lighter than the rest of his face, a sandy color. He made his right hand into a fist and faced it out toward Reverend Hoyt. He put the short thumb outside and across the fingers, then moved it straight up, then tucked it inside, all very methodically.

"S—A—M—" Natalie spelled. "Oh, he means the Good Samaritan, that was our Bible story last week. He has forgotten the sign we made for it." She turned to Esau and dropped her flat hand to her open palm. "Good, Esau. Good Samaritan." She made the S fist and tapped her waist with it twice. "Good Samaritan. Remember?"

Esau looked at her. He put his fist up again and out toward Reverend Hoyt. "S—," he repeated, "A—M—A—R—" He spelled it all the way through.

Natalie was upset. She signed rapidly at Esau. "Don't you remember, Esau? Good Samaritan. He remembers the story. You can see that. He's just forgotten the sign for it, that's all." She took his hands and tried to force them into the flattened positions for "good." He resisted.

"No," Reverend Hoyt said, "I don't think that's what he's talking about."

Natalie was nearly in tears. "He knows all his Bible stories. And he can read. He's read almost all of the New Testament by himself."

"I know, Natalie," Reverend Hoyt said patiently.

"Well, are you going to baptize him?"

He looked at the orang sitting hunched in the chair before him. "I'll have to give the matter some thought."

She looked stubborn. "Why? He only wants to be baptized. The Ecumenical Church baptizes people, doesn't it? We baptized fourteen people last Sunday. All he wants is to be baptized."

"I will have to give the matter some thought."

She looked as if she wanted to say something. "Come on, Esau," she said, signing to the ape to follow her.

He got out of the chair clumsily, trying to face forward while he did. Trying to please Natalie, Reverend Hoyt thought. Is that why he wants to be baptized, too, to please Natalie?

Reverend Hoyt sat at his desk for some time. Then he walked down the endless hall from his office to the sanctuary. He stood at the side door and looked into the vast sunlit chamber. The church was one of the first great Ecumenical cathedrals, built before the Rapture. It was nearly four stories high, vaulted with great open pine beams from the Colorado mountains. The famous Lazetti window reached the full four stories and was made of stained glass set in strips of stainless steel.

The first floor, behind the pulpit and the choir loft, was in shadow, dark browns and greens rising to a few slender palm trees. Above that was the sunset. Powerful oranges, rich rose, deep mauve dimmed to delicate peach and cream and lavender far over the heads of the congregation. At about the third-floor level the windows changed imperceptibly from pastel-tinted to clear window glass. In the evenings the Denver sunsets, rising above the smog, blended with the clouds of the window. Real stars came out behind the single inset star of beveled glass near the peak of the window.

Esau was up among the beams. He swung arm over arm, one hand trailing a white dusting cloth. His long, hairy arms moved surely among the crosspieces as he worked. They had tried ladders before Esau came, but they scratched the wood of the beams and were not safe. One had come crashing down within inches of the Lazetti window.

Reverend Hoyt decided to say nothing until he had made up his mind on the matter. To Natalie's insistent questions, he gave the same patient answer. "I have not decided." On Sunday he preached the sermon on humility he had already planned.

Reading the final scripture, however, he suddenly caught sight of Esau huddled on one of the pine crosspieces, his arms wrapped around a buttress for support, watching him as he read. "But as for me, my feet had almost stumbled, my steps had well-nigh slipped. I was stupid and ignorant. I was like a beast toward thee."

He looked out over his congregation. They looked satisfied with themselves, smug. He looked at Esau.

"Nevertheless I am continually with thee; thou dost hold my hand. Afterward thou wilt receive me to glory. My flesh and my heart may fail, but God is the strength of my heart and my portion forever." He banged the Bible shut. "I have not said everything I intend to say on the subject of humility, a subject which very few of you know anything about." The congregation looked surprised. Natalie, in a bright red robe with a yellow silk chasuble over it, beamed.

He made Natalie shout the benediction over the uproar afterwards and went out the organist's door and back to the parsonage. He turned down the bell on the telephone to almost nothing. An hour later Natalie arrived with Esau in tow. She was excited. Her cheeks were as red as her robe. "Oh, I'm so glad you decided to say something after all. I was hoping you would. You'll see, they'll all think it's a wonderful idea! I wish you'd baptized him, though. Just think how surprised everyone would have been! The first baptism ever, and in our church! Oh, Esau, aren't you excited! You're going to be baptized!"

"I haven't decided yet, Natalie. I told the congregation the matter had come up, that's all."

"But you'll see, they'll think it's a wonderful idea."

He sent her home, telling her not to accept any calls or talk to any reporters, an edict which he knew she would ignore completely. He kept Esau with him, fixing a nice supper for them both and turning the television on to a baseball game. Esau picked up Reverend Hoyt's cat, an old tom that allowed people in the parsonage only on sufferance, and carried him over to his chair in front of the TV. Reverend Hoyt expected an explosion of claws and hurt feelings, but the tom settled down quite happily in Esau's lap.

When bedtime came, Esau set him down gently on the end of the guest bed and stroked him twice. Then he crawled into the bed forwards, which always embarrassed Natalie so. Reverend Hoyt tucked him in. It was a foolish thing to do. Esau was fully grown. He lived alone and took care of himself. Still, it seemed the thing to do.

Esau lay there looking up at him. He raised up on one arm to see if the cat was still there, and turned over on his side, wrapping his arms around his neck. Reverend Hoyt turned off the light. He didn't know the sign for "good night," so he just waved, a tentative little wave, from the door. Esau waved back.

Esau ate breakfast with the cat in his lap. Reverend Hoyt had turned the phone back up, and it rang insistently. He motioned to Esau that it was time to go over to the church. Esau signed something, pointing to the cat. He clearly wanted to take it with him. Reverend Hoyt signed one rather gentle "no" at him, pinching his first two fingers and thumb together, but smiling so Esau would not think he was angry.

Esau put the cat down on the chair. Together they walked to the church. Reverend Hoyt wished there were some way he could tell him it was not necessary for him to walk upright all the time. At the door of Reverend Hoyt's study, Esau signed, "Work?" Reverend Hoyt nodded and tried to push his door open. Letters shoved under the door had wedged it shut. He knelt and pulled a handful free. The door swung open, and he picked up another handful from the floor and put them on his desk. Esau peeked in the door and waved at him. Reverend Hoyt waved back, and Esau shambled off to the sanctuary. Reverend Hoyt shut the door.

Behind his desk was a little clutter of sharp-edged glass and a large rock. There was a star-shaped hole above them in the glass doors. He took the message off the rock. It read, "And I saw a beast coming up out of the earth, and upon his head the names of blasphemy."

Reverend Hoyt cleaned up the broken glass and called the bishop. He read through his mail, keeping an eye out for her through the glass doors. She always came in the back way through the parking lot. His office was at the very end of the business wing of the church, the hardest thing to get to. It had been intended that way to give him as much privacy as possible. There had been a little courtyard with a crab-apple tree in it outside the glass doors. Five years ago the courtyard and the crab tree had both been sacrificed to parking space, and now he had no privacy at all, but an excellent view of all comings and goings. It was the only way he knew what was going on in the church. From his office he could not hear a thing.

The bishop arrived on her bicycle. Her short curly gray hair had been swept back from her face by the wind. She was very tanned. She was wearing a light green pantsuit, but she had a black robe over her arm. He let her in through the glass doors.

"I wasn't sure if it was an official occasion or not. I decided I'd better bring something along in case you were going to drop another bombshell."

"I know," he sighed, sitting down behind his littered desk. "It was a stupid thing to do. Thank you for coming, Moira."

"You could have at least warned me. The first call I got was some reporter raving that the end was coming. I thought the Charies had taken over again. Then some idiot called to ask what the church's position on pigs' souls was. It was another twenty minutes before I was able to find out exactly what you'd done. In the meantime, Will, I'm afraid I called you a number of highly uncharitable names." She reached out and patted his hand. "All of which I take back. How are you doing, dear?"

"I didn't intend to say anything until I'd decided what to do," he said thoughtfully. "I was going to call you this week about it. I told Natalie that when she brought Esau in."

"I knew it. This is Natalie Abreu's brainchild, isn't it? I thought I detected the hand of an assistant pastor in all this. Honestly, Will, they are all alike. Isn't there some way to keep them in seminary another ten years until they calm down a little? Causes and ideas and reforms andmore causes. It wears me out.

"Mine is into choirs: youth choirs, boy choirs, madrigals, antiphonals, glees. We barely have time for the sermon, there are so many choirs. My church doesn't look like a church. It looks like a military parade. Battalions of colored robes trooping in and out, chanting responses." She paused. "There are times when I'd like to throttle him. Right now I'd like to throttle Natalie. Whatever put it into her head?"

Reverend Hoyt shook his head. "She's very fond of him."

"So she's been filling him with a lot of Bible stories and scripture. Has she been taking him to Sunday school?"

"Yes. First grade, I think."

"Well then, you can claim indoctrination, can't you? Say it wasn't his own idea but was forced on him?"

"I can say that about three-fourths of the Sunday school class. Moira, that's the problem. There isn't any argument that I can use against him that wouldn't apply to half the congregation. He's lonely. He needs a strong father figure. He likes the pretty robes and candles. Instinct. Conditioning. Sexual sublimation. Maybe those things are true of Esau, but they're true of a lot of people I've baptized, too. And I never said to them, "Why do you really want to be baptized?'"

"He's doing it to please Natalie."

"Of course. And how many assistant pastors go to seminary for the same reason?" He paced the narrow space behind his desk. "I don't suppose there's anything in church law?"

"I looked. The Ecumenical Church is just a baby, Will. We barely have the organizational bylaws written down, let alone all the odds and ends. And twenty years is not enough time to build a base of precedent. I'm sorry, Will. I even went back to pre-unification law, thinking we might be able to borrow something obscure. But no luck."

The liberal churches had flirted with the idea of unification for more than twenty-five years without getting more accomplished than a few statements of goodwill. Then the Charismatics had declared the Rapture, and the churches had dived for cover right into the arms of ecumenism.

The fundamentalist Charismatic movement had gained strength all through the eighties. They had been committed to the imminent coming of the End, with its persecutions and Antichrist. On a sultry Tuesday in 1989 they had suddenly announced that the end was not only in sight, but here, and that all true Christians must unite to do battle against the Beast. The Beast was never specifically named, but most true Christians concluded he resided somewhere among the liberal churches. There was fervent prayer on Methodist front lawns. Young men ranted up the aisles of Episcopal churches during mass. A great many stained-glass windows, including all but one of the Lazettis, were broken. A few churches burned.

The Rapture lost considerable momentum when two years later the skies still had not rolled back like a scroll and swallowed up the faithful, but the Charies were a force the newly born United Ecumenical Church refused to take lightly. She was a rather hodge-podgy church, it was true, but she stood like a bulwark against the Charies.

"There wasn't anything?" Reverend Hoyt asked. "But the bishops can at least make a ruling, can't they?"

"The bishops have no authority over you in this matter. The United Church of Christ insisted on self-determination in matters within an individual church, including election of officers, distribution of communion, and baptism. It was the only way we could get them in," she finished apologetically.

"I've never understood that. There they were all by themselves with the Charismatics moving in like wolves. They didn't have any choice. They had to come in. So how did they get a plum like self-determination?"

"It worked both ways, remember. We could hardly stand by and let the Charies get them. Besides, everyone else had fiddled away their compromise points on trespassers versus debtors and translations of the Bible. You Presbyterians, as I recall, were determined to stick the magic word 'predestination' in everywhere you could."

Reverend Hoyt had a feeling the purpose of this was to get him to smile. He smiled. "And what was it you Catholics nearly walked out over? Oh yes, grape juice."

"Will, the point is I cannot give you bishop's counsel on this. It's your problem. You're the one who'll have to come to a fair and rational decision."

"Fair and rational?" He picked up a handful of mail. "With advice like this?"

"You asked for it, remember? Ranting from the pulpit about humility?"

"Listen to this: 'You can't baptize an ape. They don't have souls. One time I was in San Diego in the zoo there. We went to the ape house and right there, in front of the visitors and everything, were these two orangutangs..." He looked up from the letter. "Here she apparently had some trouble deciding what words were most appropriate. Her pen has blotted." He continued to read. "...'two oranguangs doing it.' That's underlined. 'The worst of it is that they were laying there just enjoying it. So you see, even if you think they are nice sometimes...etc.' This, from a woman who's had three husbands and who knows *how* many 'little lapses,' as she calls them. She says that I can't baptize him on the grounds that he likes sex."

He flipped through more papers. "The deacons think it would have what they call a negative effect on the total amount of pledges. The ushers don't want tourists in here with cameras. Three men and nine women think baptizing him would somehow let loose his animal lusts and no one would be safe in the church alone."

He held up another letter triumphantly, this one written on pale pink rosebudded stationery. "'You asked us Sunday what we thought about apes having souls. I think so. I like to sit in back because of my arthritis which is very bad. During the invocation there were three tots in front of me with their little hands folded in prayer and just inside the vestry door was your ape, with his head bowed and his hands folded too.'" He held up the paper. "My one ally. And she thinks it's cute to watch a full-grown orangutan fold his little hannies. How am I supposed to come to any kind of decision with advice like this? Even Natalie's determined to make him into something he isn't. Clothes and good manners and standing up straight. And I'm supposed to decide!"

Moira had listened to his rantings with a patient expression. Now she stood up. "That's right, Will. It is your decision, not Natalie's, not your congregation's, not the Charies'. You're supposed to decide."

He watched her to her bicycle through the star of broken glass. "Damn the Congregationalists!" he said under his breath.

He sorted all the mail into three piles of "for" and "against" and "wildly insane," then threw all of them in the wastebasket. He called in Natalie and Esau so he could give Esau the order to put up the protective plastic webbing over the big stained glass window. Natalie was alarmed. "What is it?" she asked when Esau had left with the storeroom key in his hand. "Have there been threats?"

He showed her the message from the rock, but didn't mention the letters. "I'll take him home again with me tonight," he said. "When does he have to go to Colorado Springs?"

"Tomorrow." She had fished a letter out of the wastebasket and was reading it. "We could cancel. They already know the situation," she said and then blushed.

"No. He's probably safer there than here." He let some of the tiredness creep into his voice.

"You aren't going to do it, are you?" Natalie said suddenly. "Because of a lot of creeps!" She slammed the letter down on his desk. "You're going to listen to them, aren't you? A lot of creeps who don't even know what a soul is, and you're going to let them tell you Esau doesn't have one!"She went to the door, the tails of the yellow stole flying. "Maybe I should just tell them to keep him tomorrow, since you don't want him." The door's slamming dislodged another splinter of glass.

Reverend Hoyt went to the South Denver Library and checked

out books on apes and St. Augustine and sign language. He read them in his office until it was nearly dark outside. Then he went to get Esau. The protective webbing was up on the outside of the window. There was a ladder standing in the sanctuary. The window let in the dark blue evening light and the beginning stars.

Esau was sitting in one of the back pews, his short legs straight out in front of him on the velvet cushion. His arms hung down palms out. He was resting. The dustcloth lay beside him. His wide face held no expression except the limpness of fatigue. His eyes were sad beyond anything Reverend Hoyt had ever seen.

When he saw Reverend Hoyt, he climbed down off the pew quite readily. They walked to the parish house. Esau immediately went to find the cat.

The people from Cheyenne Mountain came quite early the next morning. Reverend Hoyt noticed their van in the parking lot. He saw Natalie walk Esau to the van. The young man from the center opened the door and said something to Natalie.She nodded and smiled rather shyly at him. Esau got in the backseat of the van. Natalie leaned in and hugged him good-bye. When the van drove off, he was sitting looking out the window, his face impassive. Natalie did not look in Reverend Hoyt's direction.

They brought him back about noon the next day. Reverend Hoyt saw the van again, and shortly afterward Natalie brought the young man to his office. She was dressed all in white, a childishly full surplice over a white robe. She looked like an angel in a Sunday school program. Pentecost must be over and Trinity begun. She was still subdued, more than the situation of having her friends argue for her would seem to merit. Reverend Hoyt wondered how often this same young man came for Esau.

"I thought you would like to know how things are going down at the Center, sir," the young man said briskly. "Esau passed his physical, although there is some question of whether he might need glasses. He has a slight case of astigmatism. Otherwise he is in excellent physical condition for a male of his age. His attitude toward the breeding program has also improved markedly in the past few months. Male orangs become rather solitary, neurotic beings as they mature, sometimes becoming very depressed. Esau was not, up until a few months ago, willing to breed at all. Now he participates regularly and has impregnated one female.

"What I came to say, sir, is that we feel Esau's job and the friends he has made here have made him a much happier and much better adjusted ape than he was before. You are to be congratulated. We would hate to see anything interfere with the emotional well-being he has achieved so far."

This is the best argument of all, Reverend Hoyt thought. A happy ape is a breeding ape. A baptized ape is a happy one. Therefore...

"I understand," he said, looking at the young man. "I have been reading about orangutans, but I have questions. If you could give me some time this afternoon, I would appreciate it."

The young man glanced at his watch. Natalie looked uncomfortable. "Perhaps after the news conference. That lasts until..." He turned to Natalie. "Is it four o'clock, Reverend Abreu?"

She tried to smile. "Yes, four. We should be going. Reverend Hoyt, if you'd like to come..."

"I believe the bishop is coming later this afternoon, thank you." The young man took Natalie's arm. "After the press conference," Reverend Hoyt continued, "please have Esau put the ladder away. Tell him he does not need to use it."

"But..."

"Thank you, Reverend Abreu."

Natalie and her young man went to their news conference. He closed all the books he had checked out from the library and stacked them on the end of his desk. Then he put his head in his hands and tried to think.

"Where's Esau?" the bishop said when she came in.

"In the sanctuary, I suppose. He's supposed to be putting the webbing on the inside of the window."

"I didn't see him."

"Maybe Natalie took him with her to her press conference."

She sat down. "What have you decided?"

"I don't know. Yesterday I managed to convince myself he was one of the lower animals. This morning at three I woke from a dream in which he was ordained a saint. I am no closer to knowing what to do than I have ever been."

"Have you thought, as my archbishop would say who cannot forget his Baptist upbringing, about what our dear Lord would do?"

"You mean, 'Who is my neighbor? And Jesus answering said, A certain man went down from Jerusalem to Jericho and fell among thieves.' Esau said that, you know. When I asked him if he knew that God loved him he spelled out the word 'Samaritan.'"

"I wonder," Moira said thoughtfully. "Did he mean the good Samaritan or..."

"The odd thing about it was that Natalie'd apparently taught him some kind of shorthand sign for Good Samaritan, but he wouldn't use it. He kept spelling the word out, letter by letter."

"'How is it that thou, being a Jew, askest drink of me, which am a woman of Samaria?'"

"What?"

"John 4. That's what the Samaritan woman said to Jesus at the well."

"You know, one of the first apes they raised with human parents used to have to do this test where she sorted through a pile of pictures and separated the humans from the apes. She could do it perfectly, except for one mistake. She always put her own picture in the human pile." He stood up and went and stood at the doors. "I have thought all along that the reason he wanted to be baptized was because he didn't know he wasn't human. But he knows. He knows."

"Yes," said the bishop. "I think he does."

They walked together as far as the sanctuary. "I didn't want to ride my bicycle today," she said. "The reporters recognize it. What is that noise?"

It was a peculiar sound, a sort of heavy wheezing. Esau was sitting on the floor by one of the pews, his chest and head leaning on the seat. He was making the noise.

"Will," Moira said. "The ladder's down. I think he fell."

He whirled. The ladder lay full-length along the middle aisle. The plastic webbing was draped like fishnet over the front pews. He knelt by Esau, forgetting to sign. "Are you all right?"

Esau looked up at him. His eyes were clouded. There was blood and saliva under his nose and on his chin. "Go get Natalie," Reverend Hoyt said.

Natalie was in the door, looking like a childish angel. The young man from Cheyenne Mountain was with her. Her face went as white as her surplice. "Go call the doctor," she whispered to him, and was instantly on her knees by Esau. "Esau, are you all right? Is he sick?"

Reverend Hoyt did not know how to tell her. "I'm afraid he fell, Natalie."

"Off the ladder," she said immediately. "He fell off the ladder."

"Do you think we should lay him down, get his feet up?" Moira asked. "He must be in shock."

Reverend Hoyt lifted Esau's lip a little. The gums were grayish blue. Esau gave a little cough and spewed out a stream of frothy blood onto his chest.

"Oh," Natalie sobbed and put her hand over her mouth.

"I think he can breathe better in this position," Reverend Hoyt said. Moira got a blanket from somewhere. Reverend Hoyt put it over him, tucking it in at his shoulders. Natalie wiped his mouth and nose with the tail of her surplice. They waited for the doctor.

The doctor was a tall man with owlish glasses. Reverend Hoyt did not know him. He eased Esau onto his back on the floor and jammed the velvet pew cushion under his feet to prop them up. He looked at Esau's gums, as Reverend Hoyt had done, and took his pulse. He worked slowly and methodically to set up the intravenous equipment and shave a space on Esau's arm. It had a calming effect on Natalie. She leaned back on her heels, and some of the color came back to her cheeks. Reverend Hoyt could see that there was almost no blood pressure. When the doctor inserted the needle and attached it to the plastic tube of sugar water, almost no blood backed up into the tube.

He examined Esau gently, having Natalie sign questions to him. He did not answer. His breathing eased a little but blood bubbled out of his nose. "We've got a peritoneal hernia here," the doctor said. "The organs have been pushed up into the rib cage and aren't giving the lungs enough space. He must have struck something when he fell." The corner of the pew. "He's very shocky. How long ago did this happen?"

"Before I came," Moira said, standing to the side. "I didn't see the ladder when I came." She collected herself. "Before three."

"We'll take him in as soon as we get a little bit more fluid in him." He turned to the young man. "Did you call the ambulance?"

The young man nodded. Esau coughed again. The blood was bright red and full of bubbles. The doctor said, "He's bleeding into the lungs." He adjusted the intravenous equipment slowly. "If you will all leave for just a few moments, I'll try to see if I can get him some additional air space in the lungs."

Natalie put both hands over her mouth and hiccuped a sob.

"No," Reverend Hoyt said.

The doctor's look was unmistakable. You know what's coming. I am counting on you to be sensible and get these people out of here so they don't have to see it.

"No," he said again, more softly. "We would like to do something first. Natalie, go and get the baptismal bowl and my prayer book."

She stood up, wiping a bloody hand across her tears. She did not say anything as she went.

"Esau," Reverend Hoyt said. Please God, let me remember what few signs I know. "Esau God's child." He signed the foolish little salute for God. He held his hand out waist high for child. He had no idea how to show a possessive.

Esau's breathing was shallower. He raised his hand a little and made a fist. "S-A-M-"

"*No!*" Reverend Hoyt jammed his two fingers against his thumb viciously. He shook his head vigorously. "*No!* Esau God's child!" The signs would not say what he wanted them to. He crossed his fists on his chest, the sign for love. Esau tried to make the same sign. He could not move his left arm at all. He looked at Reverend Hoyt and raised his right hand. He waved.

Natalie was standing over them. Holding the bowl. She was shivering. He motioned her to kneel beside him and sign. He handed the bowl to Moira. "I baptize thee, Esau," he said steadily, and dipped his hand in the water, "in the name of the Father," he put his damp hand gently on the scraggly red head, "and of the Son, and of the Holy Ghost. Amen."

He stood up and looked at the bishop. He put his arm around Natalie and led her into the nave. After a few minutes the doctor called them back.

Esau was on his back, his arms flung out on either side, his little brown eyes open and unseeing. "He was just too shocky," the doctor said. "There was nothing but blood left in his lungs." He handed his card to Reverend Hoyt. "My number's on there. If there's anything I can do."

"Thank you," Reverend Hoyt said. "You've been very kind."

The young man from Cheyenne Mountain said, "The Center will arrange for disposal of the body."

Natalie was looking at the card. "No," she said. Her robe was covered with blood, and damp. "No, thank you."

There was something in her tone the young man was afraid to question. He went out with the doctor.

Natalie sat down on the floor next to Esau's body. "He called a vet," she said. "He told me he'd help me get Esau baptized, and then he called a vet, like he was an animal!" She started to cry, reaching out and patting the limp palm of Esau's hand. "Oh, my dear friend," she said. "My dear friend."

Moira spent the night with Natalie. In the morning she brought her to Reverend Hoyt's office. "I'll talk to the reporters for you today," she said. She hugged them both good-bye.

Natalie sat down in the chair opposite Reverend Hoyt's desk. She was wearing a simple blue skirt and blouse. She held a wadded Kleenex in her hands. "There isn't anything you can say to me, is there?" she asked quite steadily. "I ought to know, after a whole year of counseling everybody else." She sounded sad. "He *was* in pain, he *did* suffer a long time, it *was* my fault."

"I wasn't going to say any of those things to you, Natalie," he said gently.

She was twisting the Kleenex, trying to get to the point where she could speak without crying. "Esau told me that you tucked him in when he stayed with you. He told me all about your cat, too." She was not going to make it. "I want to thank you…for being so kind to him. And for baptizing him, even though you didn't think he was a person." The tears came, little choking sobs. "I know that you did it for me." She stopped, her lips trembling.

He didn't know how to help her. "God chooses to believe that we have souls because He loves us," he said. "I think He loves Esau, too. I know we did."

"I'm glad it was me that killed him," Natalie said tearfully. "And not somebody that hated him, like the Charies or something. At least nobody hurt him on purpose."

"No," Reverend Hoyt said. "Not on purpose."

"He *was* a person, you know, not just an animal."

"I know," he said. He felt very sorry for her.

She stood up and wiped at her eyes with the sodden Kleenex. "I'd better go see what can be done about the sanctuary." She looked totally and finally humiliated, standing there in the blue dress. Natalie the unquenchable quenched at last. He could not bear it.

"Natalie," he said, "I know you'll be busy, but if you have the time would you mind finding a white robe for Sunday for me to wear. I have been meaning to ask you. So many of the congregation have told me how much they thought your robes added to the service. And a stole perhaps. What is the color for Trinity Sunday?"

"White," she said promptly, and then looked ashamed. "White and gold."

Ye Who Would Sing

Alan Dean Foster

Caitland didn't hate the storm any more than he had the man he'd just killed, but he was less indifferent to it. It wouldn't have mattered, except that his victim had been armed. Not well enough to save himself, but sufficient to make things awkward for Caitland.

Even so, the damaged fanship could easily have made it back to the Vaanland outpost, had not the freakish thunderstorm abruptly congealed from a clear blue sky. It was driving him relentlessly northward away from one of the few chicken scratches of civilization man had made on this world.

If adrenaline and muscle power could have turned the craft, Caitland would have done better than anyone. But every time it seemed he'd succeeded in wrenching the fan around to a proper course, a fresh gust would leap from the nearest thunderhead and toss the tiny vehicle ass over rotor.

He glanced upwards through the rain-smeared plexidome. Only different shades of blackness differentiated the sky above. If the Styx was overhead, what lay below?

Granite talons and claws of gneiss...the empty-wild peaks of the Silver Spar Range. He'd been blown further north than he'd thought.

Time and again the winds sought to hammer the fan into the ground. Time and again he somehow managed to coax enough from the weakening engine to avoid the next ledge, the next crag, the next cliff.

No way he could get above these ice-scoured spires. Soon he was fighting just to stay in the air, the fanship dancing through the glacier valleys like a leaf running rapids. The weather was playing a waiting game with his life.

Now he was almost too tired to care. The fuel gauge hovered near empty. He'd stalled the inevitable, hoping for even a slight break in the storm, hoping for a minute's chance at a controlled landing. It seemed even that was to be denied him.

The elements had grown progressively inimical. Lightning lit the surrounding mountains in rapid-fire surreal flashes, sounded in the thin-shelled ship cabin like a million kilos of frying bacon. Adhesive rain defeated the best efforts of the wipers to keep the front of the port clear. Navigation instrumentation told him that he was surrounded by sheer rock walls on all sides.

And as the canyon he'd worked his way into narrowed still further, updrafts became downdrafts, downdrafts became sidedrafts, and sidedrafts became aeolian aberrations without names. Mobiusdrafts.

If he didn't set the fan down now, the storm would set it down for him. Better to retain a modicum of control. He pushed in on the control wheel. If he could get down in one piece, he ought to be home free.

There was a high-power self-contained homing device built into the radiocom. It would send out an automatic SOS on a private channel, to be received by an illegal station near Vaanland.

Caitland was a loyal, trusted, and highly valued employee of that station's owners. There was no doubt in his mind that once it was received by them, they would act on the emergency signal. Right now his job was to ensure they would find something worth taking back.

The fanship dipped lower. Caitland fought the wind with words and skillful piloting. It insisted on shoving him sideways when he wanted to go up or down.

There...a place where the dense green-black mat of forest thinned briefly and the ground looked near-level. Low, over, a little lower. Now hard on the stick, slipping the fan sideways, so that the jets could counteract the force of the scudding wind. Then cut power, cut more, and prepare to settle down.

A tremendous howl reverberated through the little cabin as a wall of rain-laden wind shoved like a giant's hand straight down on the fanship. Jets still roaring parallel to the ground, the fan slid earthward at a 45-degree angle.

First one blade, then a second of the double rotors hit a tree. There was a metallic snapping sound, several seconds of blurred vision...a montage of tree trunks, lightning and moss-covered earth...followed by stillness.

He waited, but the fan had definitely come to a stop. Rain pierced the shattered dome and pelted forehead and face, a wetness to match the saltier taste in his mouth. The fan had come to rest on its side. Only a single strap of the safety harness had stayed intact. It held him in the ruined cabin by his waist.

He moved to release it...slowly, because of the sharp hot pain the movements caused in the center of his chest. He coughed, spat weakly. Bits of broken tooth joined the rest of the wreckage.

His intention was to let himself down gently to a standing position. His body refused to cooperate. As the waist buckle uncoupled, he fell the short distance from his seat to the shattered side of the fan. Broke...inside...he thought hazily. Rain seeped into his eyes, blurred his vision.

Painfully he rolled over, looked down the length of the fan. The flying machine was ruined forever. Right now, the walking machine had to get away from it...There was always the chance of an explosion.

It was then he discovered he couldn't move his left leg. Lying exhausted, he tried to study the forest around him in the darkness and driving rain.

Driving rain. The fan had broken a circle in the branches overhead. It would be drier under the untouched trees...and he had to get away from the explosive residue in the fan's tanks.

It appeared to be the lower part of the leg. All right, if he couldn't walk, he could crawl. He started to get to his knees...and couldn't finish. Hurt worse than he'd first thought.

Never mind the chance of explosion...Rest was what he had to have...rest. He lay quietly in the water-soaked ruins of the fan, rain tinkling noisily off the broken plexidome and twisted metal, and listened to the wind moan and cry around him.

Moan? Cry? His head came up dizzily. There was something more than wind out there. A sharp, yes, definitely musical quaver that came from all about him. He stared into the trees, saw no one. The effort cost him another dizzy spell and he had to rest his eyes before trying again.

Nothing in the trees, no, but...something about the nearest trunk...and the one to its left...and possibly the two nearby on the other side...something he should recognize from somewhere. Too weak to raise a shielding hand, he blinked moisture away and studied the closest bole through slitted eyes.

Yes...The trunk appeared to be expanding and contracting ever so slightly, steadily. His attention shifted to its neighbors. Hints of movements were visible throughout the forest, movement unprompted by wind or rain.

Chimer trees. *Chee chimer* trees. They had to be.

But there weren't supposed to be any wild chimers left on *Chee* world, nor as many as four together anywhere, outside of the big agricultural research station.

Maybe there were even more than four. He found himself developing a feeling of excitement that almost matched the pain. If he had stumbled on a chimer forest...

Neither imagination nor intellectual prowess were Caitland's forte, but he was not an idiot. And even an idiot knew about the chimers. The finding of one tree anymore was extraordinary; to locate four together, incredible. The chance that there might be more was overwhelming.

So, finally, was the pain. He passed out.

The face that formed before Caitland's eyes was a woman's but not the one he'd been soundlessly dreaming of. The hair was gray, not blond; the face lined, not smooth; skin wrinkled and coarse in the hollows instead of tear-polished; and the blouse was of red plaid flannel instead of silk.

Only the eyes bore any resemblance to the dream, eyes even bluer than those of the teasing sleep-wraith.

An aroma redolent of fresh bread and steaming meats impinged on his smelling apparatus. It made his mouth water so bad it hurt. At the same time a storm of memories came flooding back. He tried to sit up.

Something started playing a staccato tune on his ribs with a ball-peen hammer. Falling back, he clutched at a point on his left side. Gentle but firm hands exerted pressure there. He allowed them to remove his own, set them back at his sides.

The voice was strong but not deep. It shared more with those blue eyes than the parchment skin. "I'm glad you're finally awake, young man. Though heaven knows you've no right to be. I'm afraid your machine is a total loss."

She stood... a straight shape of average height, slim figure, eyes, and flowing gray hair down to her waist; the things anyone would notice first.

He couldn't guess at her age. Well past sixty, though.

"Can you talk? Do you have a name? Or should I go ahead and splint your tongue along with your leg?" Caitland raised his head, moved the blankets aside and stared down at himself. His left leg was neatly splinted. It was complemented by numerous other signs of repair, most notably the acre of bandage that encircled his chest.

"Ribs," she continued. "I wasn't sure if you'd broke all of them or just most, so I didn't take any chances. The whole mess can heal together.

"I had the devil's own trying to get you here, young man. You're quite the biggest thing in the human line I've ever seen. For a while I didn't think I was going to get you on the wagon." She shook her head. "Pity that when we domesticated the horse we didn't work on giving him hands.

She paused as though expecting a reply. When Caitland remained silent she continued on as though nothing had happened.

"Well, no need to strain your brain now. My name is Naley, Katherine Naley. You can call me Katie, or Grandma." She grinned wryly. "Call me grandma and I'll put rocks in your stew." She moved to a small metal cabinet with a ceramic top on which a large closed pot sat perspiring.

"Should be ready soon."

Her attention diverted to the stove, Caitland let his gaze rove, taking stock of his surroundings. He was on a bed... much too small for him... in a small house. Instead of the expected colonial spray-plastic construction, this place looked to be made of hewn stone and wood. Some observers would probably find it charming and rustic, but to Caitland it only smacked of primitiveness and lack of money.

She called back to him. "I'll answer at least one of your questions for you. You've been out for two days on that bed."

"How did I get here? Where's my fan? Where is this place?" She looked gratified.

"So you *can* talk. You got here in the wagon... Freia pulled you. Your ship is several kilometers down the canyon, and you're in a valley in the Silver Spars. The second person ever to set foot in it, matter of fact."

Caitland tried to sit up again, found it was still all he could do to turn his head towards her.

"You went out in that storm by yourself?" She nodded, watching him. "You live here alone?" Again the nod. "And you hauled me all the way... several kilometers... up here, and have been watching me for two days?"

"Yes."

Caitland's mind was calibrated according to a certain scale of values. Within that scale decisions on any matter came easy. None of this fit anywhere, however.

"Why?" he finally asked.

She smiled, a patronizing smile that he ordinarily wouldn't have taken from anyone.

"Because you were dying, stupid, and that struck me as a waste. I don't know anything about your mind yet except that it doesn't include much on bad-weather navigation, but you're fairly young and you've got an excellent body, still. And mine, mine's about shot. So I saw some possibilities. Not that I wouldn't have done the same for you if you'd been smaller than me and twenty kilos lighter. I'm just being honest with you, whoever you are."

"So where's the catch?" he wondered suspiciously. She'd been ladling something into a large bowl from the big kettle. Now she brought it over.

"In your pants, most probably, idiot. I might have expected a thank-you. No, not now... Drink this."

Caitland's temper dissolved in the first whiff of the bowl's contents. It was hot, and the first swallow of the soup-stew seared his insides like molten lead. But he finished it and asked for more.

By the fourth cup he felt transformed, was even able to sit up slightly, carefully. He considered the situation.

This old woman was no threat. She obviously knew nothing about him and wouldn't have been much of a threat if she had. His friends might not find him for some time, if ever, depending on the condition of the radiocom broadcaster. And just now there was the distinct possibility that representatives from the other side of the law would be desirous of his company.

He could just as soon do without that. Lawyers and cops had a way of tangling your explanations about things like self-defense.

So in many respects this looked like a fine place to stay and relax. No one would find him in the Silver Spars and there was nowhere to walk to. He leaned back into the pillow.

Then he heard the singing.

The melody was incredibly complex, the rhythm haunting. It was made of organ pipes and flutes and maudlin bassoons, mournful oboes and a steadying backbeat, all interwoven to produce an alien serenity of sound no human orchestra could duplicate. Scattered through and around was a counterpoint of oddly metallic yet not metal bells, a quicksilver tinkling like little girl-boy laughter.

Caitland knew that sound. Everyone knew that sound. The chimer tree produced it. The chimer tree, a mature specimen of which would fetch perhaps a hundred thousand credits.

But the music that sounded around the house was wilder, stronger, far more beautiful than anything Caitland in his prosaic uncomplicated existence had ever imagined. He'd heard recordings taken from the famed chimer quartet in Geneva Garden. And he knew that only one thing could produce such an overpowering wealth of sound—a chimer tree forest.

But there were no more chimer forests. Those scattered about the Chee world had long since been located, transplanted tree by tree, bartered and sold in the first heady months of discovery by the initial load of colonists. And why not, considering the prices that were offered for them?

Chimer forests hadn't existed for nearly a hundred years, as best he could remember. And yet the sound could be of nothing else.

"That music," he murmured, entranced.

She was sitting in a chair nearby, ignoring him in favor of the thick book in her lap. He tried to get out of the bed, failed. "The music," he repeated.

"The forest, yes," she finally replied, confirming his guess. "I know what you're thinking, that it's impossible, that such a thing doesn't exist anymore, but it's both possible and true. The mountains have protected this forest, you see—the Silver Spars's inaccessibility, and also the fact that all the great concentrations of chimers were found far, far to the south of Holdamere. Never this far east, never this far north.

"This forest is a freak, but it has survived, survived and developed in its isolation. This is a virgin forest, never cut, Mr. . . ."

"Caitland, John Caitland."

"An untouched forest, Mr. Caitland. Unsoiled by the excavators of the predators, unknown to the music lovers." Her smile disappeared.

"To the music eaters, those whose desire for a musical toy in their homes destroyed the chimers."

"It's not their fault," Caitland objected, "that the chimers don't reproduce when transplanted. People will have what they want, and if there's enough money to pay for what they want, no mere law is going to prevent..." He stopped. That was too much already. "It's a damned shame they can't reproduce in captivity, but that's—"

"Oh but they can," the old woman broke in. "I can make them."

Caitland started to object, managed to stifle his natural reaction. He forced himself to think more slowly, more patiently than was his wont. This was a big thing. If this old bat wasn't loony from living alone out in the back of nowhere, and if she *had* found a way to make the chimers reproduce in captivity, then she could make a lot of people very very wealthy.

Or a few people even wealthier. Caitland knew of at least one deserving candidate.

"I hadn't heard," he said warily, "that anyone had found a way to make the trees even grow after replanting."

"That's because I haven't told anyone yet," she replied crisply. "I'm not ready yet. There are some other things that need to be perfected for the telling first.

"Because if I announce my results and then demonstrate them, I'll have to use this forest. And if the eaters find this place, they'll transplant it, rip it up, take it apart and sell it in pieces to the highest bidders. And then I won't be able to make anything reproduce, show anybody anything.

"And that *will* be the end of the chimer tree, because this is the last forest. When the oldest trees die a couple of thousand years from now there'll be nothing left but recordings, ghosts of shadows of the real thing. That's why I've got to finish my work here before I let the secret—and this location—out."

It made things much simpler for the relieved Caitland. She was crazy after all. Poor old bitch, he could understand it, the loneliness and constant alien singing of the trees and all. But she'd also saved his life. Caitland was not ungrateful. He would wait.

He wondered, in view of her long diatribe, if she'd try to stop him from leaving.

"Listen," he began experimentally, "when I'm well enough I'd like to... leave here. I have a life to get back to, myself. I'll keep your secret, of course... I understand and sympathize with you completely. How about a...?"

"I don't have a power flitter," she said.

"Well then, your fanship."

She shook her head, slowly.

"Ground buggy?" Another negative shake. Caitland's brows drew together. Maybe she didn't *have* to worry about keeping him here. "Are you trying to tell me you have no form of transportation up here whatsoever?"

"Not exactly. I have Freia, my horse, and the wagon she pulls. That's all the transportation I need, that and what's left of my legs. Once a year an old friend airdrops me certain necessary supplies. He doesn't land and he's no botanist, so he's unaware of the nature of this forest. A miner... simple man, good man.

"My electronic parts and such, which I code-flash to his fan on his yearly pass over, constitute most of what he brings back to me. Otherwise," and she made an expansive gesture, "the forest supplies all my needs."

He tensed. "You have tridee or radio communication, for emergencies, with the—"

"No, young man, I'm completely isolated here. I like it that way."

He was wondering just *how* far off course the storm had carried him. "The nearest settlement... Vaanland?"

She nodded. That was encouraging, at least. "How far by wagon?"

"The wagon would never make it. Terrain's too tough. Freia brought me in and out one time, and back again, but she's too old now, I'd say."

"On foot, then."

She looked thoughtful. "A man your size, in good condition, if he were familiar with the country... I'd say three to four months, barring mountain predators, avalanche, bad water and other possibilities."

So he would have to be found. He wasn't going to find his way out of here without her help, and she didn't seem inclined to go anywhere. Nor did threats of physical violence ever mean much to people who weren't right in the head.

Anyhow, it was silly to think about such things now. First, his leg and ribs had to mend. Better to get her back on a subject she was more enamored of. Something related to her delusions.

"How can you be so sure these trees can be made to reproduce after transplanting?"

"Because I found out why they weren't and the answer's simple. Any puzzle's easy to put together, provided none of the pieces fall off the table. If you're well enough to walk in a few days, I'll show you. The crutches I've got are short for you, but you'll manage..."

The forest valley was narrow, the peaks cupping it between their flanks high and precipitous. Ages ago a glacier had cut this gorge. Now it was gone, leaving gray walls, green floor, and a roof of seemingly perpetual clouds, low-hanging clouds which shielded it from discovery by air.

The old woman, despite her disclaimers, seemed capable of getting around quite well. Caitland felt she could have matched his pace even if he weren't burdened with the crutches. Though she insisted any strenuous climbing was past her.

Despite the narrowness of the valley, the forest was substantial in extent. More important, the major trees were an astonishing fifty percent chimer. The highest density in the records was thirty-seven percent. That had been in the great Savanna forest on the south continent, just below the capital city of Danover. It had been stripped several hundred years ago.

Katie expounded on the forest at length, though resisting the obvious urge to talk nonstop to her first visitor in—another question Caitland had meant to ask.

Chimer trees of every age were here; mature trees at least fifteen hundred years old; old trees, monarchs of the forest that had sung their songs through twice that span; and youngsters, from those narrow boles only a few hundred years old down to sprouting shoots no bigger than a blade of grass.

Everything pointed to a forest that was healthy and alive, a going biological concern of a kind only dreamed about in botanical texts. And he was limping along in the middle of it, one of only two people in the universe aware of its existence.

It wasn't the constant alien music, or the scientific value that awed him. It was the estimated number of chimer trees multiplied by some abstract figures. The lowest estimate Caitland could produce ran into the hundreds of millions.

He could struggle into Vaanland, register claim to this parcel of backland, and—and nothing. One of the things that made Caitland an exceptional man among his type was that he respected his own limitations. This was too big for him. He was not a developer, not a front man, not a Big Operator.

Very well, he would simply take his cut as discoverer and leave the lion's share for those who knew how to exploit it. His percentage would be gratefully paid. There was enough here for everyone.

He listened to the music, at once disturbing and infectious, and wished he could understand the scientific terms the old woman was throwing at him.

The sun had started down when they headed back towards the house—cabin, Caitland had discovered, with an adjoining warehouse. Nearly there, Katie stopped, panting slightly. More lines showed in her face now, lines and strain from more than age.

"Can't walk as far as I used to. That's why I need Freia, and she's getting on, too." She put a hand out, ran a palm up and down one booming young sapling. "Magnificent, isn't it?" She looked back at him.

"You're very privileged, John. Few people now alive have heard the sound of a chimer forest except on old recordings. Very privileged." She was watching him closely. "Sometimes I wonder..."

"Yeah," he muttered uncomfortably.

She left the tree, moved to him and felt his chest under the makeshift shirt she'd sewn him. "I mended this clothing as best I could, and I tried to do the same with you. I'm no doctor. How do your ribs feel?"

"I once saw a pet wolfhound work on an old steak bone for a couple of weeks before he'd entirely finished with it. That's what they feel like."

She removed her hand. "They're healing. They'll continue to do so, provided you don't go falling out of storms in the next couple of months." She started on again.

He followed, keeping pace with ease, taking up great spaces with long sweeps of the crutches. His bulk dwarfed her. Towering above, he studied the wasted frame, saw the basic lines of the face and body. She'd been a great beauty once, he finally decided. Now she was like a pressed flower to a living one.

What, he wondered, had compelled her to bury herself in this wilderness? The forest kept her here, but what had brought her in the first place?

"Look," he began, "it looks like I'm going to be here for a while." She was watching him, and laughed at that. She was always watching him, not staring, but not looking away, either. Did she suspect something? How could she? That was nonsense. And if she did, he could dispose of her easily, quickly. The ribs and leg would scarcely interfere. He could...

"I'd like to earn my keep." The words shocked him even as he mouthed the request.

"With those ribs? Are you crazy, young man? I admit I might have thought of much the same thing, but—"

"I don't sponge off anyone, lady...Katie. Habit."

She appeared to consider, replied, "All right. I think I know an equally stubborn soul when I see one. Heaven knows there are a lot of things I'd like to have done that this body can't manage. I'll show them to you and when you feel up to it, you can start in on them."

He did, too, without really knowing why. He told himself it was to keep his mind occupied and lull any suspicions she might develop, and believed not a word of his thoughts.

The song of the forest, he noticed, varied constantly. The weather would affect it, the cry of animals, the time of day. It never stopped, even at night.

He hauled equipment, rode with her in the rickety wagon to check unrecognizable components scattered the length and breadth of the valley, cut wood, repaired a rotten section of wall in the warehouse, repaired the cabin roof, tended to Freia and her colt...and tried to ignore those piercing eyes, those young-old blue eyes that never left him.

And because he wouldn't talk about himself much, they spent spare moments and evenings talking about her, and her isolation, and the how and why of it.

She'd found the forest nearly thirty years ago and had been here constantly, excepting one trip, ever since. In that time she'd confirmed much that was suspected, all that was known, and made many new discoveries about the singing trees.

They began to make music when barely half-meter-high shoots, and retained that ability till the last vein of sap dried in the aged trunk. They could grow to a height of eighty meters and a base diameter of ten.

Chimers had been uprooted and transplanted since their music-making abilities had been first discovered. At one time it seemed there was hardly a city, a town, a village or wealthy individual that didn't own one or two of the great trees.

Seemingly, they thrived in their new environments, thrived and sang. But they would not reproduce... from seeds, from cuttings, nothing. Not even in the most controlled greenhouse ecology, in which other plants from Chee survived and multiplied. Only the chimer died out.

But none of those wealthy music lovers had ever heard a whole forest sing, Caitland reflected. He'd never heard a sound like it before himself, and never would again.

Once more she explained to him how the trees sang, how the semi-flexible hollow trunk and the rippling protrusions inside controlled the flow of air through the reverberating bole to produce an infinite range of sound. How the trunk sound was complemented by the tinkling bells—chimes—on the branches. Chimes which were hard, shiny nuts filled with loose seeds.

With the vibration of the main trunk, the branches would quiver, and the nuts shake, producing a light, faintly bell-like clanging.

"And that's why," she finally explained to him, "the chimers won't reproduce in captivity. I've calculated that reproduction requires the presence of a minimum of two hundred and six healthy, active trees.

"Can you think of any one city, any one corporation, any one system that could afford two hundred and six chimers of a proper spread of maturity?"

Of course he couldn't. No system, not even Terra-Sol, could manage that kind of money for artistic purposes.

"You see," she continued, "it takes that number of trees, singing in unison, to stimulate the bola beetle to lay its eggs. Any less and it's like an orchestra playing a symphony by Mahler. You can take out, say, the man with the cow-bell and it will still sound like a symphony—but it won't be the *right* symphony. The bola beetle is a fastidious listener."

She dug around in the earth, came up with a pair of black, stocky bugs about the size of a thumbnail. They scrambled for freedom.

"When the nuts are exactly ripe, the forest changes to a certain highly intricate melody with dozens of variations. The beetles recognize it immediately. They climb the trees and lay their eggs, several hundred per female, within the hollow space of the nuts. The loose seeds inside, at the peak of ripeness, provide food for the larvae while the hard shell protects them from predators. And it all works out fine from the bola's point of view—except for the tumbuck."

"That small six-legger that looks like an oversized guinea pig?"

"That's the one. The tumbuck, John, knows what that certain song means, too. It can't climb, but it's about the only critter with strong enough teeth to crack a chimer nut. When the ripe nuts drop to the ground, it cracks them open and uses its long, thin tongue to hunt around inside the nut—not to scoop out the seeds, which it ignores, but the insect eggs.

"It's the saliva of the tumbuck, deposited as it seeks out the bola eggs, which initiates the germinating process. The tumbuck leaves the nut alone and goes off in search of other egg-filled ones. Meanwhile the seed is still protected by most of its shell.

"Stimulated by the chemicals and dampness of the tumbuck saliva, the first roots are sent out through the crack in the shell and into the ground. The young plant lives briefly inside the shell and finally grows out through the same crack towards the light.

"It's the song of the massed trees that's the key. That's what took me twenty years to figure out. No wonder bola beetles and tumbucks ignored the nuts of the transplanted chimers—the music wasn't right. You need at least two hundred and six trees—the full orchestra."

Caitland sat on the wooden bench cut from a section of log and thought about this. Some of it he didn't understand. What he could understand added up to something strange and remarkable and utterly magnificient, and it made him feel terrible.

"But that's not all, John Caitland. My biggest discovery started as a joke on myself, became a hobby, then an obsession." There was a twinkle in her eyes that matched the repressed excitement in her voice. "Come to the back of the warehouse."

A metal cabinet was set out there, one Caitland had never seen her open before. Leads from it were connected, he knew, to a number of complex antennae mounted on the warehouse roof. They had nothing to do with long-range communications, he knew, so he'd ignored them.

The instrumentation within the cabinet was equally unfamiliar. Katie ran her hand up and down the bole of a young chimer that grew almost into the cabinet, then moved her hands over the dials and switches within. She leaned back against the tree and closed her eyes, and one hand resting on a last switch, the other stroking the trunk, like a cat, almost.

"Now look, John, and tell me what you feel." She threw the switch.

For long seconds there was nothing different, only the humming of the bat-winged mammals that held the place of birds here. And that familiar song of the forest.

But even as he strained all his senses for he knew not what, the song...changed. It changed unabashedly and abruptly, astoundingly, fantastically.

Gloriously.

Something grand thundered out of the forest around him, something too achingly lovely to be heard. It was vaguely familiar, but utterly transformed by the instrument of the forest, like a tarnished angel suddenly made clean and holy again.

To Caitland, whose tastes had never advanced beyond the basal popular music of the time, this sudden outpouring of human rhythm couched in alien terms was at once a revelation and a mystery. Blue eyes opened and she stared at him as the music settled into a softer mode, rippling, pulsing about and through them.

"Do you like it?"

"What?" he mumbled lamely, overpowered, awed.

"Do you like it?"

"Yeah. Yeah, I like it." He leaned back against the wall of the cabin and listened, let the new thing shudder and work its way into him, felt the vibrations in the wood wall itself. "I like it a lot. It's..." and he finished with a feeling of horrible inadequacy, "...nice."

"Nice?" she murmured, the one hand still caressing the tree. "It's glorious, it's godlike...It's Bach. 'The Toccata and Fugue in D Minor,' of course."

They listened to the rest of it in silence. After the last thundering chord had died away and the last echo had rumbled off the mountainsides, and the forest had resumed its normal chanting, he looked at her and asked, "How?"

"Twelve years," she said, "of experimentation, of developing proper stimuli procedures and designing the hardware and then installing it. The entire forest is wired. You've helped me fix some of the older linkages yourself. Stimulus-response, stimulus-response. Try and try and try again, and give up in disgust, and go back for another try.

"My first successful effort was 'Row, row, row your boat.' It took me nine years to get one tree to do that. But from then on response has been phenomenal. I've reduced programming time to three months for an hour's worth of the most complex Terran music. Once a pattern is learned, the forest always responds to the proper stimulus signal. The instrumental equivalents are not the same, of course..."

"They're better," Caitland interrupted. She smiled.

"Perhaps. I like to think so. Would you like to hear something special? The repertoire of the forest is still limited, but there's the chance that—"

"I don't know," he answered. "I don't know much about music. But I'd like to learn, I think."

"All right then, John Caitland. You sit yourself down and relax."

She adjusted some switches in the console cabinet, then leaned back against her tree. "It was observing the way the slight movements caused by the vibrations seemed to complement each other that first gave me the clue to their reproductive system, John. We have a few hours left before supper." She touched the last switch.

"Now this was by another old Terran composer." Olympian strains rolled from the trees around them as the forest started the song of another world's singer.

"His name was Beethoven," she began.

Caitland listened to the forest and to her for many days. Exactly how many he never knew because he didn't keep track. He forgot a lot of things while he was listening to the music and didn't miss them.

He would have been happy to forget them forever, only they refused to be forgotten. They were waiting for him in the form of three men one day. He recognized them all, shut the cabin door slowly behind him.

"Hello, John," said Morris softly. Wise, easygoing, ice-hard Morris.

Three of them, his employer and two associates. Associates of his, too.

"We'd given you up for lost," Morris continued. "I was more than just pleased when the old lady here told us you were all right. That was a fine job you did, John, a fine job. We know because the gentlemen in question never made his intended appointment."

"John." He looked over at Katherine. She was sitting quietly in her reading chair, watching them. "These gentlemen came down in a skimmer, after lunch. They said they were friends of yours. How did you do on the broadcast unit?"

"Fixed some wiring, put in a new power booster," he said automatically. "They're business associates, Katie."

"Rich business associates," added Ari, the tall man standing by the stove. He was examining the remains of a skinned *ascholite* dinner. He was almost as big as Caitland. Their similarities went further than size.

"It's not like you to keep something like this to yourself, John," Morris continued, in a reserved tone that said Caitland had one chance to explain things and it had better be good.

Caitland moved into the main room, put his backpack and other equipment carefully onto the floor. If his body was moving casually, his mind was not. He'd already noticed that neither Ari nor Hashin had any weapons out; but that they were readily available went without saying. Caitland knew Morris's operating methodology too well for that. He'd been a cog in it himself for three years now. A respected, well-paid cog.

He spoke easily, and why not; it was the truth.

"There's no fan or flitter here, not even a motorbike, Mr. Morris. You can find that out for yourself, if you want to check. Also no telecast equipment, no way of communicating with the outside world at all."

"I've seen enough electronic equipment to cannibalize a simple broadcast set," the leader of the little group countered.

"I guess maybe there is, if you're a com engineer," Caitland threw back. Morris appeared to find that satisfactory, even smiled slightly.

"True enough. Brains aren't your department, after all, John." Caitland said nothing.

"Even so, John, considering a find like this," he shook his head, "I'm surprised you didn't try to hike out."

"Hike out how, Mr. Morris? The storm blew me to hell and gone. I had no idea where I was, a busted leg, a bunch of broken ribs, plus assorted bruises, contusions and strains. I wasn't in any shape to walk anyplace, even if I'd known where I was in relation to Vaanland. How did you find me, anyway? Not by the automatic com caster, or you'd have been here weeks ago."

"No, not by that, John." Morris helped himself to the remaining chair. "You're a good man. The best. Too good to let rot up here. We knew where you were to go to cancel the appointment. I had a spiral charted from there and a lot of people out hunting for you.

"They spotted the wreckage of your fan three days ago. I got here as fast as I could. Dropped the business, everything." He rose, walked to a window and looked outside, both hands resting on the sill.

"Now I see it was all worth waiting for. Any idea how many trees there must be in this valley, Caitland?"

He ought to be overjoyed at this surprise arrival. He tried to look overjoyed.

"Thousands," Morris finished for him, turning from the window. "Thousands. We'll file a formal claim first thing back in Vaanland. You're going to be rich, John. Rich beyond dreams. I hope you don't retire on it... I need you. But maybe we'll all retire, because we're all going to be rich.

"I've waited for something like this, hoped for it all my life, but never expected anything of this magnitude. Only one thing bothers me." He turned sharply to stare at the watching Katherine.

"Has *she* filed a claim on it?"

"No," Caitland told him. "It should still be open land." Morris relaxed visibly.

"No problem, then. Who is she, anyway?"

"A research botanist," Caitland informed him, and then the words tumbled out in a rapid stream. "She's found a way to make the trees reproduce after transplanting, but you need a full forest group, at least two hundred and six trees for it. If you leave at least that many, out of the thousands, we'll be able to mine it like a garden, so there'll always be some trees available."

"That's a good idea, John, except that two hundred and six trees works out to about twenty million credits. What are you worrying about saving them for? They live two, sometimes three thousand years. I don't plan to be around then. I'd rather have my cash now, wouldn't you?"

"Ari?" Caitland's counterpart looked alert. "Go to the skimmer and call Nohana back at the lodge. Give him the details, but just enough so that he'll know what piece of land to register. Tell him to hop down to Vaanland and buy it up on the sly. No one should ask questions about a piece of territory this remote, anyway."

The other nodded, started for the door—found a small, gray-haired woman blocking his way.

"I'm sorry, young man," she said tightly, looking up at him, "I can't let you do that." She glanced frantically at Caitland, then at Morris and Hashin. "You can't do this, gentlemen. I won't permit it. Future generations—"

"Future generations will survive no matter what happens today," Morris said easily.

"That's not the point. It's what they'll survive *in* that—"

"Lady, I work hard for my money. I do a lot of things I'd rather not do for it, if I had my druthers. Now, it seems, I do. Don't lecture me. I'm not in the mood."

"You mustn't do this."

"Get out of my way, old woman," rumbled Ari warningly.

"Katie, get out of his way," Caitland said quietly. "It'll be all right, you'll see."

She glared at him, azure eyes wild, tears starting. "These are subhumans, John. You can't talk to them, you can't reason with them. Don't you understand? They don't think like normal human beings, they haven't the same emotions. Their needs spring from vile depths that—!"

"Warned you," Ari husked. A massive hand hit her on the side of the head. The thin body slammed into the door sill, head meeting wood loudly, and crumpled soundlessly to the floor. Ari stepped over one bent, withered leg and reached for the handle.

Caitland broke his neck.

There was no screaming, no yells, no sounds except for the barely articulate, inhuman growl that might have come from Caitland's throat. Hashin's gun turned a section of the wall where Caitland had just stood into smoking charcoal. As he spun, he threw the huge corpse of the dead Ari at the gunman.

It hit with terrible force, broke his jaw and nose. Splinters from the shattered nose bone pierced the brain. Morris had a high-powered projectile weapon. He put four of the tiny missiles into Caitland's body before the giant beat him into a permanent silence.

It was still in the room for several minutes. After this, one form stirred, it rose slowly to its feet. A bruise mark the size of a small plate forming on her temple, Katherine staggered over to where Caitland lay draped across the bulging-eyed, barely human form of Morris.

She rolled the big man off the distorted corpse. None of the projectiles had struck anything vital. She stopped the bleeding, removed the two metal cylinders still in the body, wrestled the enormous limp form into bed.

It was time to wait for him again.

Caitland stayed with her in the mountains for another sixteen years. It was only during the last two that she grew old with a speed that appalled and stunned him. When the final disease took hold, it was nothing exotic or alien, just oldness. The overworked body was worn out.

She'd been like that on the bed for days now, the silvered hair spread out like a steel powder behind her head, the wrinkles uncamouflaged by smiles anymore, the energy in the glacier-blue eyes fading slowly.

"I think I'm going to die, John."

He didn't reply. What could one say?

"I'm scared." He took the flimsy hand in his own. "I want it to be outside. I want to hear the forest again, John."

He scooped up the frighteningly thin form, blankets and all, and took her outside. There was a lounge chair he'd built for her a year ago, next to the young tree by the control cabinet.

"...hear the forest again, John..."

He nodded and went to the console (which he'd long since become as expert in operating as herself), thought a moment, then set the instrumentation. They'd added a lot of programming these past years, from her endless crates of tapes.

The alien chant faded, to be replaced by a familiar melody, one of his and her favorites.

"I can't reach the tree, John," came the whispery, paper-thin voice. He moved the lounge a little nearer to the tree, took her arm and pressed her hand against the expanding, contracting trunk. She had to touch the tree, of course. Not only because she loved the forest and its music, but for the reason he'd discovered fifteen years ago.

The reason why she always followed him with her eyes...so she could see his face, his throat, his lips.

She'd been completely deaf since the age of twelve. No wonder she'd been so sensitive to the vibrations of the trees. No wonder she'd been so willing to isolate herself, to leave the rest of a forever incomprehensible mankind behind.

No wonder.

There was a cough an hour or so later. Gradually a coldness crept into the other hand, the one he held. He folded it over the shallow chest, brought the other one across, too. Crying he'd have none of. He was too familiar with death to cry in its presence.

Instead he watched as the music played out its end and the sun went down and the stars appeared, foam-like winking friends of evening looking down at them.

Someday soon he would go down and tell the rest of mankind what lived and thrived and sang up here in a deep notch of the Silver Spars. Someday when he thought they were hungry and deserving enough. But for a little while longer he would stay. He and the shell of this remarkable woman, and Freia's daughter, and listen to the music.

He sat down, his back against the comforting massage of the pulsing bark, and stared up into the outflung branches where loose seeds rang like bells inside hard-shelled nuts and the towering trunk exhaled magnificence into the sky.

This part coming up now, this part he knew well. The tree expanded suddenly, shuddered and moaned and the thunder of the rising crescendo echoed down the valley as thrice a thousand chimers piled variation and chorus and life into it.

Beethoven, it was...

Do Not Go Gentle

Kevin O'Donnell, Jr.

Clumsily—because even after months of adjustment she still couldn't prevent the anger-flare (*all that time I spent with him wasted*) when she saw the soul surrender its hold, and begin to diffuse into the environment—she straightened the old man's sheets, and picked up the clipboard. "I have to go now, Mr. Tomiglio." The words stumbled off her tongue, unbalanced by her close attention. If she didn't scrutinize them, a clue would slip into their midst. "If you need anything—" she nodded to the plastic box with its plastic button and its plastic-coated wires plunging into the very veins of the hospital "—just ring, and somebody will come."

I won't, she thought as she backed away, *somebody else will, but I won't*.

The withered face on the white pillow turned to follow her progress; its jutting nose, misleadingly defiant, seemed to take aim at her heart. The bloodshot eyes blinked once, blinked twice. Stepping through the greenish fringes of his spreading aura, she swung the door shut behind her.

"Giving up on old Tomiglio?" rasped a familiar voice.

"Good morning, Doctor." She half-nodded, a token bow to his token authority. Short and pudgy, he was married to a woman who'd once thought merely landing an M.D. guaranteed happiness. In consequence, he was addicted to golf and poker and anything else that got him out of the house. It was rumored that his numerous papers were less the result of a driving ambition than they were a means of soliciting invitations to faraway conventions. For all that, though, he'd never made a pass at her, or at any of the floor nurses. He should have been a monk.

He wasn't about to let her off easily. "You just gave up on Tomiglio, didn't you? I saw it in your eyes."

"Doctor, I... I don't know what you're talking about."

"Crenshire—" he took her arm and guided her into a formica-paneled alcove; a bored orderly rumbled a gurney past their heels. It left whiffs of antiseptic and anesthesia in the cool air "—I've been watching you for months."

"Oh?" she asked, coldly, to cover her sudden uneasiness. How much had he guessed? "And what have you seen?"

"I've seen you coax them back, dammit. Now, that old man in there is dying, but if you'd go in—"

She stopped listening, relieved; he had it all backwards anyway. Perception is not influence. Can a stethoscope urge on a flagging heart?

"—know you've got a lot of responsibilities, but if you'd just—"

Oversee the decay? Make sure the rainbow-hued aura dissipated properly? Didn't he know personal involvement with morgue-meat *hurt*?

"—look, I have a goddam *chart*, for Chrissakes, showing every patient you've spent extra time with, and not one—*not one*—of them died, not as long as you were still seeing them."

"And you think I'm responsible?" She didn't like the way he was clinging to his insight. Given time, he might work out the truth.

He grimaced. "Look, there is a very fine line—I shouldn't have to tell *you* this—very fine, between life and death, and it's easy, pitifully *easy*, to cross. You've got to give them a reason to stay put. And you—dammit, Crenshire, you *give* them that reason. I know you do. I've got charts."

The charts would make it difficult. Without them, she could suggest—obliquely, of course—that his memory had seized on the successes and ignored the failures. With them, she couldn't. She'd had no "failures." His charts were correct—but misinterpreted.

"Do you attribute their survival to *me*, Doctor?"

"Yes, I do."

"Solely to me?"

His mouth opened, then shut again as he pondered the implications of her question. Strangely, his after-shave was more noticeable in silence. At last, "Not *solely*, Janie—" he used her first name tentatively, as if hoping a personal rapport would bring them together professionally, "—I do a lot for their bodies, but somebody's got to take care of their...their spirits, you know? That's what counts. Christ, I've had cases come through the ER looking like so much hamburger—but if the spark hasn't gone out, if they want to keep it going—then they live, dammit. And you've got some kind of..." His face screwed up in a parody of thought as he searched through his medical dictionary for a word that wasn't there. "Some kind of power, or talent, for keeping the sparks lit. That's what I'm asking. Go in to old man Tomiglio, keep his spark going. Okay?"

She wanted to explain that her "power" affected no one but herself—that all it did was relax the automatic defense mechanism that would otherwise keep her from caring about people who might die—but she couldn't. She knew what would happen if she did. "Doctor, it won't—" catching her lower lip between her teeth, she tried to find a line that would be convincing yet concealing. "Doctor, I spend time with patients I *like*. Since I don't short-change the others, I think I have a right."

Removing his wire-rimmed glasses, he rubbed the bridge of his nose with thumb and forefinger. His naked eyes looked very vulnerable. "And you don't like Tomiglio?"

"It's not that I *dis*like him—"

"You can condemn him to death simply because you're neutral about him?"

"No, of course not! But..." Gesturing limply, half in reflection of her confusion and half as comment on the futility of arguing with a made-up mind, she tried another tack. Carefully, she said, "If I *do* affect the patients' morale, it's because they know I like them. Now Mr. Tomiglio—"

"—needs to be liked, right?"

"No!" Impatiently, she shook her head; her soft brown hair whisked gently across her shoulders. "I mean, everybody needs to be liked, yes, but—" taking a deep breath, she idly noticed that her uniform was getting tight again "—they're not dumb, Doctor. They can see right through a pose. If I hovered over him, dripping concern and all that Florence Nightingale crap, he'd know I was pretending. They always do, they can tell."

"In my experience—" he pointed a finger at her, and waggled it as though he were her father "—most cases are too absorbed in themsel—"

Again she tuned him out. She donned the mask, the one all nurses wear when a doctor belabors the obvious. It made her seem attentive and interested; it demonstrated, almost by the way, just how unperceptive he really was.

What did he know about the reality, the totality, of sickness? Even though he was one of the better staff physicians, he saw too little. To him, Tomiglio was no more than an array of symptoms, each to be measured against a series of known parameters. Quantify, that was the word, that was what he did. He reduced everything to numbers and then was blind enough to assume that the numbers were all there was.

Few of the doctors knew the winces, the hoarse voices, the suddenly moist eyes. Most hurried through—pump, count, poke, read, chart—and then were gone. Afterwards, they had the nerve to wonder "—why'd that old guy—whatshisname? ah...ah...never mind, not important—the one in 714, with the cysts, why the hell'd he Brady like that? Gotta see the autopsy on that, see what I missed. Coulda sworn I didn't, though— I mean, I worked him up *good.*"

Becoming aware that he was waiting for her to speak, she ran backwards through her memory to see if it could echo his question, No. Gone. "I'm sorry, Doctor," she said, glancing meaningfully at her watch, "I'm afraid I was thinking of something else. What did you say?"

"I said—skip it." Puzzlement, and a hint of defeat, tinged his round face. "It just occurred to me that, uh, you probably can't use this power of yours unless you really care about the person." Tiredly, he shrugged, "So Tomiglio dies. Have it your way." Spinning on his heel and striding away, he disappeared around the corner of the brightly lit corridor.

"Well, of all the—" She cut herself off with an effort. He'd mistaken her pragmatism for callousness when it wasn't, when it was simply and acknowledgment of limitations. Strength is finite, to be used where it will have an effect. For a second she was consumed by the irrational impulse to run after him, tug his sleeve and tell him everything, She fought that down, too.

Contraindicated. A nice bit of medical jargon that fit her situation. Explaining her "talent" was contraindicated. Either no one would believe her, which could cost her her job, as well as her ability to support Jimmy without crawling to her ex, or... involuntarily, she shivered. The alternative was to have her talent used, and that notion put a fluttery dizziness in the pit of her stomach.

She could visualize how they'd exploit it. They'd park her in Admitting with a pointer. She'd read the glittering, whirling, disintegrating aurae to separate the sick, the lame, and the maimed into: "Possible Survivors" and "Walking Dead." Regularly, they'd stroll her through the wards, vultures ahover for the singling out of those who would waste what they might be given.

Oh, the machinery would be smooth and oiled:not a voice would be raised, not an alibi would be missed. The gurneys would hiss soundlessly, sweeping up the imminent debris, and she...

...and she would be the Hope-Killer.

No.

She couldn't—she *wouldn't*—play that role. Everybody would be on her constantly, deferring to her judgment, canceling operations, halting medication. All on her say-so. All because she could see the—souls?—making ready to abandon the tired bodies.

Yes, there'd be a beneficial side: people could go home to die as human beings, rather than sedated lumps of machine-fed flesh. The bereaved families would be spared monstrous, useless costs. Affairs could be ordered well ahead of time.

And yet, what did she *know?* She couldn't prove her talent—she refused even to trust it completely. It was new, of some three of four months' duration, and she didn't know how long it would stay with her. She'd look a fool if she announced it, explained it, and offered to demonstrate it—only to have it fail her.

Besides. Medicine was cold enough as it was. It had been regimented and programmed until the hospital had become an impersonal, heartless superorganism. Did the world need more of that? Didn't it need, instead, caring and affection and genuine, because-we're-both-human, understanding?

The metal voice that lived in the ceiling awakened to call her name. Recognizing it as a power higher than herself, beyond appeal or even dispute, she obeyed. Her rubber soles made brisk, efficient sounds as they patted the shining linoleum; catching a coloreless image of herself in the glass of a windowed door, she pushed her hair into place without slowing down.

Martha Fedorchuk stood behind the desk, reviewing a sheaf of medication instructions. At Janie's approach she looked up, and called: "Your friend down the hall's been asking for you." Her blue eyes darted to the patient list to pick up the name. "Terry, in 318."

"Thanks, Martha," she said, pausing only to ask, "did he say why?"

"Huh? Oh, no, just that he wanted to see you when you were free."

"Thanks." She moved along the cross-corridor, letting her feet find her destination while her mind methodically refreshed itself on Terry's situation.

He was thirteen, blond, with the quick laugh and roving curiosity of the well-adjusted child. He'd fallen out of a tree, his backyard Everest; he'd somehow escaped multiple fractures, but the branch that had broken his fall had also seriously damaged his kidneys. The dialysis machine would support him until they recovered—or until he received the transplant which every member of his family had offered—and he'd seemed to be coming along nicely.

She pushed open his door. Resignation slapped her in the face. Her eyes widened, criss-crossed the small room instinctively. Her nurse nose sniffed for the smells of sickness; there were none. But Terry lay alone in a rippling blue pool of gloom that bordered on—

"No," she whispered in alarm, "no, not Terry."

Two steps took her to his bedside; gently, her index finger prodded his ribs. It was a game they played—he'd claimed, the day he was admitted, that she couldn't work for the hospital since she didn't poke him like everybody else. So she'd said, "I knew I forgot something!" and immediately shoved her finger into his side. He'd laughed, and it had become their joke.

"Stop it," he whined, "that hurts." His eyes were puffed shut, as though he'd been rubbing them; his face was flushed and hot.

"Martha said you wanted to see me." It was all she could do to keep her voice even: his aura, expanding visibly, was already past the point of no return. He'd given up. He was going to die. She could not reverse the process.

"I don't feel good," he complained.

His chart was in her hand—she must have picked it out of its box as she came through the door, although she didn't remember having done so—and she skimmed it quickly. According to its cramped notations, all signs were normal. "Would you like me to call the doctor?"

"No," he said sullenly, "he just makes me hurt more."

She licked her lips. The atmosphere was so oppressive that she wanted to flee. Terry's surrender had made everything futile—all her friendliness, all her visits, all her games and jokes and boredom-breaking gambits—all gone to waste because his thirteen-year-old spirit just hadn't been strong enough to bear the burden of his ruptured kidneys. She wasn't needed any more. Nor was she *wanted*—he'd made his choice, albeit unknowingly, and he'd chosen to reject her. So... "Would you like me to call your mother?"

"I want you to make me better, " he wailed suddenly. "Janie, please—I feel so awful—*please* make me better again."

"But, I—" How can you tell a child that there's nothing you can do? Her fingers lay on his forehead, and brushed back wisps of damp straw. Heart heavy, she braced herself. Disengaging her affections would be painful, but leaving them invested in a boy fated for the morgue would be devastating.

"*Please!*" he demanded, before she could do or say a thing.

"Terry, I—" Stalling, she walked to the window, and cranked it open. Summoning a doctor would be to no avail—he'd only express optimism, unless she explained her talent, in which case he'd be skeptical, and probably disapproving. But Terry's aura was spreading into the fresh spring air, and its foci were beginning to disassociate themselves from each other, and—She dropped abruptly to the edge of his bed, murmuring, "I'll do what I can," while her amazed mind gawked at her emotional decision.

But what could she do? She had no control over the fading of his aura—It emanated from him, it was directed by him—yet if she could make him wad it together, suck it back inside where it belonged... "Did I tell you I have a little boy?" she asked.

"Yeah," he muttered, tossing his head as if looking for comfort.

"Did I tell you what he does for fun?"

His swollen eyelids parted to reveal glazed green eyes. "No."

"Well, he—" Just in time, she remembered the difference in ages, and the vast gulf that would separate their interests. What amused Jimmy would only bore Terry.

"What's he do?"

She'd have to make something up, something that would... that would cut through his fatigue and resignation, that would give him cause to outlast it. "Well," she said, "he—he dug a hole in the backyard, and he filled the hole with water, and—"

"And he goes swimming in it?" His tone said a rich suburbanite didn't think very much of any kid who'd have fun paddling around in a mud puddle.

"Oh, no! The alligators would get him if he did that."

"The alligators?" For the first time, his eyes opened all the way.

"Yes. His uncle was down in Florida, and he sent us some alligator eggs, and they hatched, and now—"

"Why do they stay in your backyard? Why don't they run away?" He made a weak effort to lift himself up on his elbows.

Sliding the pillow under his shoulders, she invented, "We put a fence around the hole, so they can't. Besides, they're scared of our dog."

"Alligators, wow!" His voice twisted, became accusing. "You're making all this up."

"Terry!"

"You are." He raised a trembling arm, and pointed one thin finger at her. "You can't keep alligators in your backyard—what happens when winter comes, huh? You're making this all up."

Theatrically, with a hand to her throat, she sighed. "You're right. I am."

He slumped back, like a desert traveler finding that the oasis is a mirage after all. "Why did you want to do that to me?" he asked querulously.

She shrugged. "Because I didn't think you'd believe the truth."

"What is the truth?"

"No." She smoothed the stiffly starched sheets across his laboring chest. "If you wouldn't believe alligators, you'd never believe the truth, and you'd make fun of me."

"I wouldn't make fun of you, Janie, you know that. Come on, tell me."

"Uh-uh." She stood, patted his cheek—so softly, so nearly translucent—and risked a glance around. The blue pulsations held steady. "Make you a deal, though. When you get out of here, you can come over and see for yourself. You'll have to believe your own eyes, won't you?"

"I guess so," he conceded suspiciously. "But tell me now, okay?"

"Uh-uh."

"Please?" All his interest was focused on what lived in the water hole.

"I'll give you one hint." Out of the corner of her eye, she saw his aura make a hesitant move towards coalescence. She bent over, and into his ear whispered, "I'll bet you've never seen a real one before."

That did it. He was completely, utterly hooked. Even as she watched, the blue sparkles interwove themselves and retreated into safety. His underlying being had finally found a reason to bear the pain of healing.

And it stunned her. She hadn't thought it possible because her talent couldn't manipulate anything. It could only let her see. But maybe that was enough. The subconscious computers that ticked constantly maintained—with a grimace, she permitted herself to slip into jargon—a running cost-benefits analysis. The body could never forget the costs, but the soul could forget the benefits. With her talent, she could see when it was time to remind the suffering soul of what magical, fanciful, wonderful things could lie just around the corner of the future.

"Where are you going?" Terry asked sleepily. It wasn't a complaint. It was pure curiosity, exhumed by a mind that had remembered how valuable it could be.

"Just down the hall," she answered as she dimmed the lights. "There's an old man I have to talk to. A Mr. Tomiglio."

The Midnight Bicyclist

Gene DeWeese
and
Joe L. Hensley

Considering the trouble tapes have been known to cause, I'm probably crazy to record any of this, but on the other hand, I'm almost afraid not to. For one thing, it's beginning to look like this crazy scheme of mine might actually pay off—big! I've already managed to get myself some space in a half-dozen area newspapers, and there was even a wire-service man here yesterday. He shook his head and grinned a lot as he made notes, but he did make notes. More important, the watchers are starting to show up—not just the "Hi-Charlie-how's-it-going?" types, but real honest-to-God watchers, prowling around the cemetery for hours on end.

To tell the truth, it scares me, thinking how far this might go, which brings me back to why I'm putting this down on tape. If this ever *really* takes off, and the zombie . . . Well, let me put it this way: I'll need something to keep reminding me of how it really started. I'd hate like hell to get carried away with my own con job, the way a lot of others have done, and start really *believing* all this crap I've been dishing out,

So if you're listening to this down the line a few months or years, Charlie—or whatever you're calling yourself now—*don't forget!* You're nothing but a goddamned fraud, Charlie, you and your out-of-town zombie! Have fun, but don't forget what's really going on and how you—how *I*—stumbled into all this. Don't forget...

Remember, Charlie? It was just a bunch of accidents—or "serendipidity," if you want a fancier-sounding word. First, that fast-food franchise I'd been working up in Elwood went broke, despite all the fast talk of the guy who sold it to me. Then, because we were broke, we moved back to Crossville, into that old farmhouse I'd inherited from my father a couple years back. And while I was waiting for something new to develop, I took a job at the assembly plant at the edge of town—third shift, no less. Just temporary, of course, until something better came along, but I was still there six months later, and that's when Cora decided she'd had it and took off for parts unknown.Probably to her mother's place over in Illinois, although I haven't heard a word from either of them. What really griped me, though, was the fact that she took the car. But, then, if she hadn't, none of this other stuff would've happened, not to me at least, so I guess it was all for the good.

When I discovered Cora and the car were both gone, I started looking around for other transportation, but the only thing I could find was the bicycle out in the shed. It had been mine, probably fifteen years ago. I guess my father just never got around to throwing it out, and when they auctioned off all the equipment after he died, they must've either missed it or decided it wasn't worth the auctioneer's time.

To my amazement, the tires actually held air once I'd walked it cautiously to the air hose at the filling station out on the highway. Even more amazing, I was still able to stay upright on the thing, and by the timeI got back to the house, I'd decided I sort of liked it. Almost restful, in a precarious sort of way. Even that night, with a flashlight strapped to the handlebars, the four miles along the back roads to the plant were pleasanter than they had been during any of the previous six months. The next night, though...

The pleasures of midnight bicycling were already wearing a bit thin, and I was pedaling pretty hard in hopes of making it to the plant before the flashlight completely expired. Another problem was the wind, right in my face. And remember, this was a vintage bicycle, from the days when only cars had gearshifts, so a head wind was murder. And if all that wasn't enough, I kept having this creepy, tingly feeling all over my back, like someone was trailing along behind me. I knew why I had the feeling (although I've been playing it up to the papers and the rest as a "premonition"), but knowing didn't get rid of it. It had been the late show. Channel

5 was having another Golden Oldies week, and this week's theme was zombies, which could've been one more reason Cora picked this particular week to vanish. She used to like zombies, but not anymore. "*Some* people outgrow such childishness," she said often and loudly, sometimes referring to zombies, more often to just about anything she didn't care for, including me personally. That night it had been a John Carradine special. As always when he wasn't being Dracula, he was a more-or-less mad scientist, and this time he brought a couple dozen people back to life. They didn't care much for the idea, though, or for the uses he had in mind for them, and, after the usual melodramatics, they demonstrated their lack of appreciation in the last reel. Scratch one more mad scientist.

Anyway, there I was, pedaling along a couple of miles from my house, just passing Covenanter Cemetery, when Art Walters shambled across the ditch and into the road in front of me. Now this wouldn't have surprised me all that much a few weeks earlier. Art was the sort who shambled and lurched a lot, especially late at night, and he was liable to turn up anywhere during one of his binges. He'd start walking home after closing the last tavern, and since he lived as far out in the country as I did, you never knew where he'd end up. Usually Art didn't either, since his sense of direction was one of the first things to go. But like I said, that would've been my reaction a couple of weeks ago. Having him show up like that now jolted me. Or maybe *paralyzed* is the word.

Art had died almost two weeks ago.

For some reason I stopped, straddling the bicycle frame and just barely able to keep from toppling over. The sensible part of my mind was screaming that I should get turned around and get the wind at my back and get the hell out of there, but it was overruled by something else. Instinct, maybe, or just temporary paralysis.

I could see that Art was still wearing the light gray suit and blue tie he'd been buried in. I remember thinking at the funeral that it was probably the first time he'd worn it since his wedding twenty years before. His face was totally expressionless, his eyes unblinking. There were clumps and smears of claylike dirt all over him, clothes and flesh alike.

Then he spoke, and it wasn't quite Art's voice. I'm not even sure his lips moved the first time. The moon wasn't too bright, and the flashlight on the handlebars was getting dangerously dim. Anyway, the first thing he/it said was:

"Where am I?"

"You just came out of the cemetery," I said. I'm not sure if my own lips moved any more than his did. I felt pretty stiff all over.

"I know it was a cemetery!" Almost-Art's voice said, "It's always something like that, but this—" The voice was annoyed as it cut itself off and began again. "Geographically, where am I?"

"A couple miles east of Crossville, Indiana." This time my lips moved a little. Some of the stiffness was going away. Not that I was losing all fear and becoming calm, you understand, but my curiosity bump was growing by leaps and bounds. This was, after all, the first zombie I'd ever run into in the alleged flesh. Not only that, it wasn't behaving anything like I'd been late-show led to believe was typical zombie fashion. This thing was definitely interested in the world around him, not to mention being somewhat ticked off. I was beginning to have a hunch even then (I like to tell myself) that this might turn out to be a Good Thing, if I could keep from blowing it.

If I hadn't already blown it, of course. He didn't seem all that impressed with the information I'd given him. "Don't you have some kind of coordinate system?" he asked. "Latitude and longitude?"

We did, of course, but I hadn't thought about it since high-school geography class, and that was a lot of years ago. "We're in the North Temperate Zone," I said lamely, "if that's any help."

Apparently it wasn't. "You mean you don't even know—" he began, then broke off. "Oh, never mind. It's always something like this. The memory is almost totally gone, and—"

He shuddered into silence then, and looked down at himself slowly, maybe reluctantly. In the fading beam from the flashlight, I could see the blankness in his face being momentarily replaced by a tiny grimace. He brushed a bit of clay from the corner of one jacket pocket with a clawlike hand (like maybe he couldn't control all the finger joints yet), then moved a shambling step closer to the light. I caught the beginning of a pungent odor, and I wondered how many of his senses were in working order.

"I hate this," he said. His voice was definitely angry, not just ticked off like it'd been when he'd found out I didn't know where we were. "I really hate it!" He brushed at his trousers, not making noticeable headway in clearing away the grime, then at the lapels of his jacket.

Finally he gave up and looked toward me again. It was unnerving to see that, despite the tone of his voice, his face had blanked out again. "Not that it really matters, but who am I?" he asked.

"Art Walters," I said slowly, uncertainly. "Aren't you?"

"I'm sure I wouldn't have the faintest idea. For what we pay, they don't give us any extras, like a complete memory or a guide. And in this one—" His face came to life again, displaying another grimace, this one longer and stronger than the first. "—I suspect I'm lucky that even the language is still available."

"If you're not Art Walters, then who are you?"

He looked down at himself again and visibly shivered. "You wouldn't understand," he said.

"Try me," I said. Possible Good Thing or not, I didn't appreciate being patronized by a zombie, particularly one that used to be Art Walters.

He looked me over again. His face seemed to be getting closer to normal now, with not as many blank-stare interludes. I doubt, though, that Art-alive had ever managed quite the expression that was collecting on his face now. A haughty combination of distaste and superiority. Whoever or whatever was in there was at least getting better control.

He waved a hand unsteadily at the cloudless sky, dislodging a few more crumbs of dirt as he did so. "I'm from out there." The voice still didn't sound right, but this time the lips definitely moved, though maybe it was just for effect.

"And not from over there?" I asked, pointing at the rows of moonlit tombstones. This was starting to get *really* interesting. A zombie from outer space could create even more of a stir than your average home-grown variety.

"This—this *vehicle* is from there, unfortunately. *I* am not."

"Vehicle? Art's body, you mean?"

An irritated, indifferent shrug. "Call it what you wish."

"And when you say 'out there,' you mean another star? Which one?"

"How should I know? I'm hardly a scientist. If I *were*—" He stopped, apparently shifting his mental gears. "You know about such things now?"

"I know there are a few billion stars out there, and the theory is that a lot of them must have planets." I'd read enough Sunday supplements and science fiction to know at least that much.

"Well, things *have* changed, haven't they? The next thing you know—" Again he cut himself off in mid-thought, but this time he frowned in puzzlement. "There's something badly wrong with this vehicle," he said.

I could have told him that when I first saw him. "It's dead, if that's what you mean," I said.

"No, not that!" Snappish again. "It wants something. It's a sick feeling. Even at these prices, I shouldn't have to put up with problems like this. But there's definitely some sort of feeling—a craving..."

"Knowing Art, your vehicle probably wants some muscatel."

A blink. "Muscatel? Yes, wine, alcohol, these words are prominent." A musing look. "Strange..."

Not only an outer-space zombie, but an alcoholic one to boot. Great. But what else could you expect under the circumstances? The thing, whatever it was, had been using Art's body only a few minutes, but Art had been using it—badly—for forty or fifty years. I wondered how muscatel—Art's favorite because of the price—would mix with whatever was sloshing around in his veins now. Then I tried to stop thinking about that sort of thing altogether. It had been a logical thought, and I had a *prima facie* sort of feeling that logic had no place here anymore. Not that kind of logic, anyway. Besides, for my purposes, it was pointless. What I had to do was make sure the Good Thing didn't get away from me before I had a chance to—

"Where can I obtain some alcohol?" he asked, and then added, with another faint shudder: "And I really must find some way to clean this vehicle. This is disgraceful, even for—" He chopped off the thought and returned to the more urgent problem. "But first I must find the alcohol. It is really remarkable, the craving this vehicle retains."

"I could probably find you some," I said.

"Very well, let's go."

Not only alcoholic but autocratic. But maybe I could make good use of the alcoholic part... I collected my courage into a lump and plunged ahead:

"I can supply what your vehicle needs—*if* you answer my questions."

He went blank for a moment, then parodied a smile. "I'll find it myself," he said and did a shambling one-eighty-degree turn. "I believe you said your local community—Crossville, was it?—was in this direction?"

"It is, but it won't do you any good. Everything is closed at this time of night."

"Closed? Oh, yes, I see. No matter. I'll break in."

"*If* you can find the right place to break into. You said you didn't have very many of Art's memories."

He stopped shambling and looked back at me. "Very well, I'll get someone else to help me."

"Not very likely. Everyone around here knows your vehicle. And they also know it's dead. You won't get anyone else to even talk to you, let alone buy you a drink." I wasn't too sure about that last, especially if he lucked out and ran into Buck or some other drinking buddy of Art's. Most of them had been at the funeral, but there were at least a couple who wouldn't necessarily remember whose it was at this late date.

"Why not? Why should they be different from you?"

I managed an indifferent shrug. "Most of them are nowhere near as curious as I am, for one thing. And not very many of them would appreciate the distinction between you—whoever or whatever you are—and your vehicle." Probably true, especially late at night after a week of zombie movies on the late show.

"Besides," I added, "you popped up so suddenly, I didn't have time to panic and run. If I'd seen you coming..." Again, probably true, but I would've eventually gotten back within observation range, at least.

He seemed to be considering the information before speaking again, and now he sounded puzzled. "But everyone was so helpful the last time."

The last time...

I shook my head, forcing myself to keep improvising and not waste time speculating. "I don't know who you ran into last time, but I guarantee you won't find anyone very helpful around here now. And I won't give you a chance to sneak up on anyone like you did on me. I'll warn them. You don't look like you can move fast enough to get anywhere ahead of me. Certainly not if your vehicle can't move any faster now than it could when it was...alive. At best, you'll have a lot of trouble, and it'll be a long time before you get what you need. At the worst, someone will take a shotgun and blow a couple of very large holes clear through your vehicle."

Some kind of emotional battle was going on inside the vehicle's head then, that was for sure. Finally, though, he seemed to reach a decision. He was obviously annoyed, but his anger didn't seem to be directed at me.

"Very well," he said, "I agree." And then, as he looked malevolently upward, almost directly overhead: "You haven't heard the last of this, believe me! I'll have you up before the board, every last one of you, and then—" With difficulty, he cut the words off. Slowly, he brought his eyes down to look gravely at me.

"Let's go," he said. "I'll answer your questions, within reason. But no more of this nonsense about specific stars. I can't tell you things I don't know." He paused, getting his supercilious expression back in place. "It wouldn't do you any good anyway. You don't even know your *own* coordinates."

"Fair enough," I said, stifling my irritation and wondering what to do next. If I had a car, I could drive him home, but if I'd had a car, I wouldn't have found him in the first place.

Luckily, though, the bicycle had one of those sturdy, anachronistic package carriers on the back. I'd never carried a package at all, let alone one as big as this, but it might work. If it didn't, we would have a long, slow walk back to my place at the rate Art-the-vehicle shambled along. And, even at that time of night, there were occasional cars along the road. I didn't want anyone spotting us if I could help it. Not until I got my curiosity satisfied and had some time to figure out what, if anything, I could make out of all this. There had to be *something*, I kept telling myself as I showed him where I wanted him to sit. He limited himself to a couple more skyward-directed complaints and then straddled the carrier. His hands weren't quite as clawlike as before, and he was able to grasp my belt easily as I got on the seat in front of him. He seemed to have gotten control of all the joints at last.

I finally managed to get us rolling in roughly a straight line despite all the dead weight, excuse the expression, over the rear wheel. It made for heavy pedaling, to say the least, but it was partly offset by the inspiration he provided. Whenever I slowed enough for the tail wind to overtake me, I'd catch a whiff of decay that, while not as strong as it had been at first, was still enough to get my legs to speed again.

I didn't have the breath to ask any questions while I was pedaling, and he didn't volunteer anything, so the ride was made in puffing silence. I did do some thinking, though, so I was ready to have at it when we lurched to a stop and made our way into the house.

"All right," I said when I finally had my breath under control, by which time he was already tracking up the living room carpet and gurgling down a plastic glass of sloe gin, "if you can't tell me where you're from or who you are, exactly, how about telling me what you're doing here?"

He put the plastic glass down empty and looked around. "Really remarkable. I've never come across a vehicle like this before, but it does seem to be responding." He reached for the bottle, but I snatched it back.

"You said you'd answer my questions," I said, backing out of reach.

He stared at me for a moment, then sighed. "Oh, very well." Before he could say more, his eyes fell on his outstretched hand, which was still covered with several kinds of dirt. The odor, though, was definitely retreating. If it hadn't been, I doubt that I could've stayed in the same room with him. "You have some method of cleansing, I presume?"

I nodded. "And plenty more of this," I said, holding the gin bottle aloft. "But the answers . . . ?"

Another baleful glance skyward, as if he could see right through the ceiling. He muttered a couple of unintelligible syllables, then turned to me again. "As you wish, but—" A faint but ghastly smile crossed his face. "It will serve the bastards right, whatever happens! No court would—Now, what was it you wanted to know?"

"Everything," I said. "But for a start, what are you doing here?"

"It's my wife's fault, really, her and her damned—" He stopped, frowning. "Which reminds me, have you seen anyone else like me lately?"

"Like you? Someone crawling out of a grave, you mean?"

"I wouldn't be surprised. They're *supposed* to connect *before* burial, but—Well? Have you?"

I shook my head. "You're the first zombie I've ever met personally."

"Zombie? Oh, yes, I see. Amusing. Well, I'm not surprised you haven't seen her. She could be anywhere. They're supposed to get us within a few miles of each other but they're supposed to do a lot of other things, too." He closed his eyes for a moment. "Maybe this will cure her finally, if she's having as much grief as I am," he finished musingly.

"*Who* is supposed to get you within a few miles of each other? Why? And what are you doing here?"

"Oh? I thought you knew, the way you mentioned 'zombies'—"

"You mean you really *are* behind those stories? You come down here just to reanimate bodies? But why?"

"We're tourists, of course."

Tourists? No wonder he's so damned patronizing. I thought. He's talking to a mere native. But so far he'd said nothing that proved he was particularly superior—or even different. The Ugly American from the stars.

"Okay," I said, "you're a tourist, but you don't know where you're from. Do you know where you *are*?"

"With respect to what coordinates?" he smirked.

I thought for a second. "All right, never mind that. But tell me, why are you in Art's body?"

"I couldn't very well come in person, now could I?"

"I don't know. Could you? Could I—"

"Of course not! That would take years." He seemed to enjoy my ignorance.

"So you just send your minds around to different worlds, is that it? Just to look around? Do a lot of you come here?"

He shrugged. "This isn't a very popular world," he said, and then grimaced. "And there certainly aren't very many who come *this* way. The better agencies provide live hosts. It's just that my wife feels—" He stopped, grimacing yet again, managing to look a bit embarrassed and disgusted at the same time. The "no frills" flight, I thought. Or maybe it was their equivalent of traveling steerage.

He gave me a look. "I really must insist on the cleansing you have promised."

He seemed to have decided to be fairly open with the native, perhaps because he enjoyed showing off his superiority, perhaps to get in a jab at whoever had sent him here, so I led him to the bathroom and showed him how to fill the tub. I gave him another glass of gin. He tried to be dignified, but he downed it in a couple of swift gulps. Art's reflexes, I thought, and I realized that having even a tiny bit of Art still in there somewhere bothered me a lot more than whatever else was in there.

As the tub filled, he got undressed. He didn't have any trouble with the buttons, but I had to show him how the zipper worked. His only comment was a single "Ingenious!" in the same tone I might've used in complimenting someone who'd just told me he had a cat that knew how to open doors by itself.

I thought about what undertakers did to bodies and quickly took up a post outside the open bathroom door while he finished undressing and getting into the tub.

"What happens when one of you takes over a live host?" I asked when he shut off the water.

"Never having enjoyed the privilege, I couldn't say," he said coldly between splashes.

"Does the host remember anything about it?"

"They're not *supposed* to."

Amnesia, I thought. Disappearances. Judge Crater. This could explain all sorts of things.

"How many of you come here?" I asked.

More splashing, some of it a bit heavy. The gin was apparently taking effect, no matter what it was having to mix with.

"I couldn't really say. There were ten in the party I came with."

Ten... Ten zombies wandering around loose.

"And there's another tour scheduled in a few months," he went on. "My wife recruited a couple of suckers for that one, which is another reason *this* one was so cheap for us."

At least ten zombies a year, if this schedule was typical... And God knows how many live hosts for the first-class passengers. Yes, this could explain many things, particularly if all the tourists were as casual about the local laws as this one was. Possession. Vandalism. Maybe even some—many?—of the senseless killings that had been cropping up so often lately.

But was it going to do me any good? So I'd known and conversed with someone from outer space. So had a lot of other nuts. Without pots of evidence, you couldn't cash in worth a damn. Of course I *did* have the evidence, right in there splashing around in my bathtub, but how long could I hang onto it?

"How long are you staying?" I asked.

"Four of your days." A pause. "And frankly, under these conditions, that is quite enough."

Four days... What could I do in four days? How could I—

The splashing halted abruptly.

"What time is it?" The vehicle's voice was tense.

I glanced at my watch. "About one-thirty. Why?"

"I think I'm being called back, but—What *date* is it?"

"August tenth. Now what—"

"August *tenth*? Are you sure?" The voice had gone from tension to the beginnings of panic.

"I'm sure. Now if you—"

There was a huge splash. Soapy water came flying out the bathroom door, followed an instant later by a dripping, soapy vehicle.

"Those incompetent bastards!" it said as it shot past me, all traces of shamble gone. "Those lousy, fouled-up bastards! It must've taken the whole four days to just get me out of the ground! And now they're getting ready to—"

The slamming of the front door cut off the rest of the words.

I ran after him. Not only was my evidence getting away, I still had a lot of questions left.

By the time I got to the front door myself, he was gone, and so was my bicycle. Talk about bastards...

I couldn't catch him, even though I was sure that pedaling a bicycle, naked, barefoot, and wet couldn't be that easy or fast. But I didn't give up, either.

I was still a couple of hundred yards from the cemetery, my lungs and legs aching, when I saw the light. Literally. It wasn't there very long, just a few seconds, and if I hadn't been looking right at it, I wouldn't have noticed.

But I was and I did.

The light was a diffuse beam, like a faint, multicolored spotlight. It came from somewhere up in the sky, but I couldn't see how far up the light extended. Forever, as far as I could tell. And it touched the cemetery, a particular spot in the cemetery.

Something went up the beam, like a fast-moving cloud.

And was gone.

When I got to the spot, there was enough moonlight for me to see the vehicle—Art's body—stretched out on the ground next to what had been his grave. When I got close enough, I could tell that the tourist was gone. Art was beginning to smell again.

My own vehicle, the bicycle, was lying in the ditch.

I looked up into the sky, at the stars that still flickered faintly through the thin, high clouds that were gathering. I remembered the light and the ascent, and that's when the idea hit me. That's when I realized that maybe I'd gotten enough questions answered after all. That maybe the out-of-town zombie really could be turned into a Good Thing for me. If I didn't blow it. If I played it right. If I got some decent breaks for a change.

He'd said there was at least one more party coming through a few months from now. I was probably the only one in the whole world who knew about it, so...

It had worked once before, a couple of thousand years ago, so why not now? I'd be working in the one area where people were soft and gullible, where you could make them believe almost anything. All I needed was to get enough people to listen to me, to get enough people—disciples, believers, acolytes, call them what you will—to watch the graveyards of the world for me. *With* me. Certainly they'd be able to spot at least *one* of the tourists in that next no-frills group, and one was all I would need.

I'd stake my own claim at Covenanter Cemetery, of course, since that's where the precursor had appeared. I'd spend my days and nights there, probably even sleep there. And somehow I'd make people come. No more third-shift assembly line for me. No more bankrupt fast-food franchises. From now on I'd be doing my own franchising, and it wouldn't be in the fast-food business.

I wiped the water and soapsuds from the seat and handlebars of the bicycle and, smiling benignly to myself, began to plan my ministry.

The Best Is Yet To Be

M. Lucie Chin

Catherine made a somber appraisal of the face for the hundredth time since bringing it home from the hospital. Deepset gray eyes with a slight droop to the corners, what she had labeled "basic basset hound." A longish nose. High cheekbones over a squared-off jaw. The mouth had to be the best element. It undulated in a pleasingly sensuous line; ending in a slightly upward emphasis which almost balanced the eyes. Even when she laughed those eyes set the mood of her face. They were the strongest, if not exactly the best, feature. She had almost forgotten. No, she *had* forgotten.

The rest of the body didn't matter much. Whatever small annoyances she experienced after each homecoming could be adjusted to quickly enough, and one's weight could be dealt with. She wasn't too particular about that sort of thing. It was the face that counted.

What's in a face?

Nothing, if fashion is all that concerns you. But Catherine had always identified with faces, particularly the eyes. If the mind was the seat of reason, the face was clearly the gateway to the personality.

She considered the reflection in the mirror, elbows on the

dressing table, fingers laced together, thumbs supporting her chin, the mouth hidden behind a low mountain range of knuckles which peaked just below her nose. She and her image mesmerized each other in the dim light of the table lamp. The thin, gray-white tendrils of smoke from her forgotten cigarette drifted upward before the eyes, locked in contact with themselves. Sobriety seemed inherent in the structure of the face. She had become accustomed to a more pliable expressiveness. The eyes dictated too much. The state of mind with which she regarded herself was evidence enough of that.

The aroma of cigarette smoke was becoming rank. It intruded upon her attention and she looked down. She had lit it when she had sat to comb her hair and had only taken one long pull. Already over half its length was a frail, cantilevered thing of dull white fluff-and-nothing clinging together for lack of anything better to do. She unclasped her hands and gently tapped the tabletop, watching the ash collapse into the ashtray. The butt fell back onto the dressing table and she picked it up, took another drag and stubbed it out. It had been years since she had quit smoking but since coming home from the hospital this last time she had begun again without really noticing. Harvard had noticed, but then it was his business to look for such things.

"Maybe I'll get a face lift," she said to the reflection, half-aloud, "like so."

With the middle finger of each hand Catherine pushed upward at her temples. The eyebrows winged out and the droopy corners disappeared, giving her eyes a startled Egyptian sort of look. She turned her head slightly from side to side. The effect was somewhat exotic.

"If I have to live with you I may as well like it."

But Catherine knew Harvard would never agree. He would strenuously oppose anything which might threaten the fragile balance of her situation, and unnecessary surgery would most definitely head the list. If nothing else, he had his reputation to protect. How would posterity view the man who let Catherine van Dyck die? Unfortunately, history had no choices and neither did he. It was too bad he refused to believe it.

He had a vested interest in "Catherine the Great." She was a family heirloom of sorts. He had inherited her from his father who had inherited her from the generation before and once more again.

But she could feel the difference this time. Even as she left the bedroom and reached too high for the doorknob she was sure. She would take this body to the grave... or it would take her, depending on how you looked at it. Oddly, in spite of all the operations and all the frantic searches over the years of her life, the sureness of it did not bother her. She felt it was what she had been waiting for. A time for everything and everything in its time, she thought.

On the landing was a young woman, in her late twenties, blonde, hazel-eyed, and average in height. A look of anticipation was knit into her brows. "Kitty?" she said in a quiet voice.

Catherine broke into a smile, throwing her head back in a soundless laugh and waltzed a long dark shadow about the upstairs hall in the amber glow of the afternoon sun, which gushed through the windows. With outstretched arms and a smug serenity she whirled to a stop in front of the young woman.

Sara! Well, how do I look?"

She made two more slow, regal turns while Sara observed carefully.

"About twice your height and half your age."

"My dear," Catherine said in an indulgent voice, as she swept an arm around Sara's shoulders, "there isn't a functioning human body on the face of the earth that is half my age."

She reached for the banister, missed, reached again. "And I only gained eight inches."

"It must be strange seeing the world from five feet ten after so long at five feet two."

"It isn't like I haven't been here before, or very nearly. Actually five feet two took a lot more getting used to, and I only had it for twenty-eight years... but then you weren't around the last time. I must say this is a pleasantly novel experience. I haven't been able to look you in the eye since you were twelve." And she smiled and squeezed Sara's shoulders.

Sara looked at her and hung her head. "I don't know if I can get used to it, Aunt Kitty."

"What did you expect?"

"I don't know. It's been six months since I saw you and then you were my father's age. Now you are younger than I am."

"Correction, six months ago I *looked* your father's age. In point of fact I am old enough to be his great-grandmother... and you know what that makes you." Catherine was using the mock-stern lecture voice she found most appropriate at such times as it became necessary to remind people of who she was. She was well pleased with the vocal range of this body. Though it was only twenty-five years old it responded perfectly to all the nuances of voice she liked to employ. Her own enduring self-concept had always been contralto. The five foot two personage had been annoyingly soprano.

"Don't let it bother you, dear, you'll get used to it. If I can get used to it anyone can."

"But it's more important for me to come to terms with this than for most others. One of these days the responsibility will be mine and I—"

"Believe me, this time next year you won't remember what the former Cat van Dyck looked like without making an effort." They reached the downstairs hall, windowless and dusklike in the light of one antique wall lamp. "I don't know why your father likes this place so dark. It is downright morbid." She hunched up her shoulders a bit, resting her gaze on Sara. "Don't you find that a bit curious for a man dedicated to the preservation of a life?"

"I have found myself thinking about a lot of things lately, peripheral things really, but at one time they seemed to be a very vital thing...for me, anyhow...Lately I feel like a walking mausoleum. I'm not even a freak anymore—" she gave an odd smile which was at once smug and humorless. "—I'm an institution."

Sara had been watching her closely, appraisingly. "You are one of the finest human beings I have ever known, Aunt Kitty. You have been my best friend since I was old enough to know one adult from another. And even after I knew how special you were, I never had to relate to it till now."

"I have always had to."

"All the more reason for you to remember your humanity. Since the preservation of that life you spoke of is obviously not the perpetuation of any particular body, there must be something else worth keeping alive. Call it anything you want, but the person you have continued to be all this time is inexorably bound up with its own humanness. *That* is important. This seems like a hell of a time for you to forget it."

"I don't forget."

Remembering what she and her father had talked about shortly after her arrival. Sara tilted her head and looked at Catherine sideways. But Catherine had not sounded totally serious. The voice was unfamiliar but the tone it employed was light, slightly facetious. Catherine had always preferred to play devil's advocate whenever she found the opportunity. Was she playing now?

"Where is your father?" Catherine said.

"In the parlor with Chris."

"Then why are we standing here, while your husband twiddles his thumbs and your father bores him to death with the details of his latest triumph?"

Sara smiled and followed her across the room. "Oh, Aunt Kitty, you know Chris is fascinated with my father."

"God only knows why, the man only has one subject he is willing to talk about. And that's another thing...this 'Aunt Kitty' business. I was only a courtesy aunt anyway. I think, considering our apparent respective ages, it would prove less awkward if you dropped the *aunt*."

"If that's what you want, I'll do my best," Sara said.

"Just consider it another part of the Harvard family legacy," Catherine said, opening the doors into the parlor.

The room was brightly lit, with a fire dancing frantically in the heavy-mantled fireplace. It was bracketed by two floral-print couches which faced each other over a low coffee table, on which stood a massive bouquet of flowers.

Dr. John B. Harvard II stood to the left of the fireplace, harassing the condemned wood with a poker. He was of average height, a little more than average in weight, on the thin edge of sixty and handsome as all the Harvard men had been since the first John, Catherine's John, the one who had started all this. Across from him, seated on the right-hand couch, was a younger man of about thirty, taller and leaner, darkly good-looking, with bright green eyes and a quick, equally bright smile. Christian and Sara Kent had been married about five years, and Catherine liked him immensely.

Harvard heard the door and straightened at the side of the hearth.

"Ah, here we are!" he beamed.

Chris turned and rose from his seat, his right hand extended, a smile washing his face.

"Kitty..." He had intended to say something like "How are you" or, perhaps, "It's wonderful to see you again" or maybe both. But he found he could not get beyond the one word. The smile did not exactly fade, but it transformed itself into an almost clichéd expression of wonder. He stood mutely, letting his eyes find their own way from her head to the hem of her long, well-fitted gown, up to the short, precisely shaped cap of auburn hair, down again, finally anchoring themselves on her face.

"Close your mouth, Christian, you look ridiculous," Catherine said. She did a quick two-step and a spin, laughing. "The Cat has once again landed on her feet," she announced to the ceiling, arms outstretched.

"Very theatrical," Harvard said, no longer smiling. "I suggest you save that for the press and behave yourself in the meantime."

"Go to hell," Catherine replied, seating herself on the couch opposite the one Chris was once again occupying. She leaned forward and picked up the nearest glass. "What's this?"

"Scotch," Harvard said, "and you're not having any."

Catherine was ignoring him.

"I used to like Scotch," she said, setting the ice into a circling chase in the topaz liquid. The rim of the glass escaped her lips by a hair's breadth and John Harvard set the drink on the mantle and glared at her.

"I don't know what's gotten into you lately."

Sara didn't know either. She was worried. There were things Catherine had never been able to do. Strenuous exercise had always been considered risky, though some kinds of exercise were essential. Infections of all types were guarded against obsessively, her diet and medications were carefully scrutinized, her physical condition religiously checked at closely spaced intervals. Sara had never known her to smoke or drink, assuming she understood how it could interfere with the body's resistance to all kinds of things. But it was more than that. She had never heard Catherine swear before, and though she had always had a firm will where her own interests were concerned, she had never known her to be deliberately obstinate. She watched and filed things away for future reference.

"Don't be an ass," Catherine said, leaning back against the upholstered garden paths, "*Nothing* has gotten into me...it is what *I* have gotten into."

"Cute."

"I wish you'd do your homework. Your father and grandfather kept copious notes on the situation.

Harvard grunted.

"What situation?" Sara asked.

"Let's face it, no one's psyche is perfect. No matter how well prepared you may be, the experience of suddenly finding yourself thirty or forty years younger than you were can't fail to make you somewhat euphoric. The personality invariable adjusts itself to the perceived age of the body." She shrugged and smiled, "You just can't help it."

"Euphoric is hardly the word I would use to describe your recent behavior." Harvard said sternly.

"How about snotty?" She said turning to him.

"It fits."

"I thought you'd like it."

"I don't, not at all. Now you listen to me," he had the greatest urge to add, "young lady," but he caught himself and pointed a finger instead, "I don't care what you think about this time around. I have listened to you, and you have not said one word I can attribute to anything but gut feelings on your part... and you know what I think about that kind of thing. Crap! Show me something I can test, measure—"

"You won't live that long," Catherine said coolly and Sara and Chris looked startled.

"I still have another thirty-five years left according to statistics. With your track record we could well have another go around before I have to pass the problem over to Sara."

"Don't hold your breath."

"Oh, Cat," he grumbled in exasperation.

"Yes!" she said, sitting suddenly erect. Her face was stonelike. Not anger, or defiance, but the most solid sincerity Sara had ever seen; and Catherine's new face reflected it superbly. It was amazing how well she was able to know its power in so short a time. "Yes!" her voice was as sober as her face, "and I am in my ninth life."

"And I don't want to hear any more about *that*, either!" Harvard said, replacing the poker with a clank.

Chris was looking embarrassed. He was also looking at his watch and clearing his throat.

"If we don't get going soon we are going to be late for dinner," he said quietly.

"Saved by the bell," Catherine said, relaxing back against the couch.

"Good heavens!" Harvard grabbed up his coat as he hastened

toward the door, eyes checking and double-checking his own watch. "I will bring the car around. Meet me at the front door." And he was gone.

"Aunt—" Sara caught herself and began again. "Kitty, was that really necessary?"

"No, but your father is such a bloody stubborn man. His father and his grandfather used to listen to me at least. He can be so sanctimonious sometimes it's sickening. I live inside this body and I have a far better feel for what goes on in here than anyone is willing to believe...even you, I dare say." And she got up and walked out.

"Kitty!" Sara caught her just beyond the door. "I just don't want to see you two fighting. You're like a part of the family. You *are* a part of it. You know how much you mean to all of us. But especially to Dad."

Catherine relented a bit with a deep sigh.

"I know. He can't mean me anything but the best he knows how, which is a great deal. And I am grateful. You can't imagine *how* grateful. But I know a thing which he refuses to accept, and it's frustrating...infuriating! Besides, my current mode of behavior is not without historical precedent. If he could see that and place it in its proper perspective it would make things a great deal easier for him."

Catherine reached into the closet too high for the coat and missed. She shoved both hands into the draping of her skirt and glared at the ceiling for a moment. Then she stared into the closet an instant and slowly, deliberately reached for the coat again.

"Gotcha!"

Chris stood behind her, concerned.

"Catherine, are you alright?"

She laughed and handed him the coat, which he helped her into.

"Yes, I'm fine, I'm better than I have been in ages. It's just a little orientation problem. Your wife was right when she said it must be strange looking at the world from five feet ten after so long at five feet two."

"One's perspective of the world is purely a thing of the mind," she said, tapping her temple lightly with a lacquered nail. "The body has no memory of itself. One therefore relates to what one knows of the world through experience. For the last twenty-eight years I have experienced coat hangers as things which must be reached *up* for.

"It is a common problem for brain-transplant patients who are not always lucky enough to find themselves hosted by a body of the same relative dimensions as the old one."

The horn sounded on the driveway and they moved quickly out the door.

Catherine, with an occasional assist from John Harvard, continued to outline the trials and tribulations of adjusting to a new body. Chris was fascinated. Sara listened and nodded occasionally and kept mental notes.

The experience was like unexpectedly finding yourself in a whole new world. The body has its rhythms, its own special feel, which may escape notice by the conscious mind but do not elude the subconscious. It is an alien environment as potent as the ones surrounding the colonies on the moon or the research stations on Mars and must be adjusted to in much the same way. Assess everything, particularly that which the mind finds most disturbing, and assimilate it...consciously at first, later attempting to cope with things on a more reflexive level. Some people are not capable of accomplishing it. The psychological obstacles are, perhaps, too formidable or sometimes too subtle. In spite of careful screening and the medical team's painstaking efforts to find a compatible host body, the end result is not always what the patient may have anticipated. Recipients are no longer allowed to see the donor body before the event. The psychological after-effects of such meetings as did occur in the early days were devastating. *Most* people preferred not to know. Still, the suicide rate among those deemed suitable was far higher than most concerned individuals felt was within reason.

Catherine was supremely adaptable. Of the eight bodies which had hosted her brain since the death of her original one 185 years before, some had lasted far longer than others but none had failed her immediately. The first was the shortest, 5 years; the second had been 12, but the third, that had lasted for 37 years. After that some were better and some not as good, but one thing they all had in common: no matter how long the association, eventually they all moved to evict their tenant.

That in itself was not unusual. Though the rate of permanent acceptance was quite high now, there was still a significant number of initial rejections. Some of these patients were not capable of surviving a second operation, but of those that did, the vast majority never rejected again. Aside from Catherine, there was only one other known survivor of a third transplant. He had died of natural causes several years before, and the autopsy had shown that he and his host were still fully integrated. But Catherine van Dyck was unique. Not only had she survived eight such transplants, she was the oldest living human being in the world, still active in mind and fluid in character, without a trace of senility or the psychosis which plagued the lives of the less fortunate of her sort. Counting the original 25 years of her life before the chain of surgery which bound her to the Harvard medical monarch, she was 210 and sometimes, privately, she felt every day of it.

She was unique in another respect too. She was the first. The first human, that is, to come through the operation cognizant, functional, and alive more than two weeks later. She was a living legend (Harvard kept saying it was the best kind). The world at large seemed to consider her immortal, and sometime around the date of her fourth transplant (her fifth life, as she preferred to put it), she had been dubbed "Catherine the Great," by some unknown member of the press and it had stuck. She had lived through roughly four generations, and each one had felt compelled to contribute a biography or two to the myth growing in her wake. They were factually pretty accurate and all quite nearly the same.

They were also all wrong. When the time came she would leave them the story and dare them to believe it. They would probably prefer the myth. Myths are comfortable and pliable and entertaining and not filled with the dreams of the walking dead whose lives she shared through the use of their bodies. It was not a horror. It was an obligation she felt to the gift of the donor... that a person may still live as long as they are remembered. Catherine preserved all of them within her. She sought out as much as she could learn about each of the unknowns who had given her their blessing in the form of their bodies' and tried to incorporate into her life at least one of the goals they had striven for. It was a private thing. She had never told anyone, but she swore that in the end, as long as she was remembered, they would be. They were wrong about other things, too. Things she had forgotten over all the years. Things which were strangely bidden to mind lately. Things she would not forget again.

She thought about a great deal of this as John Harvard's car sensed its way to the destination he had punched into the dash panel and she sat in the back, chatting and playing cards over the small, retractable table with her three companions. She thought about it, but she talked about the initial shock of waking up to a new beginning in a hospital bed, of doing weeks of double-takes when you faced a stranger in the mirror, of reaching too high for some things or too low for others, of going shopping and trying to squeeze into something three sizes too small, learning to modulate a new voice, bouts with the psychiatrists and physical therapists, and getting used to the looks on the faces of your friends when they don't recognize you—all the things the average brain-transplant patient is likely to have to go through. But not the things that were hers and hers alone.

The dinner party was a press conference in disguise. Out of disguise, it was the sort of thing the influential people in the business of fund raising did to court the favors of the sort of money which found benefit events tacky. Money in general was never discussed, but all the right people were nestled together in a warm and nurturing environment with good food and fine wine and things were allowed to develop naturally. Lluella Harvard was imbued with an absolute genius for gathering the manna of the rich for the benefit of her various projects. Thus she was the principal fund raiser for, among other things, the Novak Memorial Hospital, which was sometimes referred to as the court of Catherine the Great. She was also John Harvard's former wife.

Lluella Harvard was like a natural force, compelling and potentially devastating. She could be no more ignored than the tide, nor could she be contained or controlled any more successfully. But she was far from arbitrary. She carried on her life with an elegant calculation firmly bound to her vested interests. What benefited Lluella benefited a great many things.

There was no animosity in the separation of one of the world's more notable couples. After twenty-nine years of marriage, they had simply had no time for each other any longer. They were both too thoroughly bound up in their own purposeful directions, and pursuing them independently seemed finally the best course. After eight years of separation they were still cordial and friendly, which is about as much as they had been for a fair part of the marriage.

Lluella was as close to Catherine as anyone had been over the years till Sara came along. Lluella had recognized very early that there was something quite special between Cat and her little daughter. Catherine she found to be somewhat more enigmatic than most people, but how can one really expect to be able to read someone who has lived *so* long, and in such a way. She knew Catherine kept her own counsel far more intimately than John Harvard was willing to recognize. He knew her reactions and reflexes and attitudes and opinions far better than anyone (with the exception of Sara), but he did not look for anything beyond what she was willing to admit to. Plumbing the depths was Lluella's talent and though she had recognized their existence she had never cared to intrude.

She watched the driveway now, feeling unnaturally fidgety. They were late and she could not restrain herself from looking for the car. It was unlike John. He was almost legendary in his promptness. Catherine, on the other hand, could be having problems. Lluella worried that Catherine might not really have been up to this quite yet after all. But this was an important evening and Cat would be well aware of it. She would probably not have declined the invitation unless there were serious complications. Catherine was hardly a martyr but she had a strong sense of responsibility, along with a certain degree of the theatrical. Her image was carefully tended.

Lluella realized, however, that the fidgets were not purely due to the lack of punctuality. In the first year of her marriage she had watched her husband's craft transform a stately, matriarchal being of slightly Wagnerian dimensions and formidable presence, visually in her late sixties, into a petite, bright-eyed cherub of thirty. They were suddenly, disconcertingly, contemporaries. If the knowledge of Catherine the Great in the fullness and power of her maturity was a cogent experience for the mind, this other aspect was subtly awesome.

When the car crunched to a stop on the drive, she felt as though she had suddenly come awake, and opened the door to greet them herself. Sara and Chris were the first up the steps, giving her a hug and kiss each, and John was making pleasantry at her from somewhere behind them. Then he stepped up, took her hand, and planted a kiss on her cheek. When he stepped aside there was a stranger at the foot of the stairs.

Lluella felt the touch of awe once again.

"Cat?"

"Hello, Lluella," an unfamiliar voice said.

"It suits you," she said and felt it was true.

"I'm more than satisfied," Catherine said, smiling, as she

climbed the stairs. "A point here or there that I might want to alter, but nothing of significance."

"Forget it," Harvard grumbled, and Lluella looked from him to Cat and back again, trying to weigh the tone of his voice and the look of defiance which flashed into her eyes.

"Who do we have inside?" he asked.

Lluella began to recite the guest list but he amended his request, asking for the representatives of the press his former wife would not have neglected to include.

"Thomas Hooker..."

Harvard looked sour.

"You may not like the man—"

"He's an idiot."

"—but he represents the best medical journal in the country."

"I didn't ask you to throw him out," he said, holding up his hands. "Who else?"

"Walter Dale, François Soufflot—"

"Ah, you've gone international."

She shot him a wifely look and finished, "—and Adella Chambers."

Harvard turned to Catherine soberly, "Watch out for that one."

"I'm hardly a novice at this," Catherine answered, archness in her voice.

"Just watch what you say. I don't want any of this nonsense cropping up in the wrong places. And this is the first wrong place."

He began to turn, but Lluella caught him with a look.

"Are you two at war?"

Harvard cleared his throat.

"If so, I want you to bottle it up and cork it tight right here. There are to be no skirmishes in my dining room. Is that perfectly clear? And I mean both of you!"

"It's all right mother, really," Sara said. "They are both rational adults, I hardly think they would be that foolish."

"They have been foolish already," Lluella said. "They let *me* see it. I don't want anyone else to."

"It has nothing to do with John," Catherine said, "except at the point where he refuses to accept what I have said to him. *He* is the one who insists upon making an issue of it."

Harvard was standing with arms folded, looking stern.

"Allow me to acquaint you with what she is capable of saying this evening, so you'll recognize it in time to head it off—if necessary," he emphasized in Catherine's direction.

"Cat has arbitrarily come to the conclusion that this is the last go-around for her. Her favorite phrase these days is 'the cat is in her ninth life.' This is her last body, she tells me...no more."

"That sounds disturbingly suicidal, Cat," Lluella said.

Catherine turned and looked silently out across the lawn. Lluella felt rebuffed. She had never known Catherine to be deliberately rude.

"If she intends to do herself in," Harvard continued, "it won't be a quiet, dignified departure. She's begun smoking, drinking when I can't catch her; the other day she took the car out, all alone I might add, and went swimming at the beach, and she has a whole new vocabulary to go with her new face. She also has an attitude problem these days."

"Which is directly related to your own, Doctor," Catherine said turning slowly. "It's *my* business. It's my life, and I know what I know. I'm not going to *kill* myself, I'm going to *live* my life. I can and I will...*this* time...and when I'm done there will be no need to go on to another. Excuse me," and she passed into the house.

Lluella realized she looked startled, standing there wide-eyed with her hand covering her mouth like that. Sara looked much the same, only a little less dramatic, with her hands in her pockets. Chris was frowning and John glowered darkly.

"Since leaving the hospital she seems to have developed this death wish," he said somberly. "It galls me, it really does. That she would throw away all the work that has been dedicated to her existence over the years, all the research done in her name, all the refinement of techniques developed to make each new phase of her life better, fuller, healthier. I'm not discounting the benefits that have accrued to mankind in general, but she has been for so long the motivation, the inspiration, the most truly compelling factor in all this—to chuck it all now—it seems downright ungrateful. Look at the years she has been given."

"Perhaps those years are becoming too much," Chris said.

"No," he shook his head, "she's clear as a bell. She's basically unencumbered by the burdens of old age."

"I was thinking more in terms of just plain being tired," Chris said.

Harvard gave a short chuckle. "She suddenly seems to have far more energy than is good for her. And that is what's so puzzling. This sudden lust for life seems at odds with her refusal even to consider another transplant operation."

"Well, look at it this way," Chris said, trying to move things toward the door, "it is only a few months since the last operation. Apparently she has taken well to the new body, she feels good, better than she has in several lives, and she *is* a little euphoric. But twenty years from now..."

"I hope so." Harvard said and turned to go in.

But Lluella was not so sure. Look deeper, John, she thought; there is more to this. She wasn't sure what, but she knew it was there. The woman at the bottom of the stairs had not simply looked like a stranger, she was one.

Down in the large, pastel-lit living room, Catherine was making the rounds, introducing herself to everyone, acquaintances and strangers alike. Lithe, tall, and attractive, she was supremely self-possessed and charming.

Sara and Chris were immediately swallowed up by a small knot of family friends. Lluella stood beside her ex-husband and watched Catherine move about the room, a smile sparkling across her face, a few inaudible words passed to someone who either looked pleased or startled. Lluella searched Cat's eyes for some clue, some hint of the secrets that eyes sometimes tease one with while the words speak of other things. But Catherine was playing a role just now and was not ready to give up anything. John was watching too but Lluella knew his signals would be different. She wished she knew what she was thinking so she could tell him to be alert to something he would normally not search out, but she could not get a firm hold on the ideas.

Half a dozen mechanical servers drifted gracefully through the assembled guests, offering up chilled champagne and *hors d'oeuvres*. As one of the sleek silver-and-pink gadgets floated by, tidbit-laden and tempting, Catherine helped herself and took up a glass of champagne, with which she toasted the man she was speaking to.

Harvard muttered something and moved to relieve her of the glass, but Lluella caught his arm. "Why bother?"

"But she *knows* better than that!"

"Precisely. So what's the point? She can't lose, John. If you start a scene she may not tear you to pieces, but Chambers certainly will. Besides," she removed her hand, "I think she knows exactly what she is doing."

"Whose side are you on?"

"No one's, except maybe my own. In all my life she is the only person besides you who did not play politics with me. I respect her. She is also the only person I can't manipulate in some way. Oh, don't look so surprised, of course I know I do that! I have to admit I find Cat more than a little awesome, especially when I look at that young, near-child of a body and think of the mind inside. Who am I to presume to dictate *anything* to her?"

"Well, *I* am the doctor!"

"And that's *all* you are. Has it ever occurred to you that maybe the family has been playing God with that woman for too long?"

Harvard looked at Lluella intensely for a moment. Then his gaze slowly began to turn introspective and finally turned away. "Not till now," he said quietly.

"Leave her be, John. She knows what she is about. She must. If the experience of life counts for anything, and we obviously believe it does or we would not work so hard to prolong hers, then what can we possibly have to say to her that she doesn't already know?"

"Not a goddamn blessed thing," he muttered as a pink-and-silver server waltzed within reach and Harvard scooped up two glasses, handing one to Lluella. The rims chimed delicately above the hum of conversation, and as Lluella sipped hers, Harvard turned to look across the room, caught Catherine's eye and raised his glass to her. She responded in kind, and as he tasted the chill of his own, he was at least reassured somewhat by the fact that she had not smiled at him.

Chris was the only member of the family who did not feel the need to scrutinize Catherine carefully at dinner. She was mercurial; exuberant at one moment and serenely serious at the next, politely fielding questions and thoroughly honest in her responses. But she volunteered nothing. She was herself searching for something. She examined the assembly as carefully and thoroughly as the Harvard clan observed her.

In the living room once again, she was immediately laid siege to by the Hooker-Dale-Soufflot-Chambers contingent. Adella Chambers was by far the most irrepressible and, though she was noted for astute judgements and an admirable lack of bias, Catherine found her totally impossible to like. It was eventually all she could do to remain civil. Though none of the others offended her overtly, she was struck by the uniform quality of their questions, or rather the lack of quality. Trivia. She felt her ire rising and let it. Chambers seemed to take notice but did not change her tack. Catherine did not care. She was earnest if somewhat cool in her answers, a departure from the pleasant though occasionally grandiose image the world had come to form of her. Catherine watched Chambers take careful note of the two cigarettes and the brandy and did not laugh at the occasional bit of humor Hooker would employ to try to lighten the mood. Finally, when Adella Chambers asked the only question of the evening with any potential, Catherine saw a place to sow the first seed.

"And what grand project does Cat van Dyck have planned for this reincarnation?"

Catherine leaned back against the sofa and saw John Harvard standing silent and sober behind Walter Dale. He would say nothing, and Catherine returned her gaze to Miss Chamber's face and spoke in quiet deliberation which matched perfectly the expression on her face.

"I'm thinking of becoming a lawyer."

A ripple of laughter from Hooker-Dale-Soufflot. "That's a formidable undertaking. Whatever for?"

"Because I *am* a lawyer. It's what I was in the first life and it is what Kate Wall was."

Chambers arched an eyebrow and smiled indulgently. "Really? And who in the world is Kate Wall?"

Slowly Catherine slid her right arm from the back of the couch and extended it before her, fingers spread, palm almost touching the journalist's nose. She held it there rigidly till the hand began to tremble with the effort she forced into it. Then she slowly drew back, balling it into a fist which she laid in her lap. She had the woman's eyes the instant her hand moved and she held them with the powerful force of her own. Chambers glared back in defiance at the affront to her dignity. But Catherine assailed her with all the awful honesty she could pack into a look and Adella Chambers retreated with a shudder. She looked down at her pad and wrote nothing. The others were silent and bewildered.

"I see," Chambers said at last, trying to shake herself back to life. "That is a noble aim. I hope you are up to it. Tell me, are you still planning to attend the opening of the ballet season in—"

"I have a question for you," Catherine said bluntly, her face carved of alabaster.

"Of course."

"What does the world *expect* of me?"

Chambers seemed satisfyingly flustered.

"Why…nothing."

Catherine nodded slowly. "That, unfortunately, is what I thought." And she stood and walked away.

They all turned to watch her leave, and in the next instant her seat on the sofa was filled with the smiling person of John Harvard. Chambers looked at him, confusion still clouding her eyes.

"A little insight can be a devastating thing, can't it, young lady?"

It was Hooker who responded. "I thought no one was supposed to know who their donors were."

"They aren't. But I have a suspicion she always does, somehow."

Adella Chambers was watching Catherine's back withdrawing across the room.

"How does she stay sane?" she murmured. "I could never—"

"She isn't Catherine the Great for nothing."

"Is she serious about this lawyer business?" Dale asked.

"I hope not," Harvard said, "but—who knows."

"I hope she is," said Adella Chambers folding her pad and rising to go.

"Adella!" Dale said. "You're not leaving! The night is still young."

"It has suddenly gotten very old for me. Besides, I have something important to do at home. I have half a dozen biographies to burn."

She walked away to another chorus of chuckles, and in short order the English language was abandoned and the conversation continued in "Medicalese."

Catherine sat in Lluella's powder room and communed with her image in the mirror for the hundred and first time.

"Too bad," she said to herself. "They just aren't ready." She stared at her own eyes in silence for another minute, then intoned in a low voice:

"The time has come," the Walrus said,
"To speak of many things;
Of shoes and ships and sealing wax
And cabbages and Kings…"

but *not*," she said jabbing the right index finger at the one which rushed forth to meet it at the glass, "why the sea is boiling hot! And certainly not what you had on your mind to tell them. *So* …you lose. You lose...I lose...we lose."

She placed the palms of both hands on the mirror, parenthesizing the face.

"So make the best of it," the mouth in the mirror reflected in reverse.

Catherine shook her head slowly, looking down at her cigarette and continuing to ignore it. "Asses." Then back to her reflection with a little half-smile. "So what else is new?"

When she got tired of waiting for the image in the mirror to answer, she crushed out the butt and left the dressing room.

Chris was waiting for her, leaning against the wall, smiling beautifully. In one hand he held a bottle of champagne and in the other a bouquet of glasses. He held the trio up before his face and studied them a second.

"They aren't the right shape, I suppose, but they are all I could swipe from the pantry and I doubt that the wine will care." He smiled again. "Madam desires the pleasure of your company on the veranda. Shall we?" he said, offering his arm.

"Why not," she said, but she took the bottle from his hand instead and led the way.

Partially roofed and flagstone-floored, the veranda embraced two sides of the huge old house. At the back it was open and balconylike, though it was on the ground floor, for the lawn sloped away close beyond it at a spectacular angle. The lake, far below and kilometers away, caught the light the moon gave up and glowed in the distance, ringed by a bodyguard of low hills black with forest. It was one of the few such views left and Catherine knew it well. Three generations of Harvards had owned this land. She felt they were survivors together, but during the day it was apparent where encroachment was beginning. Within a few years, she thought...but didn't finish it. This too was one more of the signs which marked the way for her.

Two torches flickered softly in the light breeze. Chris set the glasses on the table where Sara sat and proceeded to open the bottle. The cork was launched to the moon and the glasses filled before anyone said anything.

"To what?" Catherine asked.

"Let's see," Chris said, seating himself across from Sara.

"How about law school?" Sara said, glass uplifted.

"Or prudence, maybe?" Catherine said. "I saw you, lurking over my fireplace."

"My wife doesn't lurk," Chris said, "she's more elegant than that."

"True."

"Are you serious? About law school, I mean?"

"Yes."

"It's a lot of work, Kitty. Do you honestly think you are up to it?"

"Yes."

"I can't argue with you about it," he said, "but I'm sure there is someone else who will."

"Oh, I have no doubt about that. But it is something I have to do."

"If nothing else, it made a smashing impact with the press," Sara said. "Adella Chambers may never be the same. You hit her with rather a low blow."

"I hope she gets home and dreams about it all night...and for a long time after! It rolled off all the others like water off ducks, but with her I think I sank a barb. If it plagues her long enough maybe she will begin to understand there are more important things in heaven and earth than whether I open the ballet season or what I had for dinner the night the bandages came off. If she can see where I am coming from, then maybe she will eventually be of some use to me."

"Use," Sara said.

"Yes, use. I have something to say, but they are obviously not ready to hear it. Even my doctor does not believe me. And he, of all people, should want to."

"And exactly where, to use the archaic vernacular, *are* you coming from?" Chris asked.

"From a place very far away. From a place that died over 180 years ago. From where I call myself Cat and think myself Catherine, and know why. From across a void which has felt like eternity on the dark side of the moon. From all the lonely corners of the places my mind goes to when I'm alone in my bed. From all the people I have tried to be because I was no longer myself, and they were simply no longer."

"To where?" Sara said. "Back to the beginning?"

"To where I left off."

"What makes you think you can recapture that?"

"The fact that I have."

"How?"

"You and your father need to learn to trust a little more in instinct."

"*Something* must tell you."

"I think Kitty knows herself well enough to determine what she is and is not capable of," Chris said. He felt chilly but it was nothing his jacket could remedy. He wanted to change the subject.

"Maybe you should have gone to med school, babe," Sara said to him. "Kitty might prefer someone who believes in her every intuition just because she is unique."

"I'm unique all right. Has it ever occurred to you that I am the world's most persistent failure? I am uniquely suited to successive brain transplants, and yet I have been uniquely plagued by successive rejections. It has become a game, called keep Catherine alive. So I'm continually supplied with new bodies, new leases on life. Is that success?"

"Why not," Sara said. "Look how long you have been here. They must be doing something right."

"Ah, but therein lies the fallacy. You miss the point, as everyone does. If the transplant rejects, does that not constitute a failure? I'm not saying whose. It isn't a matter of blame. We have forgotten what we started out to do.

"So we succeed in keeping the Cat alive. Wonderful! But was that ever the point? There is no one left alive who remembers the original intention but me. What about the motivation?"

"My great-grandfather loved you. He wanted you to live forever."

"*No!*" Catherine pounced on the word. "Never! No one lives forever. The *universe* won't last forever. All John wanted was to live out his life with me...for me to live out mine with him. The first operation was a gamble. The second was desperation. By the third, the game had begun. But he never planned the relay race we have run since he passed my care along to Paul. That third operation was a changing of the guard. And all the generations of Harvards that have followed have faithfully passed the baton, but somewhere along the way they lost sight of the finish line. And I sit like a human vulture waiting for the death of a brain to leave an otherwise healthy body for me to consume and pass off.

"*Why?* Because it has always been a *medical* problem, something that surgery coud fix, over and over. They all got caught in it, that need to keep *fixing*. They forgot the incentive and so did I, till the last few weeks.

She turned to the rail and looked out across the valley, to the moonglow crisp and cold and diamond bright on the lake below. Neither Chris nor Sara could find words. Spellbound by the intensity of the voice and the gnawing hint of the rightness of the point of view, they sat mute and waited to be led where she would have them go. They felt the presence of her logic but could not yet see its shape.

The angle of Catherine's gently torchlit-moonlit face presenting itself to Sara was quiet in its expression, far away, as though seeing back through the whole measure of her time. She seemed to have forgotten they were there. But when she spoke again, to the moon and the night, her voice was low and soft and perfect:

"Grow old along with me,
The best is yet to be,
The last of life for which the first was made."

"Robert Browning," Sara said.

"And John Harvard...the first one. It was all he wanted. All *we* ever wanted. Just to grow old together. He couldn't stand the thought that he, almost twenty years my senior, might outlive me, and he found he had the power to keep me with him, and I let him. I had nothing to lose. We never expected the fourth life to last so long, but the state-of-the-art was improving and I had a good donor.

"So John grew older and passed beyond our little dream..."

"And you stayed young," Sara said, feeling lost now on the dark side of her moon.

"If you *believe that* you are hopeless, just like the rest of them," she said with a newly alert coolness in her voice. Then in a simpering, mocking sneer, "Catherine is ageless.

"Bullshit! I'm over two hundred years old and I've hit middle age as often as I have thirty." She turned and gestured in the air with her hand. "Five times I have been through menopause. Believe me, once is enough!"

Sara felt a quick trickle of a smile and submerged the urge to giggle. Once again she wondered if Catherine was playing games. What she said was, "Dad says you have a death wish. I really can't tell. Do you?"

"Maybe. I do not have a wish to continue *ad infinitum*. If that qualifies, then so be it. But it is a moot point. There will be no more operations."

"Then I have to agree with Doc," Chris said, "It sounds like a death wish. The next time you reject—"

"I won't."

"How can you be so sure?" Sara said."

"After all this time how can I not be sure?"

"Oh, I don't know. It is just one of a whole ream of things I cannot quite ignore, but it is unquestionably the least important. Your father finds it a convenient point of protest, that's all. He has the family affliction, and if this night doesn't purge *you* of it, then I shall quit trying and quietly keep my peace.

"It is an out-and-out perversity, but over all these generations the Harvard family's reputation has been based on the unattainable. Your father has achieved what none of the others could do. Yet he sees as he has been conditioned to in this one narrow area. All their failures have brought the project success and his own success he can not see as anything but the ultimate failure, so he refuses to believe it."

She was suddenly adamant, almost angry.

"I will not be forced to consent to transplant! And they can not take me from this body if it does not first move to give me up!

"I *will* die! In my own good time and however nature dictates. I am here to stay this time." Her eyes were dark and intense and her voice was passionate. "My life has been given back to me...exactly where I left it. She died within hours of the age at which I died the first time. Our dates of birth are the same, our chosen professions are the same, height, weight, coloring..." Catherine was fishing in her evening bag as she spoke. Sara watched her withdraw a folded envelope and reached for it when Catherine handed it to her.

"I brought that for the press but found the time not to be right. I was going to show it to your father but he does not want to know anymore than the rest of them. But you have to, both of you. We are going to be walking this road together and you must not only know where it leads but where it comes from."

In the envelope was a sheet of paper with two parallel lists under the names of Catherine and her latest donor. It expanded upon the similarities between the two women in extensive detail, and the comparison was uncannily striking. But what caught and held Sara was the photograph; old and cracked and brittle, fading in color, it held its image in an ancient grip. Sara handed the paper to Chris and took the photograph to the illumination of a torch.

"I wasn't sure I still had it," Catherine said. "It took me a long time to find it. That is your great-great-grandfather."

"Yes, I know. I think I must have seen a thousand pictures of him in all kinds of places."

"After the operation, when he was suddenly a genius and I was a miracle, the whole world wanted to see us, to know about us. Pictures, interviews, stories, books...rumors. But before that, when he was only brilliant and I was a new lawyer with a fresh, crisp degree, considering becoming the stepmother of his eighteen-year-old son...who cared?

"Paul took that...six weeks before the first operation. I had just turned twenty-five.

"Sara do you understand me?"

But Sara had nothing to say. She was staring at the young woman standing close beside the older man. A man she had seen in the family album and in her history and medical books. A man who had passed much of his looks down to the male heirs of his family but who remained distinct and always recognizable. Yes, she had seen that face before, often. And the woman she had seen too, but only once. She searched the somber eyes below the straight, full cascade of faded auburn bangs, looking for a sign, an assurance which she found in flesh and blood in Catherine when she raised her head and fixed upon the living face. Chris stood by his wife, peering over her shoulder. Sara's eyes trod the road from face to photo and back several times before Catherine caught and held them with her own. They *were* her own. They always had been. And Sara could not deny it, though she tried.

"I have the thread again," Catherine said in a quiet voice. "And the knot is tied. It will not come undone again. I have a life to finish."

Chris looked at the ancient picture and wondered about all the things that can happen to a life in transit...from light to light...on the dark side of the moon.

And Sara nodded and knew it was *right* ...even if it wasn't true.

On the Road

Gregor Hartmann

October is late in the year for hitching in northern California. Fog shrouded the grove when I opened the mummy bag to let my face out. My body had congealed in the night; I treated it to the last of the trail mix I'd been hoarding. Then soft across pine needles to the highway. Coast Highway 1, the nation's sinuous boulevard of weirdness. Looked like rain. It was raining, later, when I met the man who hunted aliens.

When the big green Dodge van whispered over the hill, I debated. The first law of hitching: the probability of getting a ride is inversely proportional to the value of the vehicle. Should I waste a thumb on this richie? He slowed, checking me over. My arm reflexed out and hooked him.

"Where you heading?" I asked, scanning. Short greasy hair, no beard, no moustache. Plaid shirt, but those slender arms said he wasn't a logger. About thirty-five? The runt wore a watch, like all good little clock sucking petit bourgeois worms. "North," he said.

The vibes said bore, but the rain sounded louder. So I shook off my backpack and hopped aboard the pigmobile, putting on my small-talk record. It's a hit, on the highway, where you have to reassure drivers that just because you wear a ponytail you aren't going to smoke their Triple-A trip kit. Besides, if you blab it up, it's easier to score a meal.

I opened the show with my traveling name, which usually comforts straights. Good citizens don't lie. But this dude only nodded and asked where I was going. *Wish I knew.* "Just traveling. I've bounced around the Pacific Northwest for a month." That perked him up.

"I bet you meet weird people on the road, Wendell. What was the weirdest?"

That rated a smile. He'd touched one of the reasons I hitch. Secrets. People bored with driving alone pick me up, tell me things they'd never tell their analyst, and dump me. Maybe they think I bury their confessions in a ditch. Maybe they just want to talk a hassle out. Anyway, I hear good stories. Stories I can lay on other rides. By trading road stories I can rap for hours. I'll pump you dry and never let you catch a glimpse of me.

Since he was straight, I told him about the businessman who confessed to using his waitress girl friend (he was married) to torch his Cleveland foundry. For insurance, of course. A good tale in itself. Plus it makes others more willing to discuss their own misdeeds, which seem slight in comparison. But this guy soaked it up without comment. So I used the one about the gambler who fixes greyhound races. How a gay computer programmer came out on top in a Time-Life office war. Zip.

Finally he responded. "Ever meet anyone really far out? Maybe even...an alien?"

I misunderstood, "In Modesto once I got a ride with a Cuban refugee."

"I mean an alien alien. From another planet."

H. L. Mencken once said if you turned the country on end, California is where everything loose would fall. Hitching in looney-tune land is one reason I hear such good stories. Yet this man didn't smell crazy. He drove like a machine, his speech was normal, no tics or winks. A saucer cultist? "No aliens," I admitted. "But then I've never hitched in L.A."

Silence met my little witicism. So I climbed back to check my pack, the better to inventory his van. Very porkish, the opposite of the rattley hippie VWs I usually ride in. A sofa and foldout bed, cabinets, sink, propane stove, even a fridgee. No clutter, no decals, no nothing to show a human being lived here. I upped his straight rating two notches. I washed my hands and in the guise of looking for a towel, opened a cabinet. Magazines cascaded. *Proceedings of the American Physical Society.* No reaction from the driver, so I applied more stimulus.

"You a scientist?"

"Amateur. My real profession is hunting."

"What do you hunt?"

The eyes in the mirror locked on mine. The coast sogged past, wipers whirred, he reflected. Then he told me his story.

Hunter was chasing aliens. The kind that come in spaceships. He made his living investigating UFO reports for a private organization of believers called SKYSCAN. Very matter of fact, he explained he had clues that an alien had taken up residence in the Klamath Mountains of northern California–southern Oregon. Since I was at loose ends, would I help his search? He'd feed me and let me sleep in the van in exchange for my services as interviewer.

Wow.

Lightning would have been appropriate. But only rain draped the set, so sad. I stared inland at the smooth yellow hills, so perfect that they always remind me of a model-railroad layout. They reminded me too of Jeanie's breasts, of my exile from the commune, of why I aimlessly hitch and talk to strangers.

On the left was the cliff, plummeting to a boulder beach, an ocean. Suppose this nut tried to drive on air? I stared at the hills, sensing the alienhunter's offer as a powerful karmic choice point. Was he an angel of light, to lift me from despair? Or an angel of darkness, seeking company in his obsession? His rap was practiced; that meant he'd asked others to join him and been refused.

The flaky mission didn't bother me. It would make a good tale. But I still ached from the battles in the commune, ironically named Nirvana Meadows. People=pain, one of the reasons I hitch, since on the road relationships are short and superficial. Traveling with this man would be entertaining. But even the narrowest boss-employee connection would, as days passed, be widened by the flow of shared experiences.

The rain decided me. Winter was near. I couldn't go back to my parents' dreary tract house, where conformity was the price of a place at the trough. Nor could I hole up in Nirvana Meadows, which cast me out like a germ. The alienhunter offered food and shelter. Only a fool would refuse to use him. If he got too weird, I could always grab my pack and split.

Life is a series of rides. No law says you have to take the dull ones.

Bwana and Boy, we parsed the Pacific Northwest. October crept through the forests of rain and emerged older, colder. A white-gray blanket fogged the land. Seldom did we see the stars from which our alleged quarry hailed. I had to take on faith their continued existence, just as I accepted Smith's assertion that there was indeed an alien to be caught.

Our M.O. never varied. Smith, who was frail and easily tired, piloted the van. I pounded on doors. "Hi. I'm doing a survey. I wonder if, on the night of July 8, you noticed any unusual electrical disturbances in your home? Did your TV picture distort, or your stereo make strange sounds, or your appliances or lights go off and on?"

Sometimes eyes nested in long hair would be amused. "We don't use electricity." (Proud.) More often, I learned that the Sony is fine, sorry, though the phone line clicks buzzes burrs with more ghost voices than the Saturday-night horror movie. Then I'd sidestep the country dweller's craving for a conversational fix and saunter back to the van, enjoying the soft sound of footsteps falling into forest abyss. So lovely, flowing with lonely, those half-wild mountain roads, with only the ubiquitous fence to remind me that people contaminated the land.Smith would be waiting in the van, metal box dotted with rain, only a lacquer's thinness from instant rust. "Nothing," I'd report. He'd glance at the twin compasses on the dash. Then on to the next village, tally ho.

A simple life, our sniff-sniff after electromagnetic spoor. And for the first time in my life an adult was *rewarding* me for asking questions. Even if the payoff was just a bunk and meals whenever I opened my beak. Smith never went into restaurants; as befitted a wandering kook, he ate only fresh fruit. The first few times he sent me in to dine alone I endured the hitchhiker's fear of Driver-Making-Off-With-Pack. After a few days, though, I appreciated the chance to chat, even with the bovine automatons who wag their tails in small-town cafés.

Smith, you see, made not the tiniest of small talk. His introversion was worse than Jeanie's. He wouldn't answer questions about himself, except to say he came from "back East." Family? None. If he'd held other jobs than hunting Martians, he wouldn't talk about them. Nor would he say how he'd hooked up with SKYSCAN.

Normally I wouldn't care. If a ride isn't armed with interesting stories, I'd rather he clam-up than shoot off his mouth about billboards or weather. But Smith's lip-lock was a challenge. He'd spread his wallet with little effort on my part; I ate well because he needed me able to prance up driveways. But Wandering Wendell needed mind food too.

I used every stratagem I'd tried to penetrate heads at Nirvana Meadows. I launched irrational attacks on radio newscasts, hoping that if he put me down he'd reveal his own politics. Nothing. I talked about sex, suggested we troll the parks for femflesh. Not a nibble. I told him his driving (always perfect) was atrocious and demanded a turn at the helm. He ignored me. The only response I ever stimulated came the first Sunday, when I blithely announced I didn't intend to interview toasters seven days a week, so I was taking the day off. "If you don't work I'll replace you," he said in a glacial voice. "I don't keep assistantst who don't work out." That busted that strike and that conversation.

Eventually I found the lever. Mr. Ice was upset if I lingered to talk to people I interviewed. He was hyper about publicity; chatting with the natives not only wasted time but also increased the danger of newspapers picking up the story of our bizarre quest. How ironic. To crack this secretive nut I had to socialize. I too preferred to flash past, my presence fleeting as a strobe, a back roads ghost of a hitchhiker.

But if I was to smash his shell...

Communards sprouted like psilocybin mushrooms in that northern California rainforest. My ponytail and peace-love-brotherhood rap were ticket into dozens of neo-hippie hostels. Herbs to drink, herbs to smoke. Smith simmered, but he swallowed my slowdown.

Only once did I reveal the purpose of my questions about electrical aberrations. (Californians have vivid memories of "The Two," and still debate whether they were merely wacko or conscious con artists.) It was at a commune. I was bullshitting when a girl who looked like my dead Jeanie materialized with a plate of raisin-and-oatmeal cookies. She pretended to listen but mentally was off in her own space. The conversation dribbled out and, rather than trade the pseudo-Jeanie for Smith, I decided to astound the rubes with the tale of our alienhunt.

"SKYSCAN?" one of them mused. "Must be a new one. I've heard of NICAP—that's National Investigating Committee on

Aerial Phenomena—and MUFON. That's Mutual UFO Network. But not SKYSCAN. Probably three L.A. chiropractors with a letterhead."

"It's very hush-hush," I fumbled, desperate to impress them (her).

He smirked and took a cookie. "What happens when you find your alien? What do you do?"

I flinched. Find the alien? There was no alien, just a short cell in Smith's backbrain. This was the U.S. of A., not an *"Outer Limits"* episode. But mountainman bored in.

"What makes you think it wants to talk to you? If it's here in secret, it'll probably zap you. How do you and your partner plan to deal with that contingency?"

Suddenly the chick zoomed back into our world to rescue me. "The alien is a great teacher," she announced, beatific smile fissuring her face. "I've felt him in the grove. His name is Lao Tazu and he was sent here by the Galactic Council to teach us to love. He has fourteen eyes and seven rays. Wait—I'll contact him and ask why he hides." Her two eyes closed and she hugged herself, rocking and emitting a hum.

Well. I would have stayed for the second feature but one of the big males gave me the git-go. *Must be screwing her*, I decided, as I toddled down the close-set stepstones. *Lucky bastard, to score a good-looking loonie. You can do anything with them.*

The next few communes, I didn't go in.

In Yreka I slid through a chili parlor and across the street to a library. While Smith thought I was pigging down, I was gobbling up the L.A. *Times* for early July.

For once the reactionary rag had something of use to me. July 10's "In the State" column noted:

> Coast Guardsmen at Crescent City searched for 13 hours Tuesday night and yesterday without finding a sign of a reported plane crash five miles off the coast. Three people said they saw a bright green light explode over the ocean shortly after 11 P.M. No planes were reported missing. Cmdr. H.L. Richards, who called off the search at noon yesterday, said the object was probably a meteor.

Tree gods trembled in the crackling dark, looking down on two turtles huddled in the warm breath of the campfire. Pine light flailed against pine night. Blackness flickered in and out, like waves nibbling boulders at low tide.

Stop it, I told myself, fixing eyes firmly on fire. *I'm no caveman, quivering at every rustle in the night.*

But if aliens are out there...

Another log into the fire. Smith crunched an apple, gazed at the sky. Oblivious of me, my fears. For once the stars were visible. Sparks roused by my offering to Agni soared to rank themselves in new constellations.

Why was he so sure creatures from the sky walked our world? He was no armchair theorist, citing Von Daniken or the biblical pillar of fire to prove they'd been here ages ago. He was no Carl Sagan, willing to populate half the galaxy with intelligent races as long as they couldn't cross interstellar space to get at him. Smith had deduced that they're here. Now. And set out to track them down.

Aliens. The concept gave me the creep-o's, created a whole new set of problems. It was like being a small-time suburban grass dealer and finding the Mexican Mafia wants a piece of your action. If there are aliens, there's a mysterious new force in the game. Shiver time. I didn't want to think about what might share this forest at my back. Oddball Smith was human in comparison.

Did he understand what he was getting into? What did he know about the July 8 meteor which said to him: alien. In the Klamath Mountains. He didn't argue with me. He just stated a fact. Did he really know something? Did he expect to just walk up, shake the hand/paw/flipper, ask about the weather on Jupiter? I felt like an apprentice to a magician trying to invoke a demon. What do you do if the spell works?

Crunch.

Not that he was a Merlin. Too skinny, too lethargic. And lately blotches had formed on his cheeks, subtle, like the kelp beds in the ocean off Santa Cruz. An effect of his diet? Smith was supershy about his carcass, so I couldn't tell how far the mottling had spread. I hadn't even seen him take off his shirt. I hoped he wouldn't get too sick; he was still useful to me.

Crunch. My associate's quirks were chiggers under my foreskin. He might as well crunch on my spine. But the loon was all I had, to share a nest this lonely night.

"Smith. What will you do when you find your alien?"

He swallowed. "Talk to him." *Crunch.*

"About what?" I persisted.

"Oh, where he's from. What he's doing here. Why here, out of all the places in the galaxy."

Too casual, for a man obsessed. My bullshit detector rang. It occurred to me that perhaps Smith was not the privately employed goof he presented himself as. I lie to people; why couldn't he? Maybe SKYSCAN was a front for a more ominous acronym.

A test was called for. "That's dull, Smith. I can think of a better climax to the search. If the alien came here, by definition he has transportation. A starship. Let's make him tell us where it's hidden, steal it, and explore outer space."

If I'd dropped a rattlesnake in his granola I couldn't have produced a stronger reaction. For the first time in three weeks he looked at me. Really looked. A cancerous cell about to be blasted by a laser would recognize that stare. I was so freaked that I gave him the next move.

"Wendell, why are you on the road?"

I hadn't told him about the commune. Why should I? He accepted my superficial hitchhiker personality, but if I let him see what a revolutionary I truly am, his establishment programming would take over and label me a shit. Besides, he had no right to my secrets.

He waited. Well, maybe if I made him feel sorry for me, I could score more than meals, when he got too sick to travel. Violins, please.

I found Nirvana Meadows like I found Smith: hitching. I'd just been fired from my stockboy job at Monkey Ward's (for expropriating pig property). My parents were mad at me (because I explained to Dad he was a fascist). Summer warmed the woods, so I hit the road (before my pretrial hearing). On I-5, between Portland and Corvalis, I was scooped up by a four-hippie, two-dog '57 Chevy pickup and offered a place to crash for the night. I stayed four months.

Behind the nonconformist facade, the drop-outs at Nirvana Meadows were as submissive as most AmeriKaners. The boss—they called him facilitator—was a dude name of Marcus, who'd been around long enough to get good at settling quarrels, juggling chores, and playing daddy. (He bought the land and founded the commune.) I made it my goal to knock him off his high horse. I would have, except for Jeanie.

She was OK. Quiet, which I like. (Passive as a blob of playdough. IQ of 80.) Every male in the commune would have liked to make her but I was the only one with gonads enough to do it.

I didn't bore Smith with our heartthrobs. What was significant for him, what touched off my wandering, was that my success with Jeanie enabled Marcus to use sexual frustration against me. Like most communes, Nirvana Meadows had more males than females. When she did herself in with reds, they took it out on me. At the next general meeting everyone dumped on me. (Also for dealing in town.) They claimed I endangered the commune—

"Why did the girl kill herself?" Smith interrupted.

He was supposed to be sympathetic, not interrogative. "I don't know. Maybe I gave her too many orgasms," I snapped, breaking eye contact.

But he didn't let go. "She was your mate, yet you don't know why she killed herself?"

"We weren't married. Just sharing a bunk."

"Just?" His tongue was a scalpel. "I thought sleeping together implied a more than casual relationship among the 'new people.' Was this girl a toy to you?"

"I loved her," I lied.

"That seems unlikely, Wendell," he said, twirling an apple. "Several consistent personality factors run through your narrative. One. Your contempt for people. Two. Your refusal to admit that others have needs and rights too. Three. Your preference for passive people, since you can use them.

"I have observed these already in our relationship. For instance—"

I was better off when he was brooding about spacemen. At last I remembered how legs worked and jumped up, ransacking my mind for a devastating insult. No anal-retentive bourgeois, no mewling straight could lecture the king of the hitchhikers like that. "Fuck you," I snarled, and stalked off.

A bush scratched me; I stomped it into chlorophyll paste. Had Smith followed me I would have fixed him too. But he stayed by the fire. I orbited it for an hour, smashing through the trees, afraid to go too far into the night but unwilling to tolerate more insults. That's what happens when you're open with people: they hurt you.

I was still simmering the next day when we hit Fort Jones, a hamlet of six hundred on the east side of Klamath National Forest. On the first street I found four families who remembered their

TVs or radios burning out in early July.

I was mad enough to withhold the info. For sheer spite. But I worried that the sickie might soon abandon the search and invest in something more beneficial to his health than hot meals for me.

Also, we'd been three weeks on the trail. I was bored. Might as well move to the next square.

So I told him. My reward? Convulsions.

Smith had a seizure. Luckily he was in the back of the van, parked on a quiet residential *cul-de-sac* where I'd just interviewed. His eyes rolled up into his head; his tongue erupted from mouth, brown and awful; his face turned orange; limbs twitched and he collapsed like a teenybopper on PCP.

I had the presence of mind to roll him face up. His skin was already cold. He seemed to breathe, through his nose, so I didn't fool with his tongue. I just stared at the man, shivering incongruously in the tidy van. I'm no nurse. If he died, could his employers sue me? What if the people on the street got suspicious about the strange van and called the cops? If they ran a check on me, the computer in Sacramento would shout: Fugitive. Smith sprawled, quivering. Helpless. I decided to split.

My backpack was full, my mummy bag rolled, ready for emergencies. I pulled them toward the door, so rattled I stepped on his hand. His eyes opened. I froze. But he stared vacantly into space, not at me, crouched guiltily overhead. His tongue retracted. And he began to sing.

"Hai gldno, hai reboziq, gliss raglisa wa seeh," gurgled the pumpkin-face. Or something eerie and unintelligible like that. Something so unearthly—

Awareness hit with a rush like nitrous oxide.

Smith was an alien.

It was my turn to quiver. I stared at him, lolling on the floor like a man surfacing from a drunk, chanting his outlandish song. His quirks and oddities suddenly made bizarre sense. No wonder he wouldn't talk about himself. His presence on my planet was obviously a secret.

What would he do to someone who unzipped his disguise?

Quickly as it came, my panic ebbed. Alien or human, I didn't fear this little man. I could hop, run down the street to the police station, and be a big hero. A valuable piece of information was mine. Where could I cash it in?

The government swine were an obvious source of money. But

trust them? They'd classify me and lock me in a Pentagon closet for fifty years, while they boiled Smith's brains out. Sell him to GE or IBM? They'd love an alien, but they'd cheat a poor innocent hippie too. If he carried alien artifacts, I'd consider taking them and splitting. But I'd already searched the van and found nothing worth ripping off.

Then I realized something else. Smith's search wasn't fantasy. He knew something. I stared at the hills crowding Fort Jones. Why would one alien have to hunt for other?

Was he separated from his fellows in a rough landing? That would explain his illness, his lack of supplies. Wow. Could I possibly get a reward from the other alien(s) for reuniting them?

A long shot. Too many unknowns. But obviously my best bet was to play dumb and stay with Smith. At worst I'd have two aliens, maybe a base, to cash in. I replaced my pack and sat down, cradling his head in my lap. When he came to, I'd pretend he'd thrown an epileptic fit, babbled a bit, you see it every day, ho hum.

I scrutinized his disguise. The skin was perfect. *But I know your secret.*

Lead me to that starship.

I expected him to apologize for insulting me, since I'd nursed him through his fit.

Hah. The rest of that day and all of the next he barreled around the area, nagging me to make my interviews faster and faster. Nary a word of thanks. In his monomania he assumed I could work sixteen hours a day and baby him as well.

The only think that kept me going was the knowledge that at any corner I could pull the door lever, jump out, walk to a gas station phone, and close his show with a call to the feds. Even telephones in homes tempted me. Amerika's electromagnetic nervous system was everywhere. If I but touched it, the U.S. government would form a fist and grab "Smith."

Sloshing through the night, Smith driving me to yet another place, I sat lotus-limbed on the shotgun seat and gloried in power. If only I had handled it this well at the commune. Then I would have been able to lay someone besides a dummy. Boy, have I learned.

Bumps knocked me out of my reverie. An old logging road. We slithered only a mile up it before we slithered into a hole the Dodge couldn't dodge. November rain thrummed on the van, rain perilously close to snow. In the dim cone of the headlights I could see only a few yards. "Anderson Peak," Smith announced. "The ring of burned-out appliances centers on it."

The dim dash light made it all unreal. Was he really handing me a flashlight and the twin compasses? The van was a bubble of warmth in a cold lonely night. "Now?" I protested.

"Now. Come on."

"You're crazy. The alien can wait till tomorrow. Maybe the rain will stop."

"He won't expect visitors in this weather," Smith snapped, showing emotion for the second time since I'd met him. He climbed out. I noticed he'd left the keys; then I felt his eyes on me. Reluctantly, I sealed my parka and slid into the wet.

The trail was a dashed line on the Geological Survey map, but that must have been decades ago. Now it was blocked by fallen trees, brush, slippery rocks. A nightmare. I slipped and fell and stumbled, trying to miss wet branches while keeping one eye on the trail and one on the compasses. One was a gyro, the other simple magnetic. I was to tell the alien at my back if they began to point in different directions. He kept up easily; it occurred to me that by sitting in the van he could have been saving his strength for...

What am I doing here?

"The lightning will jam the compasses," I suggested lamely. "Why don't we wait till morning?"

"At short distances the polarizer will exert an unmistakable attraction," he stated, in a voice that iced my spine. Drawn like bird to snake, I turned to stare, letting my flashlight flick across—

I dropped the light. He handed it back to me with one of the slender tentacles that now erupted from his clothing in the vicinity of his waist. Another outgrowth brandished a short dark rod. "Keep moving," he said.

I moved. Very numb, very glad I hadn't tried to peek in his shower. I thought of the other assistants he'd had until I was too frightened to think anymore. I was wearing down fast, thighs aflame, legs congealing. How could I be so hot with the cold rain soaking my clothes? Pneumonia! I had to turn back. I took the chance of telling him.

"It's not you," the creature said. "We've only climbed one mile. Ril must have set up an emotion wall to divert hikers. Keep going."

In a few hundred yards we waded from the weariness zone. My

brain awakened, hurled itself at the bars of the dilemma. The Smith-thing had me sewn up. He could be cop, criminal, anthropologist, or interstellar dealer, but what counted was the weapon posed to fry my kidneys.

Another emotion wall. Then the compass shivered to a new angle. Smith told me to follow the magnetic one, straight to the other alien. Tougher going, off the trail: blackberry thorns, vines, fallen branches to trip over. Leaf mold over my boot tops. The alien's silent passage indicated he could see better than I, but he made me walk in front.

I found out why.

It was a little glen amid Douglas fir. I stepped onto grass with relief—into a giant spiderweb.

"*Aaaaaaaaaaaargggh!*" I hacked the gooey mass with flashlight and jumped back, only to be dragged forward again. It pulled me into the center of the clearing. Where was the spider? Mother of bogs, let me out of here. Scream and fight and pull: you're trapped.

Sodden and miserable and crying, I hung for an eternity. Waiting for the giant spider fangs to pierce my rib cage. Then in an instant, the invisible webbing was gone and I fell. When I dared look up, a slender little man stood over me.

Smith shot him from his hiding place. The rod. It sizzled.

Rain on my face. Smith searched the other alien, pocketing little devices. He made me carry his opponent. Slowly we finished the peak. Another invisible web snared me. This time Smith had the key and neutralized it after a few seconds. *That's why I had to go first,* I realized. *He used me.*

The ship was like a water tank. Squat. Dark. And small. Smith opened it with another device, then motioned me in. When he saw there were no booby traps, he entered too.

I'm in a starship, I sighed. All function, like the cab of a Mack truck. No blinkers or fluorescent geegaws. Just dials, buttons, and a silver globe the size of a softball. And viewscreens. Inert now. But soon I'd look *down* on Earth. Soon I'd see the Milky Way oozing across them.

Smith dumped the other in one of the two seats and began weaving him in. When he glanced up, I saw that his eyes were slit by vertical pupils, like a cat's. Had he worn contact lenses? So many new things to learn! He tightened a strap and raked me with two words. "Get out."

"Aren't you taking me? I wouldn't mind living in a zoo. I could tell you about our culture—"

"Our anthros already know more about your world than you'll ever learn. We don't keep sentients in zoos. Out."

The rod-weapon twitched. I stepped back into the cold rain. So much for the big score. Lingering in the glow from the hatch, I realized I didn't even have the small score: his story. I didn't know if Smith was a soldier capturing an enemy, a criminal ambushing a cop, a scientist settling a private vendetta. The disguise said he or his people had been here before. What was happening? I stuck out my thumb in a desperate appeal. "Hey, going my way? Need someone to talk to to stay awake?"

"Can that crap, Wendell. I've enough responsibilities. I don't need the problems of a leech like you." As the hatch irised, choking off the light from the ship, my final vision was of the alien peeling off the Smith-face.

I hugged a tree till the starship made green light and lifted. Then I was alone on the mountain. Free to go anywhere. No place to go.

I lifted my face to the clouds where the ultimate ride had disappeared, and screamed: "My name is Robin."

Three Soldiers

D. C. Poyer

The blackness opened, and von Rheydt swam up through inky velvet to a consciousness that he had never expected to see again.

He did not move, not even opening his eyes.

Von Rheydt remembered falling face down in the snow, fingers clutching the sudden wetness in the pit of his stomach, hearing the soft crunch of millions of six-pointed ice crystals as his face sank toward the Russian earth.

Hauptmann—Captain—von Rheydt noticed, without surprise, that he did not feel particularly cold, nor could he feel anything where the bullet had struck him. He was waiting, eyes closed and mind blank, for a Russian bayonet.

The white-coated troops who followed the tanks always checked the fallen Germans for signs of life. That, he thought remotely, must be why he was now face up. One of the Red troops must have turned him over while he was unconscious, to check on the seriousness of his wound.

It must be bad if they hadn't bothered to use a bayonet, he thought. Maybe that was why he couldn't feel anything in his stomach.

Minutes passed. Von Rheydt waited. It was very quiet.

Too quiet, he thought suddenly. He could hear nothing but his heart. No machine-gun fire, neither the *tap-tap-tap* of the Degtyarevs nor the high cloth-ripping sound of the German guns. No grunting of tank engines, no shouts of "*Oooray!*" as the Red Army charged. Not even—and this was the strangest of all—not even the sighing of the wind over the plains of Stalingrad in this year of struggle 1942.

He opened his eyes, tensing himself for the bayonet. Above him was a gray ceiling.

A hospital, he thought. German or Russian? That was easy to answer. The Soviets did not waste hospital space on wounded enemy officers. So he was in friendly hands. A smile creased his thin, blond-stubbled face, and he sat up without thinking. And stared down at the crisp, unstained gray of his battle-dress tunic. No holes. No blood. After several seconds he touched his stomach with one hand. He was unwounded.

Captain Werner von Rheydt, German Army, thirty years old, educated at Gottingen...*memory's all right,* he thought confusedly, still looking down at his stomach. Had he dreamed it, then? His brow furrowed. The university...the war...the draft...the Polish campaign, then France, then Yugoslavia, and so to the Russian Front. To Stalingrad with the 44th Infantry, Sixth Army, after four years of war. To the madness of Stalingrad in winter, an entire army surrounded, abandoned, but still fighting...

No, it was not a dream, von Rheydt concluded silently. Line "Violet" had fallen; and in the fighting retreat to *Sunflower* the Soviet tanks had broken through. He had led a counterattack, and had fallen, badly wounded, on a snowy battlefield two thousand miles from home. And he was now—here.

He swung his boots over the edge of the bunk, and noticed it for the first time. It was a plain Reichsheer-issue steel bunk, standard thin pallet mattress, with a dingy pillow and a gray wool blanket.

He stood up, and the momentary sense of reassurance the familiar-looking bunk had given him disappeared. He stared around at a room that was far too strange for a dream.

It's gray, he thought, but the gray was strange. Not a painted color, but a hard shininess like the dull sheen of polished metal. But the shape—it was the shape of the room that was different. He stood at the bottom of an octagon, and at the center of one; the room had eight walls, and its cross-section was an octagon as well. He counted, came up with a total of twenty-six facets.

A pile of what looked like military equipment was stuck oddly to one of the eight vertical walls. Von Rheydt walked forward to investigate, stepped up on a slanted facet of the room to reach up—and found the pile on a slanted face just in front of him. He looked back at the bunk. It too was on a slanted face, and looked as if it should come sliding down on him at any moment.

And there was no question but that the facet he had stepped up on was now at the bottom of the room.

Queer, thought von Rheydt. He walked on, stood next to the pile. Now that facet was the floor, and the bunk hung ludicrously on a vertical wall.

Feeling a touch of nausea, he bent to the heap of equipment. It was not his own, but it was all standard army. Helmet, battle, one, white-painted for winter wear. Canteen. Pack ration. An officer's dress dagger, which he examined closely, scowling as he saw the double lightning strokes of the SS; the army and Himmler's thugs had never gotten along, and of late there had been rumors ... shadowy but horrible rumors. A dress sword, plain, but of good Solingen steel. At the very bottom of the heap he found what he had been hoping for: a Luger. A quick investigation revealed six cartridges in its magazine.

Von Rheydt smiled as he buckled the pistol belt on. Having a weapon made him feel much more confident, *wherever* he was. He buckled on the dagger, too, and began walking again, continuing around the room. His boots clicked arrogantly on the hard surface.

Halfway around—the "floor," inexplicably, still underneath his feet—he noticed a grille set into its surface. He bent to look into it.

A black, grimacing face, horribly furrowed with scars and paint, stared back at him, teeth bared. Von Rheydt recoiled, drawing the dagger. At his motion, the face disappeared, drawn back from the grille. Beyond wonder, he walked on. In the next facet of the room was a door, or hatch, set flush with the gray surface and of the same material. There was no knob or handle, and he was unable to pry it open. He went on, and had almost reached the bunk again before he saw anything else on the smooth sameness of gray.

It was another grille. This one he approached with dagger drawn, but there was no one at it. He bent and peered through it, seeing on the other side another room like his own.

"Anyone there?" he called loudly.

The quick pad of footsteps came up to the grille, and a moment later a hard-looking, tanned face stared out. A second or so passed, and then the man barked out a question.

It took several seconds for von Rheydt to realize that the strong-jawed, dark-haired man on the other side of the grille had said, "Who are you?"—*in Latin.*

Von Rheydt searched his mind for the moldy words he had struggled over at Göttingen. "*Ego sum*...von Rheydt," he said haltingly. "Ah...*sum miles Germanicus*...*amicus. Amicus*, friend. *Et tu?*"

The other man spoke rapidly; not classical Latin, but a rough, corrupt-sounding tongue with a Spanish rhythm. Von Rheydt caught a word here and there, enough to piece the sense together: "Roman soldier...Nineteenth Legion. Into the forest, the battle against Arminius...spear wound...slept." the Roman passed a hand over his close-cropped dark hair, looking puzzled, as if trying to remember something. "Slept..."

Von Rheydt started to speak in German, stopped, said in Latin: "You are a *Roman soldier?*"

"*Centurio*," corrected the man, showing a massive gold ring on his powerful-looking hand. "Junius Cornelius Casca, centurion second rank, Nineteenth Legion, General Varus commanding."

"Centurion Casca...what year is this?"

The other man—Casca—frowned through the grille. "Year? What year? Why, 762, *ab urbe condita,* and thirty-eighth year of the principate of Augustus." His heavy brows drew together. "Where are we, German? What prison is this?"

Von Rheydt did not answer immediately, for he was chasing a phrase down dusty corridors of his mind. *Ab urbe condita*... literally, from founding the city...yes, he remembered. The legendary founding of Rome, 753 B.C., the date used to reckon time by the empire. This man Casca, then, could be...almost two thousand years old?

And then something else clicked in his mind. P. Quintilius Varus, leading the Nineteenth Legion into Gaul. Sent to crush the Chirusci revolt under Arminius. *Surrounded and massacred without a survivor, late in the reign of Augustus Caesar*...

"*Non certe scire*—I don't know," he said slowly, trying to match stale school Latin to the cadence the other man used. The Roman laughed, a short, bitter sound.

Von Rheydt looked up from the grille. He looked at the bunk that stuck to the wall like a fly, at the strangeness of the gray metal walls, at the light that filled the room without visible source. He remembered the gravity that followed wherever he walked.

He had been wounded in 1942, on the frozen plains of Stalingrad. Just as this Casca, this Roman, had been wounded in the forests of Teutoburgium in 9 A.D. They had been snatched away. *But to where?* He asked himself. *And what year is it in this strange cell–9, or 1942 A.D.?*

The Roman had left the grille, and von Rheydt slowly stood up. He looked vacantly around the room, and then walked back to the bunk and sat down.

Fifteen minutes later he got up and went to the first grille, the one at which he had seen the black man. He was there again, big hands wrapped around the gray metal bars that separated the rooms. Von Rheydt wondered whether the other man was kneeling too, and if so—where did the room's gravity come from? From the gray metal of its walls?

"*Verstehen Sie Deutsch?*"

The man looked back at him without expression, and von Rheydt sat back on his haunches and studied him. The face was broad, thick-lipped and strong; though the paint stripes were obviously meant for adornment or intimidation, the scars looked like battle scars rather than tattoo or ritual mutilation. The man's hair was done up in a doughnut-shaped ring atop the wide skull, and his eyes, dark and intelligent, were studying the German with every bit as much interest as they were being given. Von Rheydt tried Latin after a time, and then French, of which he had picked up a few words during the 1940 campaign.

No luck. The man was listening intently, though, and when von Rheydt paused, he placed his outstreched fingers on his broad, bare chest and said several words in a gutteral, clicking language:

"*Ngi wum' Zulu.*"

Von Rheydt tried to understand, but ended by shaking his head in frustration. Did *ngi* mean "my name is"? If only they had a few words of *some* language in common!

"You... are English?"

Von Rheydt started. His roommate at school had been English; he had picked up a fair amount of the language. "No. German. Who are you?"

The warrior placed his hand on his chest again, and said slowly, "Mbatha. Of... the Zulu. This is... gaol?"

The language lesson lasted for about an hour.

By the time he was fully awake von Rheydt had rolled out of the bunk, and had the Luger in his hand—safety off; Stalingrad reflexes. He scrutinized his surroundings from a crouch before he stood up, holstering the pistol. The room was as empty, the light as steady as when he had gone to sleep. Only one thing was different: the door had opened.

He approached it cautiously, one hand still on the butt of the weapon.

As far as he could make out, the door had disappeared. There were no hinges, and the inside of the jamb was smooth and featureless; it could not have slid inside the wall. He remembered how impressed he'd been with the automatic doors he'd seen before the war in Berlin department stores, and grinned humorlessly.

Feeling a little like a cautious ape, von Rheydt stepped though the door. He looked to either side, down a long, narrow, gray-lit corridor, with four welcome right angles to the walls. To his left the corridor fell away into darkness; to his right it was lit with the same sourceless brightness, stretching away into the distance.

There was a high, almost musical note behind him... the sound, he realized, that had awakened him. He turned, and found the door in place, locked. He could see no way to open it.

Shrugging, he loosened the dagger in its sheath, placed his hand near the pistol and walked down the corridor to the right. He passed the outline of another door, and then another. A thought struck him, and he tried to step up on a wall; no good. The every-wall-a-floor device wasn't used in corridors, then.

Octagonal rooms... doors... square corridors... the layout of the place came into focus as he walked. Von Rheydt visualized a grid of octagons, side to side, their corners forming four-sided longitudinal corridors. The corridors would lead the length of... what? The arrangement was an inhumanly efficient utilization of space, so space must be at a premium here. He walked along, staying alert, but thinking as well.

As a boy he had read Hermann Oberth's and Willy Ley's books about interplanetary flight. Read them avidly, until his father had thrown them all away and forbidden him to read such trash. Was he aboard such an interplanetary rocket? Or... and von Rheydt felt uneasy at the thought... was he, and the Zulu and the Roman, trapped in something as far beyond his imagination as Stukas and Koningpanzer tanks were beyond Casca's?

He came to an open hatch, stepped in, and snapped to rigid attention, a look of surprise flashing across his face.

The room was gray and octagonal; but in the center of it sat a desk, and at the desk stood a man. A hard-looking man of middle age, dressed in high-collared tunic and red-striped trousers of a general of the O.K.W.—the General Staff. A man with sharp eyes and a rocklike chin, who nodded to von Rheydt's astounded salute and motioned to a chair.

"Sit down, Captain," he said, in clear, Prussian-accented German. "Smoke?"

Von Rheydt sat, shook his head. "Thank you, no, Herr General."

"Well," said the general, studying him for a moment while taking a long cigar from a box on the desk, lighting it carefully, and exhaling a puff of aromatic smoke. "You are a bit confused, no doubt."

"That is an understatement, Herr General."

"I suppose so. We expected that you would be—you and your two companions. We owe you an explanation. You are here, Captain von Rheydt, because you are a brave man."

"For Leader and Reich," said von Rheydt automatically.

The man in the general's uniform glanced at him sharply. "Yes. Of course. But tell me, Captain. Would you fight as bravely as you fought at Stalingrad—surrounded, outnumbered, abandoned by your Leader—if, say, the future of your species was at stake?"

"I beg the general's pardon?" said von Rheydt.

"How did you come here, Captain?"

"Here... I don't know, Herr General. The last thing I recall is leading an infantry counterattack against Soviet tanks..."

"Against *tanks*?"

"Those were my orders, Herr General," said von Rheydt. "And then a strange thing happened. I thought that I was wounded."

"That is not quite correct. You were killed."

"Killed... but I am alive!"

"Are You, Captain?"

Frozen, von Rheydt stared at the general's face. He felt his heart beating, felt the breath that rustled in his throat and the hunger that was beginning to stir in his bowels. "Yes, Herr General, I am alive."

"You died at Stalingrad in 1942, Captain. I am sorry."

Von Rheydt gripped the arms of his chair. "Explain yourself, Herr General. This is going beyond a joke!"

The older man chuckled. "This is not a joke, Captain. And I am not a general. Those of your time would not even consider me a man. Especially—you will pardon the emphasis—am I not a German."

"Not a German . . ." began von Rheydt, presentiment growing in his mind. "You are not of my time."

"Nor of your species," said the general. "But—just as one stoops down when addressing a child—I am addressing you in a form that you can understand, one that, to your mind, embodies authority and command. As a general officer of the O.K.W."

"What do you want?" asked von Rheydt harshly.

"Simply this," said the officer, rising from the desk. His chrome leather boots clicked on the floor as he paced back and forth, hands interlocked behind his back, a cloud of cigar smoke trailing behind him. He began to speak, looking sharply at the seated captain each time he turned. "You are familiar with war, Hauptmann von Rheydt. As are your two comrades. Well, envision, if you can, a war that encompasses a galaxy, and that has lasted for well over a million of your years. A war in which entire races are developed, deployed and used as weapons, as you develop new tanks or rifles."

In spite of what it meant, von Rheydt knew that the man was telling the truth. He shook his head. "And the fact that, as you say, I am dead?"

"You *were* dead," the general corrected gravely. "Until we intervened. But we are offering you, and your companions, the chance to return."

"How?"

"By fighting."

"Fighting for you? In this war of yours?"

"Not quite. Let me explain a little further." The general stopped pacing, crossed his arms and looked down at the captain. A wreath of cigar smoke gradually encircled the hard features. "Your race has always been puzzled by its own killer instincts, plagued by its own love for war. To you it was tragic, inexplicable. It seemed contrary to all the laws of evolution, for it killed off not the old and weak but the young and strong. Correct?"

"Yes."

"Your race, Captain, has been, shall we say, in development. Forced development. To forge a warlike race one must have wars."

"That is obvious, Herr General. The Führer has said that himself."

"Yes," said the general, looking at the ceiling. "The Führer ...we will have to recall him soon, and cover his disappearance in some convincing manner...but back to the subject at hand. Your species has developed very promisingly. It can be very useful, to us, if..."

"If?"

"If you prove yourselves to be an effective weapon in a test. Tell me, Captain, if your army had developed two types of hand grenade, and wished to determine which of the two would prove a more effective weapon, how would they go about it?"

"Well, the answer would be to conduct a comparative evaluation," began von Rheydt, and then he saw it. "There is another race of warriors," he said flatly. "Another one of your 'weapons projects.'"

"Very good!" said the general, smiling. "Correct. Please go on."

"Somehow, I don't know how, you've been able to...go back in time, and pick up the other two men, Casca and Mbatha. Roman and Zulu and German—your choice for the most warlike races of earth's history, I suppose. And now you will match us against the others, I suppose."

"Exactly," said the general, raising his eyebrows in pleased surprise, and perching one leg on the edge of his desk. "An intelligent species as well as a warlike one. Very good, Captain."

"But why pick us?" asked von Rheydt. "Front-line soldiers, all three of us. If you had all history to choose from, why not Napoleon, or Caesar, or Frederick the Great? They were true men of war."

"Not quite," said the general. He tapped the cigar into a glass ashtray and examined the glowing tip. "The men you name were leaders, not soldiers. Since, in this war, *we* will provide all necessary leadership, they would be of little value to us. No, what we value in our weapons is different. Take the three of you. Stalingrad, Teutoburgium, and Ulundi—all battles in which a body of professional soldiers, abandoned, almost leaderless, and greatly outnumbered, stood and fought to the death *because they valued obedience above life.*"

Von Rheydt sat motionless. The general went on: "We need soldiers like that. So far in your history your three cultures have shown us what we can expect from the human race at its most disciplined, most obedient, and most unthinking best."

"As you say," said von Rheydt slowly. "We are soldiers, then. But what good will our victory do for our race? Make mankind a pawn in a struggle we know nothing about?"

"It is that or extinction," said the general quietly. "To put it in army terms, Captain, the Human project is at the crossroads. It must now either be put into full production, or it must be liquidated and the resources shifted to another project. I'm sure you realize, Captain, that in total war there is no other way."

Von Rheydt stood up stiffly, put one hand on his dagger, and clicked his heels. Right hand shot out in a quivering salute.

"You will find us good soldiers," he said.

"I hope so," said the general. "Tell the others, Captain. Ten hours from now, the three of you will fight. I suggest that you all get some sleep." The high-pitched note of an opening hatch came from behind the rigid German. "Dismissed!"

Von Rheydt pivoted smartly and marched out. Outside, in the corridor, he turned. The door was not yet closed, and he caught a glimpse, not of a stiff O.K.W. general at a German army desk, but of something that sent him, mind reeling, stumbling down the corridor.

Von Rheydt's school Latin seemed to be coming back; Casca, listening at the grille, nodded slowly and frowned as he finished his explanation of the upcoming test. "I have been thinking, German. The *framea* (spear?) could not have healed like this." He drew up a dirty tunic and showed von Rheydt a smooth, unmarked chest, covered with curly black hair. "When will we go into battle?"

"About nine hours from now."

"I am ready," said the centurion. "I found some arms in my room. I will sleep, I think, before the contest of the gods."

"The gods?... Yes," said von Rheydt, realizing the inadequacy of his Latin to explain alien races and galactic wars to a man who thought the earth flat. "Yes, sleep well, Junius."

Mbatha was not at his grille. Von Rheydt drew his dagger, stuck it through the bars, and rattled it to attract the Zulu's attention. An instant later he froze as the point of a broad-bladed, razor-sharp *assegai* touched his throat.

Von Rheydt smiled as he let go the dagger, which the African took and examined critically, at last pulling back the *assegai* and returning the knife to the German.

"We must fight soon, Mbatha," said von Rheydt in English. "You, me, and Casca, the other man with us. We must win. If we lose, we die."

"Fight English? Fight you and Casca?"

"No, you do not fight us," said von Rheydt desperately, thinking that the three of them might have to act as a team in a very few hours; having one man suspicious of the other two might kill them all. The Zulu had fallen fighting white men; to him all whites were the hated English. "I am not English. Casca is not English. We three men fight three...devils."

"Devils," said the African.

"Spirits. Ghosts."

"Ghosts,' repeated the Zulu, deadpan. "Warriors cannot fight ghosts, u-Rheydt."

"We don't have a choice, Mbatha. We fight in the morning—in one sleep."

"I sleep now, u-Rheydt," said Mbatha, and left the grating. A scraping sound came from his room for a few minutes, and then silence.

Von Rheydt went back to his bunk and sat down, eased his boots off. He had a light meal of tinned sausage and biscuit from the ration pack, and found what tasted like vodka in the canteen. When he had finished his meal he lay back on the bunk, placed the Luger under his pillow, and fell into a heavy sleep.

"Captain von Rheydt," said the voice in his dream, and he jerked awake. "It is time," said the voice, and as its meaning sank in he came slowly back to reality.

He went to the grilles and made sure that Mbatha and Casca were both awake. They were, looking around their rooms; they must have heard the voice as well. As von Rheydt pulled on his boots he wondered, *in what language had it spoken to them?*

He stood up, stamped his feet into the boots, and walked to the pile of gear. He buckled on the scabbard of the dress saber over his pistol belt and stuck the dagger under it. He tightened the belt of his uniform trousers and tucked the cuffs into his boots. Finally, he walked back to his bunk, took the pistol from under his pillow, checked the chamber, tucked the gun into its holster and buttoned the leather flap over it.

He was tightening the leather chin strap of his helmet when the door bonged. With a last look around, he picked up the canteen, slung it from his shoulder, and stepped out into the corridor.

Mbatha was already there waiting, and von Rheydt's eyebrows rose.

The Zulu was big—muscular as well as tall. His broad, bare chest was criss-crossed with dark, puckered scars. A short skirt of animal pelt fell from waist to mid-thigh, and at elbow and knee blossomed fringes of white feathers. The African was carrying a short thrusting spear at his waist, a slightly longer one in his right hand, and an oval cowhide shield on his back. A necklace of yellow animal teeth clicked against his chest.

Before von Rheydt could speak, there was a rattle of metal, and the German turned to see Junius Cornelius Casca raise a hand in greeting to the Zulu.

The centurion's dirty tunic was gone, hidden by a burnished corselet of horizontal hoops of steel. Leather padding showed under half-hoops of deeply-gouged metal protecting the shoulders; the swelling muscles of his arms were bare. A coarse brown woolen skirt or kilt fell to his knees, and he wore heavy sandals. One big, tanned hand rested on the sheath of a short sword, and the other was curled negligently around a square shield, embossed with a wing-and-thunderbolt design. A short, plain dagger rode at his waist, and in spite of the Roman's short stature the plumes of his centurion's helmet nodded above the taller men. Casca reached out an arm and gripped their hands solemnly, one at a time.

Von Rheydt looked at the two of them, the tall Zulu and the stocky Roman. "If it is the fate of a soldier to die," he said aloud, in his own tongue, "to do it with such men as you is honor."

They did not understand his harsh German, but they understood that it was a compliment, and they nodded grimly. At that moment, one end of the corridor went dark, and they began to march abreast in the direction of the light. The clang of bronze and steel echoed away in front of them.

The hatch closed behind them, and von Rheydt whispered, "My God." A low grunt of surprise came from Casca. The three men stared around.

They were in a gigantic amphitheater, and it was empty. Von Rheydt looked back, seeing a high wall without a trace of the door through which they had entered. Firm sand grated under their feet, and a red sun above them cast a bloody glow over empty tiers of gray metal seats, stretched to meet a deep violet sky.

Metal scraped as Casca drew the short sword and balanced it at waist level. "In your country, German, do you have the circus?" he asked, in his strangely corrupt Latin. "That is what this is like. I have seen the gladiators fight in the imperial city. And now, we fight—before the throne of Jove."

Von Rheydt looked at Mbatha, who returned his look without visible expression. "The u-Fasimba do not fight ghosts," said the African slowly. Then the short spear pointed, with the speed of a striking snake. "But those...those are not ghosts."

Across the flatness of sand, through the atmosphere shimmering with heat, three dark figures stood against the wall of the amphitheater.

Von Rheydt unslung the canteen from his shoulder, took a mouthful of vodka, and handed the canteen to the Zulu. When Casca handed it back to him it was empty, and he dropped it to the sand and drew his saber.

Mbatha started forward at jog-trot, and Casca and von Rheydt followed, their steps thudding on the hard-packed sand. The figures opposite them swung into motion too, and the two groups, men and Others, closed rapidly.

Fifty meters apart, they both stopped, and von Rheydt's eyes narrowed.

The enemy was not human. From a distance, they had resembled men, upright, bipedal, two-armed. But from this distance the differences were horribly evident.

The aliens were taller and thinner than men, but there was no appearance of fragility. They had long legs, of a brassy color. *Skin tone?* von Rheydt wondered. Thick, small foot pads, like a camel's. The necks were long, leading to a ridiculously small knob of a head. There was no clearly defined face, though he could make out large, dark eyes fixed on the men.

A sound next to him made him turn his head. Casca, eyes fixed on the enemy, had fronted his sword and was murmuring a prayer; when he caught von Rheydt's eyes on him he grinned, but didn't stop. Mbatha had been silent, scrutinizing the enemy; but then he turned his back contemptuously to them and addressed the German.

"We fight, u-Rheydt?" he said. "You—Casca?"

Von Rheydt nodded. "We fight." Casca finished his prayer and brought the square shield up to cover his breast. Mbatha turned back; and von Rheydt, drawn saber in his right hand, Luger in his left, walked between the armored Roman and the hide-shielded Zulu toward the waiting aliens.

As they closed he could see variations in their equipment and dress. *They must be of different times, too,* he thought. One of them seemed to be sheathed in a blued-metal armor, and carried a long staff of the same material. Von Rheydt nudged Junius, pointed with his saber; the Roman nodded, teeth bared, and fixed his eyes on that one. Another was almost naked, and its weapons were two curved, glittering scimitars; Mbatha was already turning toward it when things began to happen.

In a second, the aliens seemed to shrink, from seven feet or so almost to human size. Von Rheydt blinked, then saw what had happened; the 'heads' had been withdrawn into the deep chests, and the dark eyes peered over the edge of a protective carapace like a soldier peering from a trench. *The brain must be inside the chest,* he thought. Well, a bullet would reach it even there.

And even while von Rheydt blinked, the blue-armored alien had lifted a long arm, and something swift left the long staff and fell toward him, too fast to dodge.

There was a terrifying loud clang, and a meter-long blue metal rod quivered in the sand at his feet, Casca's shield twitched back, and the centurion sent a mocking laugh at the being that was drawing another missile from a quiver on its back.

"*Gratias,*" said von Rheydt, and then the three men separated, and he found himself face to face with the third alien.

Von Rheydt's opponent stood solidly on two feet, neck stalk slightly extended, garge dark eyes fixed on the German. The smooth, brassy-looking skin was bare at the arms and legs, but the trunk was covered with a flat black garment that looked incongruously like carbon paper...

But these were details that the captain noted only with his subconscious, for his attention was centered on the short rod that one brassy hand was bringing up stealthily to cover him.

Von Rheydt fired twice, rapidly, from the hip. The nine-millimeter jolted his hand, and the flat crack of it echoed back from the circled walls of the amphitheater. His opponent reeled back, then steadied; shook itself, and stepped forward, one hand going to its chest and the other raising the rod.

Electricity snapped, and von Rheydt's whole body arced in a

spasm. He fell heavily to the sand, face up unable to move. The alien came toward him, towering up into the purple sky, and lowered the rod to point at von Rheydt's chest.

He recovered movement and brought the saber around in a whistling arc. The alien jumped back, but not in time to avoid the stroke, and the German's arm tingled as if he had struck a lamp post.

He scrambled back up, retrieving the automatic from the sand. The alien closed with him again, and the point of the saber grated against the black-jerkined chest. The alien backed off a little.

Von Rheydt looked at the saber point. Broken; the tip had gone with that wild slash to the legs. He looked again at his opponent, who was still backing away. Most likely it needed a little range to use the rod, which it was training on him again.

Von Rheydt switched the Luger to his right hand, aimed carefully, and sent four bullets caroming off the thing's torso. None penetrated, but the sheer kinetic energy of the eight-gram bullets knocked it back with each hit, and at the last shot it fell, dropping the rod.

Von Rheydt was on the weapon in two bounds, crushing it into the sand under his boot. From the corner of his eye he caught a glimpse of Mbatha and the nearly naked alien, both weaponless, straining in hand-to-hand combat. Von Rheydt reached his alien, placed the muzzle between the wide eyes, and pressed the trigger. Only at the empty click did he see that the toggle link was up; there was no more ammunition.

At the same instant, a grip of iron closed around his leg, and he was jerked off his feet. Dropping the saber and the useless pistol, he fell on his enemy, hammering with his fists on its chest. He had hoped it was the garment that had deflected his bullets, but it was too flimsy; it was the carapace beneath it that was like steel, impervious to his fists and his weapons alike.

He was being crushed in a close hug when he found the ceremonial dagger in his hand, and managed to slice it into the softer flesh of the "neck." The grip loosened, and the two fighters sprang apart and circled warily under the red sun.

Von Rheydt panted, wiped sweat from his eyes with the back of the dagger hand. Pain began to throb in his crushed ankle and in his chest. His opponent's sad eyes watched him unblinkingly as they circled, crouched, arms extended like wrestlers. The cuts on his half-extended neck gaped, but there was no trace of blood. The dark eyes flicked away from von Rheydt once, noting the ruin of its weapon, then slid back to follow the limping German.

Von Rheydt, circling to his right, stepped on something hard, stooped quickly and retrieved it; Mbatha's short spear. He held it low, pointed up at those sad, interested eyes.

This makes it a little more even than hand-to-hand, thought von Rheydt. He felt quite cool, as he usually did once a fight had started. But the odds certainly seemed to favor the alien; that metal-hard skin, its great strength he had felt in his leg, the lack of an exposed brain. The very deliberation with which the creature moved gave an impression of terrible strength. The deliberation of a tank...

Deliberation. Could it be the deliberation, not of irresistible power, but of great mass? Anything hard enough to resist a steel-jacketed bullet *must* weigh more than flesh.

At that moment von Rheydt crumpled, as if his injured ankle had given out. He fell to the sand and groaned.

The alien hesitated for a moment, then strode forward, its camel-like footpads making deep impressions on the sand.

It reached the fallen German, and the quick stride turned to a stumble as his spear entwined itself in the long legs. It began to topple over him, and von Rheydt rolled, bounding up. The neck extended as the creature fought for its balance; and then the whole frame jerked as von Rheydt swept the short spear around and rammed its butt into the back of the alien's neck.

It hit the ground so hard that little gouts of dry sand flew up. Von Rheydt reversed the spear and leaned the point into the base of the neck stalk; but the creature did not even shudder. Von Rheydt smiled tightly; there had been a major nerve from the eyes to the brain.

He glanced around for the others, and saw Casca grinning at him. The Roman was bareheaded, and blood covered his scalp and the right side of his face; but he was kneeling on the chest of the blue-armored alien, and his short sword was at its throat.

Where was Mbatha? He looked around, and saw, about twenty meters off, the last minute of *that* combat. The giant Zulu, body shining with sweat, had both hands interlocked on his opponent's back in a powerful full nelson. The alien seemed to sag suddenly; the Zulu's back and shoulder bulged with a great effort, and with a horrible tearing sound one of the brassy arms was bent far back.

Mbatha dropped the unconscious alien, fell to his knees, and was sick in the sand, his body shaking with the aftermath of his exertion.

There was a sound of clapping from above them, and von Rheydt looked up at the general, who was sitting alone on the lowest tier of seats.

"Well done, Captain!" he called down, honest admiration in his harsh voice.

Von Rheydt looked around at his companions. Casca had raised his palm in the air in salute; he looked surprised. Mbatha had risen to his feet and extended his spear arm. *What,* von Rheydt wondered, *were they seeing in place of a general of the O.K.W.?*

"Thank you," he said to the general. "And now—your part of the bargain?"

"Of course. Return to life for all three of the victors," the general said. "Finish these three off, and then..."

"No," said von Rheydt.

The general stopped in mid-stretch, arms in the air. "What did you say, Captain?"

"I said, no. This—creature—fought bravely. It is not a soldier's way to kill when his opponent, though brave, is helpless."

The general lowered his arms and laughed. "And what do your less civilized friends say to that noble sentiment, Captain?" He said something rapid, something von Rheydt couldn't catch, and they both looked at Casca.

The Roman looked down at the blue-clad warrior, slowly raised his hand, and—turned his thumb upward.

Mbatha spread his hands and walked away from his defeated opponent. Von Rheydt turned back to the general. "You see?"

"This is insane," said the general, angrily. "This primitive chivalry has no place in modern warfare. Even in your time, Captain—do your enemies give quarter to the wounded?"

"No," said von Rheydt, then his eyes fell to the sand of the arena. "Nor...do some of my own countrymen. But the best among us, the professional soldiers, do. Obedience is not our only code, general. We also have honor."

"That's enough," said the general, who had turned white. "Your last chance, Captain. Finish this matter properly. Now."

Von Rheydt stepped forward and threw the spear violently to the ground. It stuck there, quivering. "You do it," he said flatly. "It's your war." He turned, motioned to the Roman and the Zulu. They walked across the sand.

Von Rheydt felt the blackness coming, drawing closer to him, like a velvet curtain sweeping in to end the last act of a play. It reached him, and he sank into it.

He opened his eyes to the white coldness of snow against his face, and to a warmth that glowed like fire in the pit of his stomach. His eyes blinked, focused on a face. A human face. The face of a white-clad soldier, who shouted something, and who raised a submachine gun...

It had rather enjoyed the role of a General Staff Officer, and It still retained the appearance of one as It sat down to write Its report. The battered army typewriter rattled as It typed; it paused occasionally to refer to a document from the desk or to take a draw on Its cigar. The gray octagonal room gradually filled with drifting layers of smoke as It wrote:

> ...the directive embodied in paragraph [4], reference [a], was fully carried out, in accordance with standard testing procedures as set forth in Ordnance Manual, latest revision...Evaluating officer personally observed comparative combat testing and was highly impressed with performance of human soldiers. They proved the better fighters in three encounters.
>
> However, the humans evinced certain undesirable characteristics as far as suitability for front-line use is concerned. The most serious was a refusal to obey orders contrary to their primitive codes of fighting.

It leaned back in the chair and thought about that one for a while, absentmindedly blowing smoke rings. In all good conscience, It could not recommend immediate employment of the humans in the Disputed Sectors; they simply wouldn't do if they couldn't take simple orders. *But then*, it thought, *there's just too much combat potential here to simply close down and start over again with some other design.*

It thought for quite some time, and then stubbed out the cigar, tilted the chair forward again, and typed, *Recommendations.*

> What is needed now for this Project is an intensified, speeded-up program of development. To effect this, it is proposed that two great power blocs be created at the conclusion of the present war, and that a situation of continuous conflict be maintained for as long as it is necessary to produce a deployable human weapon...

It nodded in satisfaction. Just the thing. And it could stay on to

supervise, in a soft rear-echelon job, far from the Front...
It smiled, and began to change.

The Silver Man

John Kessel

Peter Wharton first saw the silver man an hour after the argument with his wife, as he walked musing through the evening-deserted halls of the physics building on the way to his office. He turned the corner into the narrow alley that led to his door, and lifting his head, saw the figure at the far end of the corridor, in front of the double doors of the laser laboratory. At first Peter thought it was a bright light, but immediately it resolved itself into a naked human figure, a man half-crouched beside the wall. He was not small or large, and his surface (you could not call it his *skin*, Peter realized) gleamed with reflections of the surroundings: the straight-lined corridor, the lavender doors with tall, narrow windows, the overhead strip of fluorescent light—all twisted bizarrely, all flashing kaleidoscopically from the curves of the man's shoulders and calves and chest and hairless, mercury-smooth skull. Before Peter could move closer, the silver man turned and vanished through the lab doors. The last glimpse Peter caught was of his own image, twisted and tiny, like a dark glass toy, reflected in the man's retreating back.

Peter ran after him down the corridor. The lab doors were unlocked; he rushed inside, but there was nothing. One of Petroski's experiments crouched on the long workbench, but aside from the clutter of stools and metal wastebaskets and a large desk covered with legal-size notepaper and cigar butts, the room was empty. The windows on the other side of the room were locked; it was the third floor, anyway. Peter did not like prowling around his colleague's lab. He felt an average man's disquiet in a dark, deserted building, and the whole thing had been a matter of a second or so, a flash in the distance that might even have been some queer, persistent glint on his glasses from the overheads. His mind had been elsewhere.

Wharton sat in his office and tried to forget about unsettling optical illusions and his teaching and his wife and the things she wanted that he had never considered as possibilities himself. The situation was more strained than he realized if he transmuted reflections and fatigue into the image of a man made of silver. A trick of the senses. He took the printout he had left on the desk in the afternoon and went over the results again. He reread the letters from the machinist on the progress of his cylinder and wondered if there might be a more efficient design for a gravity-wave detector. What he had was based on approximations, guesses on the magnitude and nature of the phenomenon he was trying to detect. Suppose gravity didn't propagate that way at all? He'd look pretty foolish listening for something that wasn't there. He'd have a great time with the department and the NSF then, and though he was a politician, no surplus of politics would make up for a deficiency in theory. It just didn't work that way.

Wharton had just been made a full professor the previous year, and for a time had seemed to be on that fair road to becoming the department's golden boy. A large NSF grant at 31. A successful series of experiments with the much older and respected Letnov at Princeton. An entertaining wife. But complications had developed over the last six months—adjustments of the theory, an embarrassing realization that his first design for the detector had been a simple-minded false start. Difficulties at home: he had thought Kathryn was pleased with her role and the direction his career was taking, but in reality he had been projecting his own feelings onto her quite distinct personality. Even his winning nature, which had enabled him to advance so rapidly in the petty morass of department politics, was, he realized, beginning to fray around the edges.

Peter could take only so much talk. How many times could you explain something to some inept administrator? What do you do with a department full of energetic adolescents who would naturally prefer to have the money themselves, to spend on their own experiments? Peter could understand how they felt. There were professorships on the line, higher-paying positions. Even fame, in a field where you'd better get your work done before you were 35, or else resign yourself to a career spent in schooling undergraduates for *their* attempts at the brass ring.

He doodled various diagrams on the yellow note pad centered in the circle of light from the desk lamp. He tried a few order-of-magnitude calculations, ones he'd done since the beginning, over and over again, long since drained of their reassurance. A silver man. He looked at the clock on the filing cabinet. 12:10. He wondered what Kathy was doing, whether she had gone to bed.

When he left the office after one, the building was as deserted and quiet as it had been when he'd entered. He hesitated after locking the door, then went back down and tried the door of the laser lab. It was locked. How cold the doorknob felt! Looking down, he saw that his fingers had left little prints on it, surrounded by moisture—like frost, evaporating.

Through the narrow window he could see only black benches and hunched shapes, and over them all the film of his reflection in the dark glass.

Peter dropped in to see Petroski the next day, after finishing the morning quantum-mechanics seminar—twelve students, half the senior physics majors in the department, and of them three were capable of doing creative work. The rest—grist for the Ph.D. mill, mathematical bottle-washers. Only in a university could you get paid for doing your hobby. It struck Peter that this was a perfect justification for the huge athletic department: it was either the popular pastime of football, or the less popular ones of English Literature, or French History, or Stellar Interiors. Hobbies.

Petroski was curt as usual; he acted as if he didn't approve of inter-specialization conversations. Peter tried to be casual in his mention of the silver man, but how do you work such a fantasy into a casual conversation? Say, Alan, how's the holometrics work going? Did you know I saw a chrome statue walk into your lab last night? He froze your doorknob.

Absurd.

"Well, Peter, I'll tell you," Petroski said in his infantile, mocking tone. "I'm not so good on the color silver. Red is more in the laser line." Peter refused to laugh.

Petroski nervously tapped a pencil on the black vanes of an amplifier. Something was on his mind. "Of course, you invent a nice silver skin cream and you can eliminate sunburn from the beaches of the world. Then again, you'd eliminate suntan with it. And you'd freeze some people to death, painting them with a perfect reflector." He smiled and stared. Peter should have known better than to talk to him, a smug mediocrity who wouldn't let any weakness he spotted be.

"Let's cut the crap, Peter." The change in Petroski's tone was sudden and sharp as a knife. "You were in here last night, weren't you?"

"Ah... well, yes."

"I thought as much. You shouldn't have disturbed my desk—that was stupid. If you needed something, it could have waited until this morning."

"Look," said Peter, "I just told you—"

"Sure. I didn't know you went in for idle speculation. I thought you dealt in hard realities—like your gravity waves."

Wharton forced his anger down and returned to his basement lab.

He was *sure* he hadn't touched Petroski's desk. Someone else must have been there.

Later that afternoon the aluminum cylinder arrived and the workmen maneuvered the truck around the parking lot, preparing to move the bulky rod downstairs into Peter's lab, into the cradle that lay waiting to receive it. Several physicists and chemists emerged squint-eyed into the spring sunlight to watch the proceedings. Walter McGrath, chairman of the department, was there to chat with Peter, to nervously break the ground for a few new worries with his talk of the state legislature and the university budget. In McGrath's glasses the cylinder drew itself into a silver line that slashed across his eyes. The image waggled as he spoke. Peter found himself staring at the reflection and ignoring the man's words. He caught himself—couldn't he concentrate?—made some polite small talk, then turned to fuss over the men who were awkwardly lugging the cylinder through the door. In the basement they suspended it in two canvas slings from the bolts in the ceiling while it was lowered into the floor trough which contained the cradle of detectors.

Outwardly, Peter hovered over the maneuverings, insisting the men be careful. In the back of his mind stood the silver man. He speculated, detached for the moment from the gravity experiment, which was more important because it was real. Petroski was wrong about silver being a color. The ideal silver—total reflection—was an absence of color, like black, only the opposite. The silver man would have no color of himself—he would merely reflect everything which impinged on him. A perfect silver man would reflect *all* radiations . . . true, he might freeze. But then if his silver skin reflected in as well as out, his body heat would kill him in short order. Therefore, assuming such a man had a mammalian body temperature, he would have to radiate heat out *through* his silver coating. He would glow, like a man, in the infrared.

And not only that! If all light were reflected he would not be able to see.

The men had all left; he was sitting alone on the workbench. He shook his head, set to work mating the cylinder to the instruments. But he thought of other things all the while.

Blind—certainly. But oh, how the silver man would shine with their reflected light!

"I ran into Phyllis Spiegel today," Kathryn told him. "She and Ted want us to come by Friday evening. She asked whether we were still interested in that oak table they have in the basement."

"Uh-huh." They were sitting in the living room listening to classical music. The television had just been turned off, and the cat lay sprawled atop it, batting with its paw at the phantom paw in the dead gray screen. On Peter's lap an old issue of the *National Geographic* lay open.

"Well?" Kathy persisted. Her voice held a skittish challenge in check, barely.

"Yes?"

She turned in her chair. She spoke quietly, unsteadily.

"You don't ever listen to me, do you? You don't care what I do or want. You don't even have the courtesy to make a show anymore."

She didn't cry because she never did. Peter's eyes remained on the color photograph before him, but he felt flushed.

"Can't you even put down that damn magazine for a minute?"

Peter put the *Geographic,* still open, on the end table beside him. He had not been reading; he'd had trouble reading lately. He'd been looking at the pictures. The cat leapt off the TV with a thump and attacked its scratching post in the kitchen. Peter finally turned to Kathy, but strangely, she would not look at him. She rushed up, stumbling, to the bedroom. He heard the door close upstairs.

"I'm sorry," he said.

His glance fell on the picture again, a glossy photograph from an article on an archeological find in mainland China. Excavators for a new public building had unearthed the tomb of an ancient Chinese noblewoman. Her corpse had been found in a two-thousand-year-old sarcophagus, marvelously preserved. Her skin was still soft and there was blood in her body and the doctor who ran an autopsy could tell what she had had for breakfast on a day so long, long ago, when the Orient morning breeze had sparkled through wind chimes, and spring blossoms fell gently to pools which embraced and gave back the rising sun like lucid mirrors.

Suppose you could put a field of total reflection around a man without killing him. What would be the use of it?

If such a second skin—mirror membrane, force field—could be made to reflect everything—gamma rays, ultraviolet, visible light, radio, heat—and particles, too—alpha particles, fast neutrons, accelerated protons, electrons—the man would be absolutely immune to many killing forces. He could walk unharmed through a reactor core—if he didn't breathe. A silver man would be a void in the universe of radiation. Totally indifferent to everything! He would be indispensible in dealing with high-energy technologies. He could, for instance, travel at speeds near that of light and be unaffected by the flux of high-energy particles and radiation to which such a passage would naturally give rise.

This was Peter's reasoning.

And if a silver man were to survive, he would indeed radiate in the infrared.

Feeling slightly foolish, Peter slipped the goggles down over his glasses. The office became a dream-duplicate of itself. The desk lamp still glowed, illuminating the room with a paler whiteness than before. The heating pipes glowed like a fluorescent lamp behind the baseboard. He shut off the lamp and its heat faded very slowly. His right hand shone with a ghostly light of its own. It was three o'clock in the morning, and Peter Wharton was ready to stalk the silver man.

He started on the fourth floor and worked his way down, turning off the corridor lights before he entered so that he saw only by the heat from ventilators and water pipes in the walls. They had used a more sophisticated form of these goggles in Vietnam, Drake had told him that afternoon in the military-science building. They had hunted men in the jungles and picked them off at long range while they crouched under what they thought was the cover of darkness. So Peter hoped to catch the silver man—if he existed. He would not be distracted this time by the man's astounding reflection of the light around him. Peter used the passkey he had coaxed from Sally Barker, the department secretary, to get into the offices that lined the hall. He disturbed nothing in the vacant rooms he found.

Occasionally he heard the sound of steps, but when he stopped to listen he could discern nothing clearly. It would be damned embarrassing to be caught by some nosy grad student while snooping around with a ridiculous pair of goggles on in the middle of the night. But he felt he had to go through with this and get the nagging image out of his mind, so he could get back to some serious work.

After an hour or so he had reached the basement and stood outside his own laboratory. In spite of himself his heart was beating quick and hard. He clamped his mouth shut and drew a couple of slow breaths before he turned the doorknob and swung in.

The long room was silent and empty. Everything looked normal—but a light shone around the corner from the alcove at the other end of the L-shaped room. Peter moved uneasily toward it, along the instrument cavity, resting his hand occasionally on the work table along the south wall. Half-afraid to look, he cautiously peeked around the corner. Something very bright shone in the top left corner of the empty desk he kept there! He had a moment of sharp panic before he realized it was his coffeemaker. He must have left it on. Grimacing at his own girlish fright, he flipped the switch off. So much for supernatural intruders.

He turned to leave and almost stumbled in shock. Behind the rack of equipment that Peter had been working on that very afternoon stood the figure of a man. His naked body glowed with strong phosphorescence, like certain fish whose rotting corpses shine from the sea's surface at night. His nimble fingers played among the leads and open circuit boards.

Peter swayed and put his hand out to touch the wall. He closed his eyes, shook his head. When he opened them the man was running out through the opened door. Peter raced after, saw the man turn left at the end of the corridor. He ran down the hall, his feet thudding softly on the carpet, and turned the corner just in time to see the figure disappear behind closing elevator doors. Grinning tightly, Peter rushed through the metal fire door to the stairs. The elevator was notorious for being the slowest on campus. His steps rang hollowly in the stairwell as he took them two at a time. When the elevator doors opened on the ground floor he was standing out of breath in front of them. He lurched in and grabbed the man by the arm. The man struggled to get away. "Let go of me! Goddamn it, let go!"

Peter realized then that the man was fully dressed, and did not glow in the way the intruder had. He pulled off the goggles as his captive twisted out of his loosening grip.

"What the hell do you think you're doing?" the hefty, middle-aged man said, rubbing his shoulder through his green work shirt. It was one of the janitors.

The janitor's name was Arthur Baldwin. Normally, he would not have been in the physics building in the middle of the night, but on this occasion a problem with the heating system and two pints of Southern Comfort had kept Arthur and his colleague, Willis Ivy, up late in the mechanical room. Willis had left earlier in a belated attack of conscience at the memory of his wife. Arthur had no wife. He could care less about going home to stare at his cluttered apartment's walls, but he couldn't sleep on concrete.

So Arthur, too, had been on his way out when, stepping into the basement hallway, he discovered that somebody had turned all the lights off. Damnfool energy savers, not saving a damned thing. He pulled his flashlight from his belt and headed for the elevator.

It was then that he caught a flash of something in the beam of his light. He didn't know what it was; it was almost as though someone had flashed a light at *him.* Or maybe the flashlight beam had bounced off the stainless steel doors of the elevator. But hadn't it moved?

He wasn't about to worry at it. He got on the elevator; when the doors opened on the first floor, he was grabbed by some one of those professors who cluttered up the building. Like he was some thief! He was frightened, and the liquor burned in his gut. The guy wore goggles, like a spaceman.

Arthur was just ticked off enough to tell off one of the office secretaries the next day. Damnfools—couldn't tell what they were looking at, when they were looking right at it.

The experiment was going badly. If theories were reality, it would work like this: the long, solid cylinder, a column of absolutely motionless matter, is resting in its cavity in the bowels of the physics building. Twice a day the earth, in her rotation, would orient the cylinder in a direction perpendicular to a line drawn from Peter's device to the Sagittarius arm of the galaxy, 0° galactic longitude, the direction of the galactic center. Gravity waves, presumably strongest from the galactic core, would impinge on the dead column, causing it to resonate in time to the disturbance. The periodic vibrations would be registered by sensitive detectors. And so, over a period of time, data would be accumulated to demonstrate that gravity did propagate in waves.

It didn't work.

The problem was extraneous vibration. A truck would rumble by on the highway, the classes would change upstairs and a hundred students would walk through the hall, a sparrow would fall somewhere in the continental United States, and each time the detector would record the vibration. Peter had hoped that sinking the device in the ground would solve that, but it did not. At first the upset had destroyed his free, openhanded manner. But he was somehow able to gain a new detachment in the face of the gentle chiding of McGrath and his colleagues, and Petroski's suggestion that Peter sell his contraption to the Geology Department as the most sensitive seismometer ever created by the hand of man.

He tried various means of cushioning the device. He considered immersing the entire detector in a tank of silicon lubricant, but after a few tests realized that even this would not seal the system off from all noise. He considered the theory of interference. What he really needed was something to generate vibrations exactly the inverse of the ones which were disturbing the experiment, which would then cancel out the incoming wave and create a dead space inside. Certain surfaces had the property of vibrating so readily in response to incoming electromagnetic waves that they turned them back on themselves. Mirrors.

Peter called on Butler in engineering and, working together, after several months they constructed a "mirror" for mechanical vibrations.

The incidence of recorded signals was thus greatly reduced. Peter's hopes rose, but still he occasionally detected impulses at times he should not have, when the detector was not oriented perpendicular to any source. Perhaps he had discovered some new astronomical phenomenon? He consulted the astronomers. The random signals could not have originated with the sun, or any of the planets, or even with some distant galaxy. They had to be some further interference.

Through all this, instead of growing more frenzied, Peter grew less so. Sometimes he would not meet his classes, and when he did he did not teach well. He ignored the students. At the end of the summer session, before the fall semester began, he went to visit Letnov at Princeton. He did not take Kathryn with him. They didn't go anywhere together anymore. Kathy would occasionally visit their friends alone and try not to act worried. Her stiff-upper-lip routine was transparent to all but Peter.

Letnov was old and curiously remote, and Peter had worked under him as a graduate student. Peter felt they had much in common though he could never really talk to the old man. Letnov was friendly, to be sure, but like some pre-revolution Russian patrician he did not mingle well with brash young men. You spoke to him, and he responded exactly the way you expected every time, as true as a billiard ball bouncing off a cushion. Letnov had been working on a similar detector. Peter suggested they harness their machines in tandem, over long distance, so that they could coordinate their results as they came in and eliminate impulses that registered on one detector but not on the other. In this way they would filter out any local terrestrial disturbances.

The machines were connected. The two scientists, young and old, listened through the declining months of the year. Nothing was heard. They had filtered out all the noise, and there was nothing left.

McGrath began to offer fumbling advice whenever he saw Peter. Wharton didn't care. In the evenings now he often did not go home. He did not work. He slept on a cot in the lab; he drank coffee and prowled the halls of the building at night.

The silver man was tampering with his experiment. And he was beginning to suspect that the subtle influence of this creature on his life did not stop there. Peter struggled, however, not to let the suspicion show, for on certain days it seemed the whole thing was mere disappointment and paranoia, and the world around him would climb back onto its well-ordered tracks.

But Peter had *seen* him. He had *seen* the silver man lurking at night about the darkened building, present in the salt sound of metal on metal heard in an adjoining corridor, in the occasional smell of ozone near the elevator. In liquid glints of light caught unawares by the corner of his eye.

Suppose a race of beings exists on another world in our galaxy. Suppose they are not quite human in the way that we are human. They do not think as we think. They do not consider contact with others, whether of their kind or another, to be necessary. They are remote and aloof. They are subtle. They possess technologies of which we can only dream. Of *their* dreams we can know nothing.

This was Peter's reasoning.

Indian summer had just failed that afternoon: the wind had shifted from the south to the northwest, bringing with it clouds and cold air and the threat of a freezing rain. Peter listened with satisfaction to the rustling of dry leaves on trees and in the gutters, as he walked home from campus late that evening. The moon, full and high, was visible only occasionally through breaks in the clouds. His footsteps tapped dryly on the sidewalk. Halloween weather.

The living room was clearly visible through the latticed window at the front of the house; as usual, Kathryn had forgotten to draw the drapes. He remembered how he'd chided her about that when they'd first started living together. How trivial it seemed now! The recollection drew him momentarily out of his musing, and when he unlocked the door and entered the room he was almost grinning. She was sitting in one of the armchairs, doing needlepoint. She looked up nervously as he entered, then bowed her head once again. Her fingers worked the needle and thread with tight, angry jerks.

The room was cold, so he sat down in the chair opposite the window without removing his jacket.

"Hello," he said.

"It's late." She didn't raise her eyes.

"I guess I lost track of the time."

The needle jerked more furiously.

"I've been working pretty hard," he continued when the silence grew ominous. For the first time in months he felt like trying to break through the ice between them. "You've been working on that bedspread for a long time," he said. "It seems like years."

"I'm almost finished now." She spoke very quietly.

Another silence.

"The experiment's still not going well." His voice sounded

absurdly loud to him. "I think I know what the problem is, though. I want to recalibrate—"

Kathy clenched the bedspread tightly in her fists and sat upright. "Oh Lord, Peter! I don't care about your machines. Tomorrow I'm...going away." She sounded very tired.

Panic began to constrict Peter's throat. He twisted his head from her and looked at his broken reflection in the rectangles of the dark window. He looked the same as always. It was when he forced himself to face her again that he first saw, behind her tears, the strangeness of Kathryn's eyes. He held his breath: was she the same woman?

"Peter...please say something. Don't just sit there." Her voice was timid, afraid. Kathryn, *his* Kathryn, was a strong woman.

"I think I'll go to bed."

She pulled her legs up into the chair, huddled with her face pressed into the bedspread. He went upstairs, undressed, put on his pajamas, brushed his teeth. He noticed in the mirror that he hadn't shaved for several days. The bedroom was, if anything, colder than the downstairs.

He lay awake in bed, listening after Kathy, trying to make out what she was doing. She was not acting normally. Through the darkness and the rustling of the trees outside his window, he heard small metallic taps that might have been the ticking of the furnace, that might have been the sounds of something infinitely stranger moving through the rooms of his home.

Once a month the Committee on Departmental Research met. In his earlier, activist days, Peter had sought a position on the committee; now he merely attended meetings, sat mutely, and voted merely arbitrarily whenever questions were called. The other members undoubtedly had noticed this, and knowing of his marital and professional problems, ascribed the change in his behavior to worry about his possible failure. Only Peter himself knew the real reason: his search for the silver man.

It was late November and the windows of the conference room were tightly closed against the whiteness outside, but still Peter felt a chill. He thought he might be coming down with something. He looked at the minutes of the last meeting and the agenda that lay before him. It looked boring. For some reason the light at his end of the table was dim, making the reading difficult.

"The first order of business," said McGrath, the chairman, after the polite chatting had died down, "is that eligibility matter of last month. Paul Glass was going to check up on that for us, so we'll listen to his report first." McGrath nodded appeasingly to Dutton, the aggressive low-temperature man on his left, "We'll get to the matter of the budget after this preliminary stuff is cleared up, Willy. Hang on."

Peter was not paying attention. He regarded the entire meeting as a phenomenon, like a solar eclipse or a change of state, which was strictly predictable and therefore trivial. He wondered why he'd ever taken it so seriously.

But the silver man! Peter had almost cornered him the previous night near the cryonics lab, Dutton's lab, but the fool had shown up for some reason and his throwing on the lights had washed out everything.

Glass droned on. Peter decided he'd have to quit the committee. Even though they no longer asked him to do any work, it was too much bother.

McGrath was speaking again. "...the apportionment of departmental research funds for the coming fiscal year. Note the table of last year's appropriations on page three..." More of the same. Peter couldn't read page three; the light was too dim. Overcast outside.

Where did the silver man come from? Why and how did he interfere?

Dutton had the floor now. "...some of these items should be dropped. They can undoubtedly subsist on their NSF funds, if they can continue to justify them—" People were shifting in their chairs. Perhaps they were cold, too. "—but we should not spend money on research that has proved fruitless and which threatens to remain fruitless, when there are better projects—I'm sure we all agree on this—" Dutton looked around the table like a lawyer in summation, "—which deserve the funds."

Peter realized they were all looking at him. Something about irresponsibility. Uncooperativeness.

Dutton looked down the table at Peter. His face was growing more flushed—the man would have a heart attack one day, it was clear—and he struggled for words. Peter felt completely calm.

"Peter, don't give us the old excuses," Dutton said defensively. "How do you explain your meddling with every piece of research being conducted in this building? Your own troubles offer no justification. I won't be the person to tend charges of sabotage, intellectual or otherwise, but who else could have caused—"

"Willy, *please*!" McGrath interrupted. "I've asked you not to bring up any wild, unfounded..."

They all looked as though they were sitting a hundred thousand miles away, dead gray, on the moon. Strangely, it did not matter that they might cut him off and leave him apart from them all. He was suddenly excited. The experiment had served well enough: it had led him on to the mystery of the silver man. Perhaps—perhaps that civilization was out there, a civilization of men who knew how to control gravity the way we control electromagnetism and light. Perhaps, Peter said quietly to himself, seated at the conference table while his colleagues voted to discontinue the funds for his research, and their cold eyes in the cold room lay on him alone—perhaps they fear that they will be detected by us—why not?—and so they have sent an agent to me, to prevent me from learning what they have learned, from becoming what they alone have been able to become!

With a thrill of fear and anger and power, he looked up to see, in the darkening room, the shining form of the silver man. He stood silently behind the man at the other side of the table. Peter stared at the absurd tableau. The committee members did not turn: were they hypnotized? The silver man's sightless mirror eyes were fixed on him; even his eyelashes were delicate silver wisps.

"Look!" Peter shouted. "Will you look!"

Flashing twisted images as he turned, the alien creature of light fled the room.

Paul Glass blinked. "What's that?"

"What's what?" Dutton.

"Is it cold in here, or is it just me?" McGrath asked.

The embarrassed men stared as Peter Wharton stumbled from his chair and rushed out into the corridor.

It's so cold, so dark! Peter thought as he chased the silver man through the halls of the building. Has the power failed? The lights?

It was 4:40, and classes would soon let out, but the hall was empty. Peter heard the drone of lecturers through open doorways as he rushed by. Why don't you help me? he thought. He'll escape!

Light from the windows at the end of the corridor glanced obliquely from the polished floor tiles. Polarized. He hit the stairwell seconds after the man, slamming the fire door open with a hollow crash. Two, four steps at a time; don't fall!

On the basement level a reflection, a quicksilver motion told Peter that the silver man had dashed into the men's room. How absurd! How clever! The sublime to the ridiculous—the last, desperately simple hiding place. The alien in the room for men.

His hands and feet were numb. The corridor grew darker as Peter hesitated outside the door, frightened before the confrontation that he knew would answer all questions, remove all doubts. He pushed clumsily through—he could hardly see or even feel the door in its remoteness—and inside he spotted a movement opposite him in the room. He moved forward—it was growing darker, darker, little light, no warmth in the home of the silver man—and as he advanced the creature at last moved *toward* him instead of away. Peter came to the mirror above the washbowl in the midnight lavatory, and at the very last, before everything became blackness and separation, he saw the face of the silver man there, reflecting back and forth and back again, and there was no color or substance to him, merely light—trapped and twisted and shrunken duplications of his surroundings gleaming from his totally discrete and inviolate surface, which gave nothing of its cold self back to the objects which it distorted.

Walter McGrath located Peter in the men's room in the basement. He was standing ramrod straight, eyes clenched shut, in the center of the tiled floor. He swayed slightly, and if you looked closely, you could see that he was trembling.

"Peter." Walter stepped forward, hesitating. Should he call for someone else?

"Peter," he said, "what's the matter? Are you ill? I'm sorry about the meeting; I didn't realize how cruel we could be when we all…"

He stopped talking; Wharton's shakin had increased. He was trying to speak.

"Can you *see*?" Peter finally gasped, pointing awkwardly across the room.

Somehow Wharton's tension had rubbed off on him; nervously the older man looked where the other pointed.

He saw only their reflection in the mirror above the washbowls.

He put his arm around Peter's shoulders, but the man refused to budge. Eventually he was forced to leave him to go get help. Some people from the university hospital arrived in short order; through the numbers of curious onlookers outside the washroom, they carried Peter out to the ambulance.

McGrath tried to contact Kathryn Wharton, but she was not to be reached anywhere. The department chairman sat in his office on into the evening, brooding over the young man's collapse. Was he in any way responsible? Could he have prevented it? He felt very old.

It was late when he decided to leave. As he locked the door to his office, he was taken by a sudden impulse. With furtive steps, half-amused and half-frightened by his own curiosity, he went down to the basement-level men's room. There was no one there. He glanced with embarrassment into the stalls, then, as though saving it for last, as though he could not bring himself to do so without working his way up to it, he turned to the mirror above the sinks. He looked hard. What an old face he had!

Then he noticed that the mirror was slightly warped, and more than that, there had to be something wrong with the silvering on its back—for behind the reflected image of himself, he saw a kind of shadow image of another face. Like two layers of glass, half-silvered. A flaw.

My god, it was cold down there! He shivered, turned out the light, and left.

The Children of Cain

Eugene Potter

Jane Benamou pushed the high-powered rifle up on her shoulder so it didn't jab her back. The weapon was a nuisance, but she could not visualize going anywhere without it in the Lower Pleistocene African savanna (with who knows what kind of predators about). She spoke into the microphone of her notetaker.

"*Day 150. Lower Pleistocene Expedition One, Southeastern Research Synod. 0900 Hours.* The troop is watering at the lake. Their 'guardian' stands away at a distance of about fifteen meters—"

She started at a footfall and looked up to see the guardian beside her. The creature's two-and-a-half-meter frame stood easily, one horny hand resting at the end of an impossibly long arm flat on the ground, the other fastened in what anatomists call the "power grip" around a short, curved spear like an assegai. The sunlight was bright and the creature's normally blue skin appeared light, almost green except where the dark shadows under its enormous jaw colored it violet. It made a slow, lazy blink with its beady eyes.

"Do you talk to your people now, little sister?" it said.

"Yes, you might say that," said Jane, marveling again at the creature's use of English. It had not spoken at all for a long time after their first encounter, but had appeared to listen closely and religiously to her frequent log entries.

"I listen," said the creature.

"Certainly," said Jane. She realized that this was its way of learning her language.

The creature turned to watch the troop as Jane brought the microphone back to her mouth.

"The troop does not post observers while watering," she said. "All fifty enter the lake at once, bathing and drinking. Several individuals appear to gather shellfish. They seem to place complete faith in the guardian." She stopped.

"Guardian?" she said to her blue-skinned companion.

"Yes," said the creature without turning to her.

"Do the little brothers and sisters eat shellfish very much?" she said.

"Yes," said the creature, the muscular protuberance at the back of its neck throbbing with some unknown chemical process. "It is permitted to eat creatures of the lake."

"Do you eat shellfish, guardian?"

"No," said the creature. "Guardians do not eat any other creatures. Your world is rich and we find food enough among the trees and bushes."

Members of the australopithecine troop splashed each other in the lake shallows, making loud noises like laughter. Jane had to guard against anthropopathism in her work and so made no attempt to interpret the expressions on the beetle-browed australopithecine faces. She saw a small herd of strange bovids walk carefully from the nearby brush to the lake shore about half a kilometer further down. Horned ungulates with antelope-like grace.

"Have you ever seen animals like those, guardian?" she said, pointing to the bovids.

"Yes,'" said the creature.

"That's the sixty-seventh new bovid I have observed," she said. "I am at a loss to classify them all."

The guardian said nothing.

Jane decided to bait him a little.

"It is permitted to eat those bovids?" she said.

"Bovids," said the creature. "No," it said and turned to face her. "I told you before, little sister. It is not permitted to eat creatures of the land."

"Yes,' she said, "you told me before. I just don't understand.

How can the troop survive on shellfish and fruit?"

"Guardians survive on less," said the creature, turning back to watch the splashing troop. Then it added: "The troop is happy. My function is met."

Jane was about to ask it more about its function when they both noticed a disturbance in the lake. The playful splashing stopped as the troop members turned to watch the floundering and bubbling of one of the juveniles, obviously over its head in the water. They stood and stared.

The guardian laid its assegai on the grass and began to trot toward the lake on its stubby legs. It assisted the fully striding (but still almost penguinlike) gait with its horny hands, laying the alternate palms on the ground about every three steps. It ran for all the world like a mobile windmill. Jane ran, too, but knew the guardian had the matter under control.

As the blue-skinned creature waded into the water, its neck protuberance pulsing, Jane began to wonder if she wasn't also coming to depend on the guardian. The thought appalled her, dredging from her mind a certain amount of contempt for the pitiful "family" of inept australopiths.

Heedless of its trousers and toga, the guardian marched into the water up to chest height and reached a long arm out to the struggling young ape. It seized the juvenile in a precision grip, an act of which Jane had not known the creature was capable. Then it carried the "child" back to shore, draped over the palm of a gargantuan horny hand. The other australopiths went back to their play while the guardian, toga and trousers dripping, set the young one down and rubbed its fur lightly. The young ape appeared to revive sufficiently to strike at the guardian, a blow which the larger creature hardly noticed.

Jane walked back to the rock where she and the guardian had spoken, thinking to retrieve the creature's spear. She began to pick up the weapon and heard the footsteps of the owner's peculiar foot-foot-foot-hand gait. The large hand pulled the heavy curved spear from her grasp.

"You may not have weapons, little sister," it said.

"I was just going to get it for you," she said.

"Little brothers and sisters may not have weapons," it said.

"Why haven't you taken away my rifle, then?" she said.

The guardian just stood there without speaking, blinking the heavy lids of its small eyes. She knew the reaction from whenever she used an English word for the first time. She also knew from before that the next time she used the word the guardian would understand it. As far as the creature was concerned, two contexts established the meaning of a word. Its rapid assimilation of English consisted of just such an endless series of linguistic triangulations. She resolved not to use the word "rifle" again, but puzzled over this obvious deficiency in the creature. Surely it must have figured out the function of the rifle, but it certainly did not behave as if it had.

"What I cannot understand," she said, "is how none of these spears has ever been preserved down to my own time. I expect the haft to deteriorate; it is just wood. But the blade must be a hard substance."

"Yes, hard," said the guardian, "but it is a belief among guardians that we can leave no signs of our presence. The spear is an unstable material."

"What could it be?" said Jane.

"We make it from sand," it said.

"Sand? You don't mean sandstone?" she said.

"No," it said. "We heat the sand."

"Glass?" she said. "You mean that spear tip is glass?"

"Glass," said the guardian slowly. "Glass. It is the only thing we know which is hard and is yet unstable." It turned to watch the troop coming out of the water. "No more talk of weapons."

"If you must leave no sign of your presence, guardian," said Jane, "what will you do about me? I know you are here and I will return to my own time."

"You will not return," said the guardian.

"What?" said Jane, not a little angry.

"I will keep you here. You will be happy," said the creature.

"Like hell you will," said Jane.

The creature did not respond and she knew that she had used a new word.

"Well, I'm sorry to tell you, guardian," she said, still angry, "that I happen to know you will leave traces. In my time, we have found fragments of the bones of your people. We classified you as *Australopithecus robustus* because we thought you were closely related to the little brothers and sisters."

The guardian snorted and Jane wondered if it were laughing. "My people go away to die," said the creature, "and we live longer than you can imagine. You must be mistaken. You could not have found our bones. We are not of a type with the little brothers and sisters."

"We *have* found your bones," said Jane. "We have found the portions of about fifty individuals, the best specimen being a complete skull. Some we have found beside the bones of little brothers and sisters."

The guardian snorted again. "We are fifty individuals on your planet. Each of us has a troop of fifty little brothers and sisters. There are fifty guardians and two thousand five hundred little brothers and sisters." Then the guardian appeared to reconsider, looking closely at Jane. "Two thousand five hundred and one," it said. "Your people are few."

"We must have found all the guardians," she said.

"No, little sister," said the guardian. "You cannot find our bones. We go away when we know we shall die."

"How do you know when you will die?" she said.

"We know," said the guardian, turning to her, "unless we are killed." The creature snorted.

"Maybe every one of you will be killed," said Jane.

The guardian snorted again and Jane had the fleeting impression that the creature had not had so much fun in five hundred years, as if it were listening to a stand-up comic. "There are no creatures here to kill guardians," it said. Its eyelids swung closed lazily, then opened again. It snorted.

The guardian laid down the assegai again and began to strip matter-of-factly of the wet trousers. Jane got a fairly good (scientific) look beneath its toga and noticed a lack of genitals. She wanted to make a note of it, but wanted more to continue the conversation.

The troop had begun to shuffle, after the manner of australopiths still imperfectly adapted to upright locomotion, toward the brush. The guardian left the trousers on the ground, picked up the spear and began a lopsided windmill stride after them. Jane hitched up her rifle, which had begun to slip, replaced the recording unit in her shoulder bag; and followed.

"Guardian," she called, "please slow down."

The creature appeared not to hear her, but continued its purposeful stride, adjusting direction constantly to compensate for the use of one arm as the other carried the spear.

The sun grew hotter, but nothing like it was at Olduvai before she left the twenty-first century. She concluded early in the expedition that she had entered a pluvial and, as a matter of fact, the grass was much more lush than the Serengeti she knew and the brush was fairly succulent. Berries and fruit abounded, leaves were broad and green. The ecology of grassland and even woodland-savanna is based on a large biomass/land–area ratio due to the fact that grazing ungulates can breed so easily, and open areas are conducive to herding. That was why Jane had cataloged sixty-seven new bovids since she had arrived.

Ungulates—like so many other animals—survive, not by defending themselves, but by breeding in profusion. And that means the grasslands produce predators as well, which was why Jane carried the rifle everywhere she went. The Serengeti of her own day boasted carnivores in abundance, including jackals, hyenas, leopards, cheetahs, and lions. There was no telling what kind of predators had evolved at this time, before the environmental cataclysms of the Middle Pleistocene. And Jane wondered if she would ever be able to fill in that gap of her research on the Lower Pleistocene. She had not seen a single predator since she had been here. She knew it was because of the guardian, but she did not feel she could leave the australopithecine troop because of the importance of human history to the Research Synod.

She had been just a little hesitant about the rifle before she embarked on the expedition, having read so many science fiction novels about the dire consequences of "altering the timestream." The temporal physicists at the Research Synod, however, had assured her that there was nothing to fear, that there was indeed no such thing as a "timestream." She had never been able to understand it, but she was a paleobiologist, not a physicist.

They picked their way through the brush until they came to a spot obviously favored by the australopiths. Although the area was occupied by another new type of bovid (which she tentatively classifed as *Gazella gazella benamoni*), the troop stopped to eat beside the browsing gazelles. The australopiths picked berries among the bushes and low trees, the gazelles munched leaves. There was very little interference between them, but occasionally one of the larger troop members would push a gazelle away from a bush and the creature would simply comply and move on.

The guardian stood on stubby legs and rested its left hand on the ground. (Jane had noted fifteen days previously that the guardian carried the assegai with its right hand and used it with the left).

"Guardian," she said, pulling out her recording unit to tape any answer, "why are your people here and where did you come from?"

"We came from another world, little sister," said the creature, blinking. "We are here to teach your people."

Jane almost shivered at the reminder that she was so close phyletically to the wretched berry-eating apes around her. She took a food-concentrate bar from her bag as the guardian continued its explanation.

"To any question," said the guardian, "there are many answers. We wish to teach you an answer."

"Is that why you protect them?" said Jane.

"We must protect you," said the guardian, "that you need not protect yourselves."

"But if they don't learn to protect themselves," said Jane, continuing her disassociation from the australopiths, "they'll never build a civilization."

The guardian stared at her without speaking. It blinked.

"Civilization is when people live together in very large groups," she said. "We build permanent dwellings, use tools, have extensive communications."

The creature just stared and she decided to slow down. "We live together in very large groups," she said, "and produce more together than any of us could by himself."

"Your world is rich," said the guardian. "Your troops are happy." One of the australopiths had apparently started an altercation with another and a howling went up as they faced off, addressing their one-meter, forty-one-kilogram frames to each other. They looked like brawling ten-year-olds. They bared teeth.

The guardian trundled over to them and reached out to smooth the fur of one and it struck the blue-skinned creature repeatedly with its open hands. Both apes began to strike at the guardian, which took very little notice of the blows, but smoothed the fur of one combatant until it calmed down. With one of them calm, both returned to their berry-picking.

The guardian walked back to stand beside Jane, and she wondered if the creature, in its detached way, had taken a liking to her. It certainly showed no reticence in their conversations, although it did seem to harbor the belief that it could hold her here even when her launch window came up. It was almost as if explaining things to the "little brothers and sisters" was part of its purpose.

"I can guess," she said, picking up the previous discussion, "that the question is how to survive."

The guardian was silent and she realized it did not know the word "guess."

"The question," she began again without embellishment, "is how the 'little brothers and sisters' can continue to live."

"Yes," said the guardian. "On some worlds, creatures live by killing other creatures. They kill as they grow and when they have grown enough, they threaten other worlds."

Jane bit off a piece of her food-concentrate bar and thought that she never heard the guardian speak at such length. Then again, if the creatures lived as long as this one claimed, it must have been here for almost a thousand years with nobody to talk to.

"My people will show your people that they can grow without so much killing," it said.

"They must kill in self-defense," said Jane.

"No," said the guardian, "when they are threatened, the guardians will protect them so they will not learn to kill."

"What will happen when the guardians are gone?" she said.

"At that time," said the guardian, snorting slightly, "your people will be guardians."

The hominids began to chatter and scream and the two of them looked over at the troop. The fifty members were addressing all manner of australopithecine abuse at an intruder of their own species. The strange ape carried a small stick like a club and it hissed and spat at the nearest members of the troop, eyes narrowed and teeth showing.

To the extent Jane could read the guardian's strange body language at all, it seemed to be very alarmed as it stepped over to stand between the troop and the intruder.

The troop members intensified their vilification and screamed louder than ever from the cover of the guardian's bulk. Some of them began to throw excrement.

The intruding ape, for its part, treated the guardian with contempt. It struck at the blue-skinned giant with its ineffectual club, bared its teeth, and tried to scratch the leatherlike skin with its fingernails. The guardian endured the blows without difficulty, all the while scanning the horizon as if it were searching for something.

The guardian did not rub the intruder's fur the way it did when it tried to calm a member of its own troop. Jane wondered if its calming influence extended only to its own "family."

The ape finally struck the guardian's knee furiously with its stick, so that the implement broke. The guardian dropped its spear and, while it held its knee with one hand, it used the other to keep the intruder from getting any closer to the troop.

The ape seemed to calm down after its club broke and finally turned and left. Jane supposed it was going off to look for another club. The disgusting little yahoo.

The guardian limped back to where Jane was standing, using both of its long arms like crutches, dragging the assegai on the ground with one hand.

"Is your knee hurt?" said Jane.

"It will be well before the day ends," said the creature, its neck protuberance rippling and pulsing.

"Where was the guardian of that strange little brother?" said Jane.

The guardian became very contemplative and did not speak.

The troop, apparently exhausted from its encounter, began to nap, most of them stretching out in the shade of the higher bushes, some climbing short trees. The bovids had long since left, and Jane listened over the prevailing buzz of a katydid (or its Pleistocene equivalent) to her notes regarding the three varieties of non-bovid artiodactyls she had classified. She judged the guardian was involved in some healing process for its damaged knee and that it might not even be able to move for the rest of the day. She wanted to consider the problem of the lone ape (could the guardian be wrong about all australopiths having troops and all troops having guardians?), but these periods of troop inactivity were the only chance she ever had to classify the flora.

She laid her bag on the rock where she was sitting and adjusted her rifle strap. She wanted to go to the meadowlike hillside beyond the brush to examine some of the grasses and tried to arrange the rifle for instantaneous use. She did not even know if she was entitled to the guardian's protection (since the creature did seem to be able to discern the difference between her and the australopiths), but she certainly did not want to be without protection while the creature might be immobile. Its healing process would require less than a day, but the guardian's time sense was imprecise by Jane's standards and that could be fifteen minutes or six hours.

She might be able to depend on the creature. It had treated her paternalistically ever since she had insinuated herself into the troop (after two months of observation) ninety days before. And if it enjoyed anything, it certainly seemed to enjoy its discussions with her.

Pondering the imponderable, she shrugged on her shoulder bag and strode off through the bush toward the clearing she knew to be fifty meters north.

When she emerged onto the hillside, she was mulling over the varieties of predator and prey of this prehistoric grassland. She continued to let those thoughts percolate in the back of her mind while she knelt in the grass to get a complete root system. And she was not all that surprised when she heard a swishing noise like a faint breeze and looked up to see the most enormous felid she had ever observed standing about thirty meters away in the meadow. Her heart beat faster when she realized it was staring at her.

She laid her piece of grass beside her, unshipped the rifle, and thought of a line from Milton about eyes like carbuncles. The felid probably massed 3500 kilograms and it hunkered down as it stared at her, seeming to try to bunch most of its body up behind its shoulders. Jane, fighting for calmness, pushed a shell into the breech of her rifle, aimed at the cat's forehead, and squeezed the trigger as the monster sprang into motion. Nothing happened.

Her heart missed a beat as she saw the beast bearing down on her like an express train and she dodged to the left (though the cat was still ten meters away) as she tried to reset the rifle. Then she noticed stumpy blue legs beside her and looked up to see the guardian. It was poised with its spear in an impossible grip and its legs obviously healed and anchored to the ground like gnarled trees.

Jane dropped the rifle, rolled clear, and looked back in time to see the spear enter the leonine forehead with a splintering sound. The guardian picked itself nimbly off to the right with its elongated arms to avoid being crushed by the enormous body.

Jane realized that the giant's detached boasting had been justified. There was no creature on Earth which could challenge a guardian. That cat had been at least three times the size of her savior.

Jane walked over to the inert form of the carnivore, meeting the guardian, who studied the broken spear point it retrieved from the ground, the bulk of the point having been imbedded in the cat's head.

"My rifle didn't work," she said.

"Rifle," said the guardian.

"Yes," said Jane, picking up the jammed weapon, "this thing."

"A weapon," said the guardian. "The rifle."

"Yes," said Jane. "Did you know it was a weapon?"

"Yes," said the guardian. "Little brothers and sisters cannot have weapons. I altered the device to prevent killing."

"Oh, God," said Jane. "*I* could have been killed!"

"You have a guardian," said the creature. "Little brothers and sisters cannot be killed as long as there are guardians." It turned back toward the brush and stopped.

Jane turned also and saw the entire australopithecine troop facing them from the edge of the bushes. The hominids shuffled slowly toward them and took positions around the felid carcass. Finally one of them touched it. Another touched it, then one struck it. Another struck it. They began to scream and chatter and beat the dead form.

The guardian walked patiently around the body, pulling enraged australopiths away and frequently receiving ineffectual blows for its efforts. Jane retrieved her equipment, sat down on the hillside, and watched the orgy of cat flogging and the guardian's pathetically gentle efforts to stop it.

Eventually, the australopiths tired and walked back into the bushes to pick more berries. Jane and the guardian followed. "The little brothers and sisters," she said to the guardian, "have tasted violence."

The creature did not respond and she assumed it did not know the word "violence," although she found it hard to believe she had not used it twice in the past ninety days. It continued walking and Jane began to fall behind.

"Guardian," she shouted to it.

It stopped and turned toward her.

"I must leave tomorrow, guardian," she said.

The creature said nothing, as if it did not wish to hurt her feelings.

Jane realized with a start that the guardian was actually capable of keeping her in the Lower Pleistocene. It had been capable of a lot of other things.

"Others will come," she said. "It takes hundreds of these expeditions to make a complete picture. You cannot control every one."

The creature did not respond. She decided she had better cease prattling and began to walk toward the berry patch again. The guardian fell in beside her. She could hardly understand herself. Here was a creature bent on holding her against her will and she insisted on keeping company with it. It was as if she believed the guardian knew what was best for her. She understood better than the australopiths what a wonderful creature the guardian actually was and she felt herself beginning to understand its obscure pronouncements on violence and life.

They heard screaming at the berry patch. They picked up the pace to investigate the disturbance and arrived to find another troop of about thirty individuals in possession of the area. Their troop stood off, chattering and screaming.

With the scientist's intuition, Jane knew this was a troop without a guardian, that the stranger they had encountered previously came from among these creatures. She hardly had to tell herself what had happened to the twenty or so missing individuals.

Jane noted that some of the intruders carried things: sticks, rocks, and short clubs which looked like bones. They didn't chatter and scream as much as her own troop, but seemed to take up a sort of formation around their half-dozen juveniles. She noticed an infant clinging to a female and realized she had never seen such behavior in her own troop, where the guardian did much of the caring for the young.

A young individual of her own troop got close enough to an adult intruder to throw excrement and was dispatched by a hand-held stone struck to the point of the jaw. The young ape appeared to be killed instantly. The guardian was visibly agitated as it waded in among the enraged creatures.

There were too many in its own troop for it to control them and the strangers began to pelt it viciously with their weapons. Several of the australopiths in Jane's own troop were killed shortly, obviously demoralizing the remainder. The guardian scanned the horizon anxiously while it sustained the blows of the weapon-bearing creatures. It tried to hold some of the intruders away from its own troop, but—even though their troop was understrength—there were too many for it to deal with individually.

It reeled when one of the intruders, creeping up behind, struck square in the center of its neck protuberance with a chipped stone. The rest of the strangers closed in immediately and rained blows on the guardian while Jane's troop fell back in shock, juveniles clinging to adults, and adults shuffling away backwards. It was a scene as she had witnessed not an hour before: enraged hominids flogging a larger beast and continuing long after it ceased to move.

The first thing Jane Benamou asked for when she returned to the twenty-first-century base at Olduvai was coffee. The officials of the Research Synod knew the syndrome and were glad to cater to her wishes. They gave her a complete breakfast in a sumptuous suite and told her she would have a full thirty days to finish her report. She did not want thirty days, however. She wrote the report immediately after breakfast and said simply:

"Our world is rich, yet we are the children of Cain."

The Oak and the Ash

John Alfred Taylor

The lines keep running through MacKay's head:

> O the oak and the ash and the willow tree
> And that's the end of the infantry!

And maybe it is, MacKay thinks, looking down at his charges in the dull red floods, darkroom-dim to save their night sight. They'll need it, with this overcast. Must cover half-Georgia. Big darkroom. See what develops. As if there was anything else to do now.

J. Fred Muggs II flips his sensor visor up and down, up and down, Boadicea whimpers and scratches under her weapons harness, MacKay moves upon silence like a long-legged fly surface tension keeps from drowning—

From drowning in the memory of Korea, of killing gooks efficiently and never calling them gooks, of coming back to become the Yeats of the Fifties, and ending up other end man (thasso, Mr. Interlocutor?) (thasso, Mr Bones) assistant trainer for the chimps at the Zoo.

And liking it. *St. Louis chimp, with your rhinestone rings, lead your trainer round by his apron strings.*

Before separation, when the Army cut the cord, by chance and by the absolutely predictable accumulation of days that was the same thing, he and his corporal had met again in the same repple-depple. Simms had been an Ohioan and run a farm before he was drafted, butchering thousands of chickens and a veal or two a month, but had seen enough blood. His last postcard had been from Garrett Theological Seminary in Illinois.

And MacKay had had his chimps learning to play the piano and ride bicycles.

Until St. Cyr asked him to join up again, to train chimpanzees for another kind of show. And MacKay had. He'd signed the devil's book with ball-point ink, not blood, but still he signed.

But the Devil hadn't looked so ugly then. St. Cyr's original idea—at least as he had explained it to MacKay, though who ever knew what St. Cyr was really thinking?—had been more humanitarian, less brutally empirical. Though of course with sufficient military value to get a grant.

As a graduate student involved in teaching chimps American Sign Language, St. Cyr had recognized the possibility of studying the roots of war. Chimpanzees were every bit as aggressive as men, but their aggression was individual and unorganized. Was it man's ability to use symbols that led to war, the way he could fight over a word?

Originally St. Cyr had planned to train two teams of chimps to play a kind of football, with all the discipline team sports demanded, but more important, he wanted to see if he could produce absolute partisanship among the non-playing chimps, if he could turn them into football fans. That would be the moral equivalent of war. And of nationalism.

And for the first year that had been the project's goal, a goal both generals and pacifists could find worthwhile, though for different reasons. But the Pentagon wanted something more immediately applicable, and the man who pays the piper calls the tune. Remotely piloted vehicles were big, and the Navy was leading dolphins into temptation.

So St. Cyr came back from Washington one night and announced that the whole thrust of the project had been changed. MacKay almost quit that night, but St. Cyr argued him around. They were his chimps, he felt responsible for J. Fred and Cleopatra and the others. Besides, though MacKay would barely admit it to himself, he wanted to see if they could do it. So he stayed on in the real world, the world of secret funding and "need to know."

DOD, DOD, shine your ever-loving light on me. Read my writeup, skip my math, pour your pointless cash on me.

Weird, having St. Cyr up in D.C. so often now, ringing his beggar's bell for all his pride. But then it was his idea, even this version, and you couldn't blame him for sticking his neck out to save it.

St. Cyr had taught the chimps to talk and hate. One led to the other, but it had been complicated, inventing chains of logic to make them face loud noises, making up curses in sign language.

One of his real inspirations had been the Hate Sign. A red triskelion, it gradually became an almost instant trigger for the manly instincts of Cleopatra, Wellington, Molly Pitcher, Ally Oop, Bonnie and Clyde, Mother Courage and the rest. He could superimpose it on a color slide or film of a man in any uniform, and the chimps would begin to smile their humorless smile.

Weiss had taught them how to use the rifles and grenade launchers Nakashima adapted for them. And MacKay had taught them how to charge and kill and die, just as he had taught other chimps how to beat out "Roll Out the Barrel."

Disgusting, but less disgusting and more interesting than gabble about "detente" and "bargaining chips" or about "running dogs" and "wars of national liberation." That was hot air, empty wind for the public; this was the reality.

St. Cyr had even considered gorillas, when they were demonstrated to have equal or superior linguistic ability, but they were too expensive and tricky. Putting together the immunization package for the chimps had been hard enough.

But now it's the real thing, with live ammunition rather than laser simulators, the test that makes or breaks the project.

And up there next to St. Cyr stands Major General Masterson, so distant he makes St. Cyr seem human, looking at the test area in the starlight scope while St. Cyr tells him what he sees. Everything rides on what those small, shrewd eyes see tonight.

Yet for all his commitment MacKay feels oddly detached. Tonight he's only a watcher. The automatic sequencer has been started in the control bunker, the monitors are warming up, the clock is ticking. The triggers to the pop-up targets and the laser-simulator guns are armed.

St. Cyr stubs his cigarello out on his boot, field-strips it automatically, says something quick to the general. The chimps are waiting. He pulls on his fluorescent gloves.

When he gets down in front of them, the chimps all pull down their sensor visors, stand easy on three paws, their M-16s or grenade launchers at the ready. Not exactly a drill sergeant's dream, but soldiers.

St. Cyr starts the Hate Signal strobing on the screen in the pit, begins his hand talk. The chimps watch attentively, without jittering.

Then he makes his final gesture and the first five move out into the dark, Ally Oop in the lead. Then the next five and the next.

"We've given them forty-five seconds to reach Target One," St. Cyr calls up to Masterson.

MacKay looks out at the forest, more tangible than visible, barely distinguishable from the overcast above. Nothing happens.

Then suddenly the whole night explodes with tracers and the tinny counterfire of the simulator speakers. Ghost shapes appear on the repeater screens down in the pit; a chimp—he can't tell which—looms on one, silhouetted by muzzle flashes. Smile, you're on Candid Camera.

He'd been against issuing live ammunition, but St. Cyr had overridden him. "Damn right I know your chimps are valuable, but this is for real. Besides, you taught them not to shoot each other, didn't you?"

Then the nightscape is silent again, except for the ringing in his ears.

The loudspeaker from the control bunker says, "We score that as overwhelmed—one minute eight seconds and counting."

"Now for the hard part," yells St. Cyr. "The next target would be alerted; it's programmed pretty lively."

Pyrotechnic charges flash among the trees, outlining branches like black lightning. The pale red whips of laser simulators play back and forth.

On a repeater screen MacKay sees a chimp jerk, throw up its rifle, and collapse. A massive tranquilizer injection triggered by a laser hit. He'd argued against that too, but St. Cyr had insisted it was the only way; if the chimps were only scored as casualties by the computer they'd still be moving upslope, confusing the automatic defenses.

Another chimp staggers, distorted by the fisheye lens of the image intensifier, rolls into a ball. Which was that?

"Subjects six and eleven scored casualties." Molly Pitcher and—and J. Fred. MacKay realizes he's no longer detached. Even and—and J. Fred. McKay realizes he's no longer detached. Even though it's only a game, he feels emptied. What if it were real?

The tracers hose through the trees, grenades thump, the chimps charge grinning on the screens.

"Target Two scored overwhelmed. Two minutes fifty-one seconds and counting."

MacKay feels a surge of pride. They're making it, they're doing almost better than expected.

St. Cyr: "Target Three is considered fortified. They have to enfilade and use demolition charges."

More pyrotechnics and lasers. The chimps are doing their version of the infantry crawl, or moving in a squat while firing continuously. Branches between them and the fisheye lenses move and shift like tentacles. A chimp rises to his feet, throws. A large charge, then the last few shots.

"Target Three scored overwhelmed—five minutes thirty-one seconds and counting."

They're almost to the top of the hill. It's steep now and they have to crawl. MacKay strains with them, keeps his head down.

"Target Four is the hardest and last. The enemy has a clear field of fire of almost 120 degrees."

There are no trees between MacKay and the pyrotechnics now, the lasers are a flickering web of light, the M-16s bark like insane terriers.

It's even worse on the screens. The chimps seem to be crawling on a lunar landscape. They rise, rush, drop, rise. Two fall almost simultaneously, and MacKay feels his belly contract sympathetically. They rush again. Another casualty. Another.

"Subjects five, eight, twelve and thirteen scored casualties." Wellington, Boadicea, Bonnie and Clyde.

Grenades, the rifle fire rises to a crescendo and moves up the hill.

"Subject one scored casualty."

Mother Courage, but what the hell, they're almost there, you can see on the screens they're going to take the hill. MacKay is laughing without knowing it, St. Cyr is trying to hold in his excitement.

"Final target taken. Elapsed time nine minutes and twenty-four seconds. Casualty count seven. Recovery and revival team dispatched. Monitors shutting down."

St. Cyr lets go. "They did it, they did it! I knew they could!"

MacKay has run down and slaps him on the back. They hug each other.

St. Cyr looks up at Masterson. "Well, what about it? I told you they could do it."

The General's face is like a red stone. "They did it. And damn well too. But—"

"But what?" bleats St. Cyr.

"The program is terminated."

"Terminated? Terminated? You saw what they did—"

"Yes. But the decision was made today. And I concurred."

"Why?"

The General's red-washed face crinkles into a smile, if anything that cold can be a smile.

"Men are cheaper."

813.08
S

c.2

Starry messenger: the best of Galileo / by Charles C. Ryan.

5/80

NEW HANOVER COUNTY
PUBLIC LIBRARY
Wilmington, NC 28401